PROPHECY OF BLOOD:
A SUPERNATURAL PSYCHIC THRILLER

WRAITH HUNTER CHRONICLES: BOOK 2

By John R. Monteith

I0640466

Prologue

Diane dreamt of a human figure burning on a cross, blood pouring from the blurry apparition's chest. Time stopped, accelerated, and slowed again as the surreal nightmare unfolded.

An unseen wind flapped a milky gown over a ghost of feminine form who spoke with a young woman's voice. "Heed my warning."

In her ethereal vision, Diane responded with her human voice. "This isn't happening again."

"You knew it would."

"I'm not ready. I'm still exhausted from last time."

"You will see horrors born of mankind's deepest evils, and you will suffer with the victims."

Flashes of stabbings, beatings, and mutilations assaulted Diane's mind. "Why didn't this stop after I killed the wraith?"

"You defeated one of many. You must now face one more insidious than the one you defeated."

"How can that be?"

The ghost's black orbs narrowed. "He enjoys killing."

"That's disgusting."

"He kills whom he must to survive, and he kills others for sport."

"What should I do?"

"You learned to defeat a wraith by defending yourself. Now you must endanger yourself for others."

"You want me to go through this again for strangers? I barely survived last time."

"You will grow stronger."

Diane sensed something odd. "You're not the same maiden, are you?"

"You are observant. I am another."

"What's your name?"

Ignoring Diane, the apparition whispered as she faded. "Avenge me."

CHAPTER 1

Major Edric Tuncay watched the massacre.

Having perfected the techniques in prior cleansings in Upper Mesopotamia, his Ottoman Turk soldiers worked through the assassinations with mechanical efficiency.

From the hotel in which they'd corralled them, Edric's soldiers ushered Assyrians into a courtyard in small groups. As the terrified and hungry captives lumbered towards the pit of bodies, their executioners selected women to extract for abuse in harems and other lewd crimes.

The remaining captives stood in line and then fell atop the bodies of their brethren as rifles cracked. Blood flowed in streams above the pit, forming pools of crimson around the feet of soldiers who brought forth the next dozen souls.

Edric watched the subsequent victims walk forward with his men selecting sex slaves from its ranks, but an Assyrian woman screamed her objection. A guard backhanded her, but after recoiling from the strike, she doubled the volume of her shrieks, and her flailing arms eluded the soldier's grasp.

The major marched to the conflict. "What's wrong?"

The soldier pointed at the defiant woman. "She says she'd rather die than serve us, sir."

Eyeing her, Edric found her desirable, and her feistiness made him want to tame her. "She's not the first to beg for such mercy. I shall not grant it."

Fire in her brown eyes, the woman surprised Edric with her calm and strong tone. "Are you in charge?"

Unable to resist her questioning, he answered. "Yes." Unsure if he'd overindulged in hashish or if his evening's intake of wine deluded him, he sensed a foreign presence in his mind. He wanted to flush it from him, but it clawed its way to a stronghold.

Its identity became obvious as he heard the unspeaking woman's voice. "Release my people."

Obeying her became his second nature. Disobeying her took effort. She held him in her gaze, and he writhed in pain.

The soldier glanced at him. "Sir?"

He tried to speak, but his throat tightened.

"Sir?"

Edric withdrew his pistol, jammed it into the captive standing beside the woman, and pulled the trigger. The old man collapsed, and the emotional shock created a moment of cerebral separation from his telepathic invader.

Her eyes welled with tears, but she found the resolve to retain her connection to his mind. "Then you will kill me."

"Yes, I will kill you." He elevated his pistol.

But her telepathic commands continued. "No, probe my groin."

He returned his weapon to its hilt, shoved his fingers under her dress, and ran it between her legs. The supple flesh of her inner thighs excited him, but when a slicing pain hit his index finger, he understood her intent.

He withdrew his arm and examined the cut. The knife strapped against her upper leg was sharp, and he sent his hand back under her dress to retrieve it.

He grasped her hidden knife by its handle, slid it from under her dress, and gazed at it. Made of solid cast bronze, it shimmered with a coppery glow, and it imbued him with an urgent rush of power. An ancient will resided within the metal, and by holding it, he'd become the divine dagger's chosen champion.

The knife's power resonated within his bones, but possessing it brought servitude to the enchanted weapon and to the spirit residing within it. And servitude brought resentment and anger, increasing the internal conflict within the already disturbed man.

He lowered it and stepped forward. "Do you think you can bribe me with this old relic?"

Her lips remained motionless while her voice penetrated his inner ear. "No. You will kill me. I will not be defiled."

The dagger became a sentient being in his hand and agreed that he would kill her–and two more of her people.

He addressed his soldier. "Bring me two more women."

"Old or young, sir?"

"Young. And attractive."

While the guard grabbed two women and dragged them to his commanding officer, Edric glanced at the late evening's moon. The fullness of its phase seemed part of the cause behind his new dagger's uniqueness.

He aimed the bronze point at the younger of the two women his guard had grabbed. "Hold her arms."

The soldier restrained her, and Edric rammed the knife into her beating heart. Letting his newfound servitude and anger drive the thrust, he pushed with vigor.

To his amazement, the dagger glowed sanguine while blood spread over the woman's dress. With supernatural insight, he interpreted the reddish glimmer as a confirmation of proper tribute to the knife's deity.

The guard released the collapsing victim, and then he grabbed the next. Edric killed her the same way, and the blood-covered weapon's illumination increased.

He then taunted the woman who had invaded his mind. "Do you choose their fate over servitude?"

She withdrew from his mind and answered with her bodily voice. "I do. My salvation is nigh."

He scoffed. "So be it."

With both hands, he rammed the blade into her flesh. Covered with the blood of three tributes, the weapon's red glow became a beacon, and he glared at its radiance. With a newfound unearthly reckoning, he knew the crimson fluid fed the dagger, which in turn promised him power.

The third corpse collapsed at his feet, and he issued an order to his guard. "Bring flame and oil and set them ablaze. Make haste."

Within minutes, fire consumed the trio of tributes.

"If another selected woman begs for death, set her ablaze without the mercy of killing her first. Burn her alive as an example."

As the soldier agreed and saluted, Edric suffered a new, haunting consideration.

Why had she offered him the weapon of her own murder, and what devilry resided inside it?

Four weeks later, during the next full moon, he formed an execution squad outside the largest hotel of another village.

He waited for women to beg for death instead of subjection to sexual servitude, and he gathered the first three who obliged. As with the prior village, he stabbed their hearts and burned their bodies.

Then, during the subsequent full moon, he repeated the serial murders on three more tributes.

Having killed nine women in three months, he sensed a change in the dagger's demeanor as his troops entered the village of Urmia under the subsequent full moon.

Though he'd been the weapon's slave during the first three ritualistic crimes, the knife felt like a treasure as he marched into the northwest Persian city, and he knew a gift awaited.

Having fled for spiritual refuge, the Assyrians simplified their capture by convening within the city's church. With the windows boarded and most doors barred, Edric stormed through the front portal.

Inside the building, his men corralled the frightened people.

He walked towards the altar where priests and deacons led the condemned through prayer. Examining women in the pews, he saw flickering lights from his soldiers' torches backlighting somber scenes in the stained-glass windows.

When he reached the altar, the holy men spread their arms and pleaded. With an order to one of his captains, Edric begat the massacre. "Remove the holy men first and shoot them. Then take the rest outside row by row. Move the women selected for leisure to the courtyard."

"Yes, sir."

The dagger demanded his attention, and he withdrew it. Under its power, he aimed its point at a maiden in the congregation. While he ogled her, energy flooded his body, and a red aura rose around her. The sanguine light blossomed, and the woman's life force became his complete world.

When the red illumination receded, he updated his intent. "Except her."

"Yes, sir. Shall I have her bound in waiting for you?"

The enchanted weapon conveyed its desire to Edric, who looked at a wooden crucifix mounted against the front wall. "No. Bind her wrists and ankles to that cross. Immediately."

Minutes later, he stood alone before the restrained woman, ignoring her pleas. Although the language he spoke was foreign, something reminiscent to him as an ancient form of Arabic, the dagger whispered words into his mind for him to speak aloud.

He recited an incantation to the knife's living spirit, which he recognized as his Master spirit as he clutched the dagger. He squeezed the handle and held his breath while the blade's sanguine luminescence appeared before him for the first time without a victim's blood upon it.

With instant comprehension, he understood the prior full-moon murders offerings to the dagger's deity. The payback for his servitude, for harvesting a trinity of trinity of souls, was this… ritual. Convinced of a pending prize, he ran his free fingers down the bound woman's flesh, counted bony contours from her collarbone, and turned the blade sideways under her fourth rib.

He slid the metal into her heart.

Like flame, pulsating crimson light shot from the blade, and Edric bathed in its oscillating glow. A dizzying rush of euphoria overcame him as he ingested her life.

Ingesting her life–taking her years from her. That was the reward. Incredible. Addicting. Revitalizing. "Thank you, Master."

The dagger's light receded, and he sheathed the weapon.

He checked the church and noticed his men satiating their perverse needs to control and kill. Nobody had grasped the significance of his new ritual, which began his new life of solitude.

Marching away from the crime, he gave his captain a final order before walking alone into the night. "Burn the church, starting with the dead maiden on the cross."

Fifty years later, Edric remained physically unchanged. As the dagger's god had fulfilled his promise of unnatural longevity, he'd adapted to seeing his thirty-three-year-old face in the mirror for half a century.

Unsure of his mortality, he'd placed increasing value in his life. Its extended span made him cherish it, inflating his selfishness and his paranoia. To protect himself, he'd crossed the Bosporus into Europe to study modern weaponry and martial arts. His muscles had committed movements to memory over decades of work and had built him a repertoire of firearms and hand-to-hand skills.

While in Europe, he'd also learned the major languages and had made respectable incomes translating documents–a safe job for someone guarding his life. Western banks had provided the compound interest that yielded him a fortune, allowing him to quit working, in pursuit of leisure.

The dagger had rested inside a safe he'd moved from home to home while he'd spent countless hours sampling the best opium, hashish, and alcohols. The knife's master–his Master– had brought him spellbound women as play toys. He'd also become nomadic, relocating twice per decade to avoid attention as an ageless man. Though alone, he enjoyed satiating his lusts–killing more so than sex–and his ego.

As the semicentennial anniversary of his enduring youth had approached, he'd sensed a change. Playtime was entering a temporary pause, and months of work awaited.

His Master had urged him south to offer another trinity of trinities as tributes. He'd headed to Jordan to resist Israel in the War of Attrition. Though his Arabic was weak, the dagger's spirit had given him supernatural help while he'd fought with the Palestinians. After stabbing nine Israeli women during raids over three full moons, he'd earned his sacrifice.

Under July's full moon in 1968, he and a fire squad of three other rebels stormed a house in a kibbutz of Beit She'an Valley.

Determined, he moved with the small team room to room, sending rifled rounds into the parents and two adolescent boys before reaching the daughter's room.

Hiding under the bed, she gave off the red glow he remembered from a maiden in church in Urmia fifty years earlier.

He realized her aura was invisible to the others. "Lift the bed."

The team leader scowled. "You're not in charge. You're not even from Palestine."

Edric smirked. "But I sympathize with your people and hate Israel. I've trained with you, and I've killed for your cause."

"Tell me your plan. We must strike more houses before the Israeli military arrives."

His Master offered the unspoken promise of his sacrifice, giving him confidence. "If you help me kill her my way, I promise you that you'll see a death like never before."

The leader returned the smirk. "How do you want her?"

"Bind her to the underside bed boards like a crucifix. I will handle it from there."

The young woman howled her protests while the raiders bound her. Edric removed the dagger from its sheath in his jacket, and he held his breath while the blade glowed red. Silenced, his audience gasped at the otherworldly luminescence.

Before Edric could strike, the ghost of Urmia appeared. The one who'd given him the dagger blocked the path to his sacrifice.

An unseen wind flapped a milky gown over the misty apparition's frame. Once stabbed and burned, she appeared unblemished and clothed in dignity in the afterlife. Her eyes were black orbs, and her voice carried deep, haunting tones. "Why are you here?"

His companions gave no sign of seeing her.

"Silence!" He moved through her ethereal mist, making her disappear. He ran his free fingers down the Israeli woman's flesh, turned the blade sideways, and slid the metal between her ribs.

Like flame, pulsating crimson light shot from the blade, and he ingested her life. Renewed strength blossomed within him. "Thank you, Master."

The dagger's light receded, and he sheathed the weapon.

While the stunned onlookers gazed in disbelief, he opened the window and crawled into the night. His boots hit the dirt, and then he trotted in the safest direction he could conceive.

Wearing the same milky white gown as the Urmia ghost, the new ghost of Beit She'an appeared in his path, blocking him. Her black, dead eyes stared into him.

Her words were in Hebrew, but he understood them. "Why did you kill me?"

"Silence!" Terrified, he lowered his head and ran through her, cutting her cool mistiness and resisting the curious urge to look back.

Then he recognized the whiz of a bullet and fire erupted in his right leg. Clutching his leg, he hobbled forward and looked over his shoulder at his assailants.

From a hedge, two rifles shimmered in the moonlight. Thinking himself doomed, he cringed as the automatic weapons shifted towards his fallen position on the earth. Two human-shaped auras of azure and blue pulsated behind trees, marking the gunmen as people Edric could only guess were his supernatural enemies.

While questioning their identities, their reason for attacking him, and how his eyes could view their colored energy fields, firearms cracked from a neighboring yard. He looked to see a platoon of Israeli soldiers gunning down the enchanted duo who hunted him.

Pushing to his feet and then breaking into a limping sprint, he left the armed men to fight amongst themselves. Alone, he escaped into the darkness.

CHAPTER 2

Diane knelt in the first pew of the small Irish church. Beside her, the handsome hunter also went to his knees, and for a moment, she fantasized about joining him in that same posture at their wedding.

She'd taken a liking to the young hunter, Liam, as he and his father had rescued her from a killer three weeks earlier.

Handsome and well-built, he'd risked his life for her like a chivalrous knight, taking two bullets in his arm and countless rounds into his body armor. The cast on his upper arm provided a reminder of his commitment. Despite the violence, the romance was taking root in her head and heart like a fairytale.

Next to her new heartthrob was his age-defying father, Connor, who moved with the strength and agility of a man much younger than his mid-seventies.

At the altar, a single priest moved through a ceremony reminiscent of the Catholic Mass she'd long ago attended in her Eastern Rites Chaldean Church. But the ritual seemed abridged, and the recitation happened beyond her understanding, in Latin.

Other than her two companions and the priest, the sanctuary was empty.

Frowning, she wanted to protest flying across the Atlantic Ocean to attend a Catholic Mass in a foreign language, but she thought better of it. She remained silent and reverent to the reading.

The action began.

Wearing a red robe with a white cross as a coat of arms, the priest waved his audience forward. Unsure of her role, Diane watched the men rise and hoped to remain a bystander.

The hunters stood, and Liam called to her. "Come on."

She rose to her feet and followed him. Climbing a few small steps brought her to the priest, and she somehow ended up in the middle of the trio, a hunter flanking each shoulder.

With her hands clasped in front of her, she listened as the priest shifted to English with a thick Italian accent. "And you, Diane, have been chosen to wield the blessed sacramental against all powers of darkness."

The robed man twisted and grabbed a wooden box from the altar. He faced her again and revealed the contents.

Her dagger.

And it was hers. When she'd held it three weeks earlier, it had shown a life of its own. Overcoming a martial arts expert in hand to hand combat, she'd used the artifact as a mystical, superior weapon.

The priest closed the box and handed it to her. "When you touch the weapon, it calls upon divine powers. But it also attracts the unwanted attention of darkness. Use it only in times of need."

She found the advice logical. "I understand."

The priest twisted and grabbed another box from the altar. He turned and handed it to the older hunter, Connor.

Diane gazed upon the second dagger as the lid flipped open and revealed a copy of hers.

Half the straight blade reflected the room's light, while the other half showed its coppery color. A crossguard protected the user's fingers on the handle, which was cast with grooves to tighten the grip.

Engraving in an ancient language labeled the dagger, but Diane sensed something odd in the Aramaic lettering. Although unable to read the old writing, she recognized the characters as something different than those on her knife.

"It's a rare honor to stand before knights who have defeated the enemy. It's an even more rare honor to have a surviving virgin sacrifice present with the dagger."

Frustrated by the fixation on her sexual history, Diane wanted to yell at the men to stop announcing her chastity. But since they revered her for it, she focused instead on the priest's other point–knights. If she could keep Liam's interest, if it existed outside her head, she could date a man with a cool title.

Unfazed, the elder hunter-knight answered while Liam presented the robed man with a box he'd held under his arm.

"My son and I acknowledge the rare honor of inheriting the weapon of our fallen comrades. We also consider it a rare honor to retire a cursed dagger."

The priest intoned a prayer in Latin while drawing a crucifix in the air with his hand. He then placed on the altar behind him the box Liam had handed him.

When he faced his audience again, the robed man held a vial and moved in front of the younger hunter. He traced a cross of oil on the hunter-knight's forehead with his thumb. "Liam, I bless you in the name of the Father, the Son, and the Holy Spirit. May God protect you and guide you in all your dealings with Satan and the other evil spirits who prowl the world for the ruin of souls."

"Thank you, Father."

Diane lowered her head and accepted the same blessing.

"Diane, I bless you in the name of the Father, the Son, and the Holy Spirit. May God protect you and guide you in all your dealings with Satan and the other evil spirits who prowl the world for the ruin of souls."

She wasn't sure about a triune deity and a devil with pointy horns, but she figured the good wishes couldn't hurt. "Thank you, Father."

After the priest blessed Connor, he brought the ceremony to a quick end.

"Congratulations again, to all of you. It was truly a pleasure meeting you all, but I must leave you now."

In the Land Rover, Connor drove while Diane sat alone in the back seat. The three-story shops of the Glengarriff downtown distracted her from the questions pervading her mind. As the last store passed, revealing the southern county's lush green hills, she gazed at the high rugged mountains.

Turning towards the backseat, the young hunter anticipated her confusion. "You've taken in a lot the last few days."

His sparkling green eyes impressed her.

She remembered being held captive for a ceremonial sacrifice before he'd broken into her prison with the enchanted dagger she'd used to overpower her kidnapper. She also recalled ghosts visiting her to coach her through using her newfound psychic powers. "I've taken in a lot in the last few months."

"Months, yes. I stand corrected."

He seemed interested in her. Had he gone above chivalry? Did he feel a connection to her, as she hoped? "But yeah, I'd like to know what just happened."

"I'm still learning. I think Father is also."

"Indeed, I am, strangely. I believe we've been so successful in our endeavors that we're entering uncharted waters."

"Uncharted for us, but not for your order."

"It's our order, lad, since your first hunt is complete and you've been knighted within it. Technically, Diane is a lady of the order as well, for her courage, strength, and initiative."

The elder hunter removed his eyes from the road, which appeared to disappear over a rocky cliff into the Atlantic Ocean. "But you're under no obligation or expectation to render service to the order, young lady. You're free to return to your life."

She pondered her apathy, even her reluctance, to return to her pre-Liam life.

Connor aimed his weathered face back to the windshield and continued with a somber tone. "You've been through enough."

She jumped on the premise of his statement. "But you and Liam are under some sort of obligation?"

"For us, the ceremony in the church was also a commencement."

"I thought that was just a celebration?"

"Yes and no. Yes, we are celebrating. We accomplished a rare feat by defeating your wraith. But we're not the first, and for those who succeed... well, the reward for good work is more work."

"What sort of work? You told the priest you were honored to inherit the dagger of the fallen comrades."

"I can probably explain it best by showing you at home."

At their house, Diane followed the hunter-knights through a living room with a high ceiling and a stone fireplace while the lifeless eyes of wall-mounted animal heads stared over her. Square windows gave a view to a verdant slope leading to the rocky County Cork coastline.

The men's strides were long, like children hastening to a tree on Christmas morning, and Diane trotted to catch them. She tripped over her small feet but regained her balance at a heavy oaken door.

Connor unlocked a latch. "We call this room the observatory."

Inside, the stone cylindrical silo struck her as being incongruent with its name. The only views in the windowless alcove were four vertical lines of whitish mortar set ninety degrees apart, marking what she assumed were cardinal directions. A waist-high circular limestone table rose from the cobblestone floor.

Installed in ancient recesses that once held torches, electric diodes illuminated the space as Connor took charge. "Diane, please take the blessed dagger and place it in the center of the table."

"How accurate do I have to be?"

"Don't worry about it, young lady. It will take care of itself. Just point it that way, towards Israel. It's best to aim at the last known location."

He handed her the wooden box and then turned his back to her, as did Liam. If her memory served her, the hunters needed to avert their eyes to avoid invoking life into the charmed knife.

She opened the box, wrapped her fingers around the handle, and felt nothing but hard bronze. It relieved her to grab a dagger that didn't attach itself to her. Holding her breath, she leaned forward and placed the weapon on the surface, trying to center it. "Okay, guys. It's on the table."

The hunters faced the knife, and it assumed a reddish glimmer.

"Let me turn down the lights a bit." The elder hunter-knight dimmed the bulbs, and the sanguine illumination looked brighter. In the low light, Connor's wrinkles revealed his age, and the tight space's mustiness smelled stronger.

Liam noticed discrepancies. "It shouldn't be glowing red."

"Not unless there's still a victim's blood on it, no."

"Shouldn't it also be moving?"

"Patience, lad. It might be moving too slowly for human perception. There's definitely something amiss. Give it time. I don't know if this is a silly theory, but perhaps it's wounded."

"A heartbroken dagger, Father?"

"Imagine how our old dagger, Diane's new dagger, would have reacted had we died rescuing her in Traverse City."

"I don't think I can imagine a piece of bronze having emotions, no matter how blessed it is."

But Diane could, believing in her dagger's living spirit. "That makes sense. It might even be scared, if its last hunters were killed."

The elder hunter's tone was reverent. "Five decades ago, they were close to victory, but horrible luck saw them gunned down by an Israeli Defense Force platoon. Their wraith was hiding with PLO raiders, and our brothers were unfortunate victims of the Israeli retaliation in a Beit She'an kibbutz."

"And now their dagger is your dagger?"

"Indeed. And their wraith is now our wraith. While we're waiting for him to move, perhaps now's a good time to mount the compass."

"Of course, Father." Liam reached towards a metal annulus leaning against the wall and hoisted it over the table.

The ring of metal appeared made of bronze and designed as a perfect fit over the table. Four small grooves in the flat surface aligned under notches in the annulus, setting its orientation. As Liam slid the metal over the stone, Diane noticed engraved ticks on the bronze, marking it as a compass.

Connor pointed towards the ruler laying against the wall. "Place the straight edge over it. Perhaps we can measure imperceptible movement over time."

"Yes, Father." Liam rested a meter-long wooden ruler over the dagger to add precision to its measured direction.

Though she found the tool crude, she realized the ruler would reveal if the blade rotated.

Connor clarified his expectations. "The dagger will adjust to the last location where the wraith offered tribute. The order suspects he's drawn blood recently."

The order remained a mystery to Diane. A hasty church ceremony had shed little light, generalities from Connor were cryptic, and Liam seemed as confused as she was. "So, we know nothing about his location?"

Connor frowned. "That's unfortunately correct, although we do know his schedule. By divine providence, we were able to defeat our wraith in Michigan with spare time to face this new threat."

The young hunter stepped back from the stone table. "He means that we have an opportunity to save other potential victims. The timing with this wraith places him in his killing cycle right now."

"And you both just became available to hunt him?"

"Yes, and we're needed. Apparently, being a hunter is something special, and there aren't many of us. Right, Father?"

The elder hunter clasped his son's shoulder. "We can only be replenished from our own lineage, and that's a bit of a murky history. We don't know who our successor is until the order finds an infant with the possible connection and tests him for candidacy."

The statement confused her. "How do you test an infant? I mean, today, I'm sure they can use DNA tests. But when they brought Liam to you twenty-five years ago, it was still a new science."

The elder hunter-knight removed his hand from his son. "Right again. The tests are secret exercises in divine discernment to assign the son to the father. There was also divine discernment used in our inheriting the responsibilities of the broken hunter line. The order didn't just assign this to us out of desperation."

She glanced at the unmoving dagger. "But you think this dagger you inherited is broken because it's not pointing towards the site of your new wraith's attacks?"

Showing optimism, the elder hunter smiled. "It's resisting for the moment, but it will oblige us in due time."

The younger hunter sounded anxious. "It needs to hurry. We were following a twelve-month schedule while looking for Diane. Our new wraith works in a four-month window. He's active now and will seek his sacrifice on the full moon in July."

Connor took a stern tone. "The dagger will help us when we need the help."

"Yes, Father."

"And this is a young wraith. He'll make mistakes. He's only had his dagger for one hundred years."

Diane had absorbed enough. "How can I help?"

"You're under no obligation, young lady, and I can't bear the thought of saving you from one savage only to have you victimized by the next."

She needed to be with Liam, whatever it took. She'd find a way to meet her obligations, such as paying the rent and caring for her autistic brother, Josh. "I want to help you hunt him. I know what it's like to be the next victim."

The elder hunter surprised her with his resistance. "But how could you help?"

"I'm not sure, yet. But I have an enchanted dagger that reacts only to me, and I have some pretty good telepathic powers. You guys need me."

Liam was nonchalant, hopefully hiding his excitement about her joining them. "She has a point, Father. We never would've succeeded without her last time."

"Don't argue, lad. I appreciate your youthful exuberance, but my ruling is, that as a survivor of a past wraith's attack, Diane cannot again be placed at risk."

CHAPTER 3

An hour before making a late evening pot of tea, Liam had mounted a camera over the new dagger and had run an Ethernet cable under the observatory's door. As he heated the water, he checked the knife's view in his phone.

Lifting the device's weight stimulated the dull throbbing under his cast, but the hairline fracture of his humerus allowed him freedom to use his elbow. Wiggling his thumb across the touchscreen imparted unexpected torques across his broken bone, causing deep stings.

He bore the pain, but seeing the unmoving dagger incited his swearing. "Bloody hell."

Reflecting upon the knife's apparent resistance, he developed a hunch. A hope.

He marched to the observatory and tapped keys on the laptop he'd balanced on the bronze compass. Quick work captured the stored video and allowed him to run it at one hundred and twenty times the speed of reality.

His hunch was right. The dagger was moving.

Starting where Diane had placed it, as close to bearing one-zero-four as she could, it still pointed towards Israel. But during the hour, the blade had rotated an eighth to a quarter of a degree–his eyes lacked the precision to quantify it–and its counter-clockwise creeping provided a clue.

The dagger's fractional motion ruled out Portugal, Spain, Africa, and the Americas as the location of the wraith's latest triple homicide. Coaxing more information from the knife could help find the killer's prior crime, but even if Liam could determine the location, he'd still be guessing about the next attack.

He hated hunting from two steps behind his prey, but prior success boosted his confidence.

In stopping the savage who'd sought Diane, he'd proven his effectiveness to himself. Based upon the extended, full-year killing cycle, he'd saved nine innocent lives by killing her wraith. He'd hoped to learn he'd set a record among his brethren, but the priest, the only member of the still-semi-secret order he'd met, had been curt with the accolades.

He didn't complain about the lack of glory, humility being a requisite of his calling.

Chastity was also a qualification, and it became uncomfortable as he returned to the kitchen and saw Diane's curves jutting from the stove.

When she turned in his direction, her long straight black hair bounced. He noticed her pleasing face, with expressive thoughtful bright eyes, and sharp and long nose. He liked her defined lips, long neck, and her soft, smooth skin.

Then he noticed the whistling pot he'd ignored. "Bloody hell. Sorry about that."

She scolded him, but it seemed affectionate, like the mother he'd never known or the wife he couldn't have. "I swear you two need a lady watching over you so that you don't burn this place down. And would it hurt to update the curtains? They're older than your dad. Your interior design needs a lady's touch."

"I couldn't agree with you more. About your touch. I mean, a lady's touch, I suppose."

He pursed his lips to stop yammering. Although he'd grown up with young women in his school and social life, he'd sensed a divine force giving him the strength for curbing any romantic desires.

But Diane unsettled him. "If I stay long enough, I may make some improvements."

"I'm sure Father would approve."

She poured water into waiting cups. "Where were you?"

"Oh, yes. I almost forgot. It's almost imperceptible, but the dagger's moving."

"No kidding?"

"No kidding. You can't see it with the naked eye, but the video shows it."

"We need to tell your dad."

After he'd developed the rescue plan and had placed himself in front of bullets to save her, he'd expected her respect. But she seemed to overlook him in favor of paternal authority, and he questioned if he'd become hypersensitive to her signals.

"Fine. Follow me." Diane walking behind him, he entered his father's study. A plethora of shelved books covered the room's walls. Liam considered the collection outdated, but he knew some old volumes carried valuable secrets, like the ancient tome of his lineage and that of Diane's that shared a decryption scheme despite descending through different lines for centuries.

Behind a huge oak desk, his father sat at a keyboard and monitor. "What can I do for you?"

Liam disbelieved the news as he shared it. "The dagger's moving, imperceptibly."

"Without our presence?"

"It must be a delayed reaction. It's been moving slowly or trying to move since we last saw it. It's also been trying to hold its red glow, but I think its light is fading." He knew of machines that could measure luminous power, but he thought better of investing time into gauging the knife's glow. All that mattered was the direction, which their new dagger seemed handicapped to provide.

"That's spectacular."

"It's true. I can show you on your computer. I uploaded the video to the cloud. I can walk you through it."

Connor stood. "Why don't you handle this?"

Liam sat in the elder hunter's armchair, looked into the screen, and grabbed the mouse. He brought up the video and started it as Diane and his father watched over his shoulders.

Diane broke the short silence. "That's so cool. I held my dagger's magic power, but I've never seen one move completely on its own."

"Rules are rules, young lady. To us, this movement is as predictable as the laws of physics, or it was until this new dagger. Its behavior is quite peculiar."

"I don't suppose our order gave you any warning about this?"

"Unfortunately not. But we have time to figure this out. The next full moon's due to rise June twenty-eighth, is it not?"

Liam did the quick math. "Yes, but today's the nineteenth. That's hardly a week away."

"Even at an eighth of a degree per hour, three degrees per day, we'll probably get our proper bearing to his prior kill before then."

Liam rolled back the chair to face his audience. "But we won't be able to travel and triangulate the location with a dagger on life support."

"True. I was trying to be optimistic. Something's amiss with the premise of our mission. The order wouldn't present us with an impossible starting point. We must be missing something."

Diane interjected her concerns. "What are the rules with the dagger, again?"

Liam feared that catching her up would slow him, but he reconsidered. She had magic, and she could help. He needed to share everything. "During the wraith's killing year, when there's a victim's blood on his dagger and a hunter looks at its blessed twin, the blessed one will glow, and it'll point towards the location of the murder. After the blood's cleared off the cursed dagger, our dagger stops glowing but still points to the location."

"As long as one of you is looking at it."

He appreciated her absorbing the rules. "Right."

"So, it's just a hunk of metal when you or your father aren't looking at it?"

He liked her directness. "Right."

"Why do you think the dagger only moves and glows when a hunter looks at it?"

He'd never challenged the premise and shared the first concept that came to his mind. "I guess it's like the double-slit experiment."

"What's that?"

"It addressed the nature of light and matter to behave as particles and waves, but the conclusion I'm referring to is that an object being observed gets its existence from the interaction between itself and the observer."

"Slow down, Einstein. I'm a marketing major."

She was going to make him think about the application of his knowledge, instead of reciting memorized data, and he liked it. "Something doesn't exist until an observer observes it to collapse it from a cloud of probabilities into reality."

"You're getting closer."

"Um… we make our own reality by observing it."

"Okay, I get that. That's cool. I've always thought that. The power of positive thinking, our moods, harnessing the universe's energy. I mean, it's all related somehow, right?"

"Right. Related somehow… maybe… it all falls apart at masses greater than the quantum level, but back to our dagger. Like Father said, we're missing something. It should be pointing to the last spot where he killed a tribute, but it's struggling to move."

"But it is moving, even without you or Connor watching it."

"That's why I think there's a delay in its reaction to our observation, in addition to its slowness."

The elder hunter shrugged. "I'm at a loss to explain it."

Liam was also lost. "I have no idea, either."

Diane gave him a look suggesting that everything would be okay. "Well, I do."

Liam was open to anything. "What?"

"Are men really that dense? Your dagger's obviously sick, and I'm going to nurse it back to health."

"How?"

"I'm not sure, but I've got a few ideas. Let me sleep on it and show you tomorrow. It's late and I'm tired, and this is going to take a lot of energy."

CHAPTER 4

The next morning, as Edric examined the young women–some of them girls–through his phone, their seller's marketing of them as sex slaves struck him as odd.

He questioned how men crumbled under their rampant desires for sexual conquest, when killing women was so much more satisfying.

Like any man with an itch, he'd enjoyed his share of lustful encounters during his last hundred years, but he considered sex a distraction. His primary rush was murder, asserting godlike control over another human, and exercising his will to dole out death.

As he'd amassed his small fortune over the decades, his ease of purchasing victims through human trafficking had grown. Outpacing inflation with his investments had also granted him comfort and access to modest real estate.

When the new year had begun, he'd sensed his Master urging him home–within the industrial section of Istanbul's Bayrampaşa district, a few hundred miles from where he'd begun his military training in the Ottoman Empire long ago.

The building that suited his needs was an unused warehouse he rented north of the European side of the city. The yellow paint on the upstairs bricks was peeling, and grime covered the industrial gray of the ground floor, especially near the eight unused loading docks on the windowless southern side.

As his boots clapped against the concrete floor, they echoed throughout the warehouse's open space. He lifted his phone towards his mouth, tapped the 'unmute' button, and mentioned his intent. "They're fine. I'll be there for the first bid."

He stepped through the warehouse's side door into the humid midday heat. Sunglasses on, he scanned his surroundings and saw no one. The remote commercial location far from prying eyes provided him with his requisite solitude.

He strode to his white van, which he'd bought from a downsizing delivery fleet and blended in with thousands like it. He entered the cargo hold and checked the restraints he'd welded to the floor. Eight stainless steel chains held eight shackles. After shutting and locking the back doors, he climbed into the driver's seat and headed towards the neighboring working class Esenler district.

The street he stopped on was livelier than he'd expected when he'd first visited the site. Beside the restaurant and bar that fronted the backroom auction block, a thriving deli enjoyed frequent customers, and a hairdresser across the street was busy. As he lifted his phone to his cheek, he saw a patron walk out of a wireless carrier store holding a box with a new headset.

The voice of a guard issued from the speaker. "Yes."

"I am client thirty-three. Let me through the gate."

"You're rather demanding for a client."

"Do you want my money or not?"

The phone went silent and then a motor rolled open the rusting chain-link gate to the parking lot. He drove the van into the fenced perimeter and then turned behind the building where he hit a three-point turn to back his vehicle to the loading dock.

With three vans parked ahead of him, he expected competition for the woman he intended to buy, but he knew, with his Master's silent assurance, he'd head home with the lives he needed.

And if he got lucky with his bids, he'd bring home some extra entertainment as well.

As Edric stepped from his vehicle, he wondered if any of his competing buyers intended to snuff the lives they bought.

When he entered the building, the worn red carpet smelled musty, and the air-conditioned atmosphere cooled his skin. The first armed guard raised his palm, stopping him. "Hands against the wall."

Remembering the routine, the wraith obeyed and spread his legs while thick hands probed his uncomfortable places.

"You're clear."

He continued down the corridor, passing restrooms, and stopping at the hallway's end. Admiring his seller's technical sophistication, he pressed his thumb against a fingerprint reader and waited for the latch to click open.

As he passed into the main showroom, the scent of perfumes from the properties hidden behind a curtain assaulted his nose. Another locked door at the room's far wall issued to the main restaurant and bar area that he avoided.

The first man to greet him brushed back shoulder-length black hair, extended his hand, and offered a salutation in Turkish. "Welcome. Can I get you a drink?"

"Not while I'm working." Edric shook his hand and moved beyond the lackey to the boss.

The seller was short and barrel-chested. Combed forward, his coarse gray hair contrasted the ruddiness of his face. The wraith smelled the spicy sweet scent of his cologne, and the shape of his head reminded him of a melon. The coldness of his eyes suggested a monster lurking behind them. The seller, broker, boss, or whatever he thought of himself greeted his client with a deep, gravelly voice. "It's always a pleasure. I trust that today's inventory interests you?"

"I plan to take a few of them."

"Excellent. You're the fourth to arrive. We're still waiting for two more."

The wraith checked the room for the other buyers and recognized four groups of two to three men. Their garb varied from designer sweat gear to suits. A few of them talked, presumably about the traits they sought in the women while probing each other for the prices they were willing to pay, but most of them stood in impatient and anxious silence.

They weren't the type of people who tolerated waiting.

Wearing an eastern European imitation of an Italian-cut, a single client entered the room and greeted the seller and his minion.

The minion climbed to the stage and addressed the crowd. "We were waiting for one more client, but the late shall suffer for their tardiness. So, we shall begin the festivities." His long hair brushed his back as he stepped to the side of the stage. "Today's beauties hail from Aleppo, Syria with ages ranging from fifteen to twenty-seven. You've seen their videos. Now get ready to meet these jewels, starting with number one."

Bright spotlights lit the stage as a young woman appeared from behind a curtain. Wearing skimpy shorts and a tight tee shirt, she squinted and raised her arm against the lighting.

The minion waved his hand downward. "Lower your arm, dear. Now turn around all the way. That's it. Keep going. Now face us again and stop."

She obeyed and then stood in coy uncertainty. Even while slouching, she looked tall, thin, and without curves. Her nose was wide, and a reddish birthmark covered her right cheek.

Edric knew the other buyers would consider her a low priority, like all the first products displayed on auction day. The first, less desirable women on the block gave him his best bargains.

The minion swept his arm towards the woman. "The bidding begins at one thousand liras."

The audience remained silent.

"Come now, who will bid one thousand liras for this young woman with such long legs?"

The last client to arrive raised his finger.

"Excellent. Now who will bid twelve hundred? Twelve hundred liras?"

The wraith lifted his finger.

"I have twelve hundred for this Syrian doll. Who will bid fourteen? Fourteen hundred liras?"

The buyer in the imitation Italian suit made his second bid.

"I have fourteen hundred. Who will bid sixteen hundred liras for this healthy girl?"

To add drama and throw off his competitor, Edric waited.

"Will no one offer the pittance of sixteen hundred liras for this gem? Fourteen hundred going once. Fourteen hundred going twice."

Edric pounced. "Sixteen hundred."

"Sixteen hundred! I have sixteen hundred. Do I have seventeen? Seventeen hundred?"

The competing bidder became stone.

"Sixteen hundred going once. Sixteen hundred going twice. Sold, to client thirty-three."

A guard escorted the young lady offstage, and then the next woman passed through a curtain onto the stage.

Like the first, she wore cheap, revealing clothing. She was short, buxom, and below average as measured by the beauty metrics most buyers considered.

With minimal competition, Edric bought her.

Then he bought the next one to complete his trio for the upcoming full moon.

Having found his three bargains, he bought a fourth–a plaything.

When the auction ended, he waited his turn behind the buyers of the more expensive girls to load his possessions.

As a repeat customer, he received help loading the women into their shackles of his van. His new properties ranged in age from eighteen to twenty-two, if he believed the advertising, and they were all perfect for his needs.

With sullen faces, they sat cross-legged in the back of his vehicle. As he closed the doors, he sentenced them to short and horrific fates.

CHAPTER 5

Diane realized she appeared overconfident to the men, but the concept seemed obvious.

Feed something weak from the abundance of something strong.

She wondered why the men had missed such an easy observation. Perhaps it was woman's intuition, but men baffled her with their denseness when they missed simple clues.

Sitting with the hunters at their kitchen table, she watched their housekeeper, who'd arrived early to cook, lay out a breakfast of bacon, sausages, black pudding, poached eggs, fried potato wedges, and brown bread. Diane sipped a tea with a robustness that reminded her of the cardamom-infused drinks of her Chaldean people, but which tasted blander.

After a week as the Irishmen's houseguest, she knew better than filling her plate from each dish the stocky housekeeper placed before her. While her hungry colleagues wolfed down monstrous mouthfuls–Liam especially–she tallied an impossible sum of calories ingested. But their daily training regimen burned them all.

She moved sliced melon wedges, which she'd requested to add fiber to her meals, onto her plate. Biting into its juicy sweetness, she glanced at the young hunter.

He swallowed an enormous hunk of sausage. "Did you ever come up with a plan?"

Raising a white cloth napkin to her mouth, she cleaned her face. "I was thinking about it last night. I have a feeling about what I need to do, but nothing detailed."

"So, this is an empath thing? You just have an intuition?"

"Yeah. I'm going to see if I can use the energy of my dagger to nurse yours back to life."

"Huh. Like jump-starting a car battery?"

She'd never jump-started her car, since her younger brother had proven capable and since she often protected her craftsmanship after painting her nails with elaborate, multi-colored designs. It was okay, she figured, to let men handle occasional dirty tasks. "Sure. I guess."

"You want to try it after breakfast?"

"I want to clean up first, but after that, yeah."

Showered and wearing fresh jeans and a tee shirt, she finished making her bed in the guest room. She then pulled open the top drawer of her dresser and saw the plain wooden box containing her mystical dagger. Keeping the knife concealed, she carried it downstairs to Connor's study, but she found an empty room.

She turned and walked to the observatory door. Finding it locked, she knocked.

Connor unlatched and swung open the heavy wood. "Sorry. Force of habit."

Within the room, Liam faced a computer. "I think it's speeding up. But it's still too slow. Maybe a half a degree per hour now."

She looked at the dagger on the circular stone table. Its reddish glow was a faded light. "Well, I'm ready to try it."

"Let me get a final measurement." Liam stooped over the knife and eyed the straightedge. After seeing the blade's bearing, he grabbed the bronze handle and then lay the weapon in its box on the floor. Clasping the wooden case like it stored lightning, he lifted it and looked to the empath. "Where do you want to do this?"

"I have no idea what's going to happen. So, it's got to be some place safe."

"This whole house is safe, depending what you mean by 'safe'."

"I'm not sure what I mean. All I know is that I fell asleep for days the last time I tried something new."

"Let's get you lying down then, just so you don't fall over and hurt yourself."

The elder hunter raised a finger. "I'll get the first aid kit, just in case."

Lying on the couch in the living room, she noticed the huge wooden crossbeams and the white stucco ceiling. Kneeling beside her, Liam wore oven mitts.

She thought he looked silly, given her assessment of his nonexistent culinary skills. "Are those really necessary?"

"Nobody else has touched your dagger with their bare hands since you beat your wraith in Michigan. Let's keep it that way."

"Okay, I'm as ready as I'll ever be."

She extended her right hand, and the hunter pushed the bronze handle into her palm. As it gave off a bluish glow, its energy pulsated into her, infusing her with the sense of infinite possibilities. Resting it on her chest, she extended her other hand. "It's not as blue as the last time I grabbed it."

Seated on the edge of a coffee table behind his son, Connor explained it. "That's because it doesn't need to be. Before you, it had been a millennium since a virgin held a dagger, but the order's learning suggests that its energy is reactionary to the virgin."

Diane disliked the labelling based upon her sex life. "Can we stop calling me 'the virgin'?"

"I'm sorry, young lady, but it's the term we've always used. I'm happy to use a different term, if we could conjure up a better one."

Liam's candor surprised her. "We're all virgins here."

"Really? I didn't know you guys were... sworn to it?"

The young hunter preached, like he was reminding himself. "It's a valuable and vital virtue of our lineage."

"Well, isn't it silly that a bunch of male virgins call the woman they try to rescue 'the virgin'?"

Connor blushed. "I've always believed it to be a matter of reverence. A woman gives up so much more by foregoing the ability to grow life in her womb."

"I guess, but I still don't like being called 'the virgin'."

"She's 'the empath', Father."

"So be it. Diane is our esteemed empath."

"Cool. I like 'the empath'."

The young hunter smiled, displaying a knight's charm that had escaped her. "You were special. You are special. You deserve a special term."

She thought she might be happy with "Liam's wife" if she could get to know him.

"Get ready for the next dagger. Here we go." Liam lowered the lethargic knife into her free palm, and its feeble sanguine glimmer became a darker, chocolatey red.

While the bluish-azure weapon felt weightless in her right hand, the sickly one was an anvil in her left. She grunted.

Liam extended his oven mitts over her. "Let me help you."

"No, I've got it."

"You're sure?"

"No. But I have to try. It feels heavy and cold, but it's okay so far." During a minute, nothing changed. No matter what she thought or felt, the glow of each dagger remained constant in color and intensity.

"Is anything happening?"

"I don't think so. I'm holding two daggers that want nothing to do with each other."

"Should you think about energy moving from one to the other?"

"What do you think I've been doing?"

"Sorry."

After Liam's apology, she admitted to herself she hadn't been truthful in her claim. As she reflected about her recent thoughts, they'd been exploratory. She'd been subconsciously probing each dagger to learn about them. Shifting her purpose from exploration to control, she imparted her will upon the bronze items, commanding energy to flow from one to the other. Still nothing.

Connor shifted his weight on the table. "I fear this is bearing no fruit."

"Let's not give up so easily, Father. Diane, do you remember anything about your mindset when I threw your blade to you and you were fighting the wraith in Michigan?"

Of course, she did. She replayed the memory multiple times daily, and her subconscious mind rendered varied distortions of the episode during her sleep. "Yeah."

Kneeling closer to her, Liam blocked his father from the conversation. "Well, how about recreating those thoughts or feelings? That's when your dagger produced some amazing magic."

"I was pissed off and scared, but I don't think that's going to help anything right now."

"But what about your feelings towards the dagger?"

Being unaware of the answer, she had to reflect upon her regard for her weapon when she first met it. "When you first threw it to me, when it changed colors from red to blue and moved under its own power in mid-air, I was exhilarated."

"Yeah, so was I. What else were you feeling?"

"Hope?"

"What about love?"

Ugh. Love again. She'd nearly died trying to love an enemy as she'd invoked her telepathic power over her prior wraith. Advice from a ghost had guided her by reminding her of love's constituent parts–acceptance, patience, kindness, empathy, selflessness. She could feel all those emotions for anyone.

Or anything alive.

As she reflected upon her first encounter with her glowing blue dagger, she realized it had a life, and she'd loved it from the moment she'd clutched it. "Yes, love. It saved my life. I love my dagger."

"What about ours? The sick one?"

Her honesty struck her as she spoke the words. "I resent it."

Liam's words eased her guilt of harboring the negative emotion. "Understandable. We're all struggling with the new burden it represents and its inability to help us."

"I need to love your new dagger, the one that failed your predecessors fifty years ago."

"I think so."

"I'll give it a shot."

With her high emotional intelligence, she shifted her perspective of the ailing weapon from condemnation to empathy. The rapid switch opened a channel to her acceptance, her love of it, and the effect was instant.

The blue light pulsated, as did the dark chocolate red, locked in opposing phases. When one lit the room, the other swallowed light, and in rhythm, energy flowed from right to left across Diane.

Her breaths shallow, she forced a faint whisper. "It's working."

Reminiscent of her prior first attempts at new empathic tricks, a supernatural force drew her into a deep slumber.

CHAPTER 6

Liam removed the blood pressure cuff from Diane's arm. "Normal. A bit low actually, probably because she's resting so calmly. That aligns with her low heart rate."

"We assume so, but we should've measured her vital signs beforehand as a baseline."

Somehow, he knew she was okay, but his father had insisted on checking her. He gave the cuff to the elder hunter, who handed him a small flashlight.

Liam lifted her right eyelid and saw a round, dilated pupil. He shined the light, and the dark circle shrank. He removed the light, and the pupil widened. "Looks good." He checked her left eye, stimulating similar results. "They both respond to light, both have normal roundness, and the sizes are the same. No sign of neurological damage."

"A CT scan would confirm that."

His success in stopping Diane's wraith gave him the confidence to challenge his father. "Don't you think you're overreacting?"

"Perhaps, but I don't like her helping us. We spent our entire lives preparing to save her, and we did so three weeks ago. I don't want her placed at further risk."

"She's fine, Father. She looks like a sleeping..."

"Angel?"

"Yeah."

"I think you're becoming emotionally attached to her."

"Careful. She's an empath. She can probably hear us. Her consciousness may be hovering in this room laughing at us."

"You're confusing her with a ghost. Per my reckoning, an empath needs a host to reside in. To hear us, she'd have to be inside one of our minds."

With a strong attraction to her, Liam wondered if he'd notice her invading him, but he kept that possible vulnerability hidden from his father. "You're right. I'm sure I'm just being paranoid."

"I'm sure you are."

Liam reassessed the empath as she held both knives. The luminous pulsations continued as energy flowed from one, across their comatose conduit, and to the other. "Do you suppose I should remove our dagger from her hand?"

"That might interrupt the process. It seems to be working, or at least she said it was before she drifted away."

"Yeah, but what about her? What's this doing to her?"

"Like you said, she's resting calmly."

"I don't like it, Father. She could be in pain. This could have long term effects we don't know about."

"Now, who's overreacting?"

"Fair point."

"Bah. Don't let an old man scare you. It's all conjecture at this point. Do what you think is right."

Liam put on his oven mitts and grabbed the tip of Diane's left finger. Like all her digits, it was slender and elegant, and it yielded to his lifting.

After he'd peeled her hand open, he lifted the dagger, and when its contact with her skin broke, its pulsating dark light yielded to its familiar weak reddish glow. "I'll set this on the observatory table."

"Right. Take it directly in. I'll keep an eye on her."

"Can you at least unlock the door for me?"

"Oh, yes. Sorry. Stay with her while I tend to it."

The elder hunter darted off with impressive agility for an old man, and Liam hoped the distant ancestry connecting him with his adoptive father had gifted him similar genes.

He checked on Diane, and her breathing remained slow and regular. To free his hands, he lowered the dagger into its box. He then reached back to the empath and tested her grip on her knife, which had ceased pulsating but maintained a light blue glimmer.

Her fingers were vice grips.

"Bloody hell, Diane. Nobody's ever going to disarm you."

His father's voice rang from the observatory. "What?"

"I was talking to Diane."

"I don't suppose she can hear you, but that's open for debate, isn't it?"

"Here, Father. Try opening her hand." He extended his mitts towards the elder hunter, who approached him.

Connor pulled them from his son's hands, put them on, and tested Diane's grip. "Good gracious. I can't budge her fingers."

"That's why I was talking to her. I couldn't help but remark about something so, well, remarkable."

"Right, then. We'll have to remember this."

"I don't think I could forget."

He reached for his dagger's box but remembered it was his weapon, belonging to his lineage, within his rights to touch. He grasped its handle, stood, and walked to the observatory.

He steadied the knife on its last bearing of one-zero-zero and stepped back. Thinking his eyes tricked him, he saw it move. "Father! It's moving!"

"Coming." The elder hunter entered the circular silo and closed the door. He watched the dagger keep its sanguine luster while rotating counter-clockwise. "It's slower than a healthy dagger, but it's trying. I can see it move without your time-lapse video, now."

"It still seems sick, though."

"It is, but it's much more alive. Let's take turns watching it to make sure it doesn't quit."

"Can you take the first watch? I'd like to look after Diane." After his father's affirming nod, Liam walked to the empath and knelt by her. Alone with her for the first time without an agenda, he wondered who she was.

What music did she like? What were her political views? Why did she sacrifice her needs behind those of an autistic brother? What were her career goals?

Did she want to get to know him better?

Unless she woke up, he'd never know, but he expected her full recovery. He'd lost her to supernatural slumbers while she'd been imprisoned in her wraith's Michigan basement, the longest outage lasting a week and a half.

She'd always returned from her sleeps unharmed, but this was the first time she–or anyone, to his knowledge–held two enchanted daggers. He could only hope she'd recover. With her empathic work proving draining, he questioned if his father's doubts about her chasing the next wraith had merit.

Long before meeting her, his purpose had been saving her, and rescuing her from one wraith should have been the end. But it felt like a beginning, a first protective step of many.

But then he remembered his ordained duty was protecting the next virgin, the one sought by a wraith who'd caused the death of two hunters of his lineage. Duty trumped feelings, and the fear of being forced to choose between Diane's safety or that of a stranger weighed upon him.

Though unnecessary, he palpated her wrist and enjoyed the warmth of her smooth skin. He tried three times to count her pulse, but his attention wandered, and he gave up.

He closed his eyes to quiet his thoughts and let himself notice if she sought a telepathic link with him. He'd communicated to her several times through links with other people, but she'd never been inside his head. With her slumber placing her beyond his communicative reach, he missed her company.

But within his mind, he sensed only himself, and she remained motionless except for her basic life functions.

"Liam!"

"Yes, Father."

"It's stopped."

"Coming." Liam trotted to the observatory and saw the stationary dagger. With his father's silent approval, he rotated the straightedge over the blade and noted the orientation. "Bearing zero-nine-seven."

"We must map it."

With the Ethernet cable feeding the laptop on the table, Liam typed the numbers into a page showing bearings originating from his home in Glengarriff. After tapping in the direction, he watched the line curve across a flat rendition of the earth. "That crosses or approaches the borders of nearly half the nations of Europe. Then it passes through half the nations of the Middle East."

"That's accurate only if we trust the dagger. I'm not sure what to believe, but I will report this to the order for confirmation."

Liam's instincts made him optimistic. "I'm sure they'll agree it's accurate. After Diane helped it along, I can't see it failing."

"We'll know the accuracy as we tighten the location."

"I'm sure of that, but we'll face the same old problem of stale data. By the time we find where he killed his last tribute, he'll be long gone."

"Tributes."

"What?"

"Tributes, lad. Three per full moon, with only three full moons of homicides preceding the life-stealing virgin sacrifice."

"What'd I say?"

"You mentioned only one tribute, which would refer to our prior mission saving Diane. Our new duty is to catch a savage beast who operates on a different killing cycle."

Liam found his father's stating of the obvious patronizing, but he feigned reverence. "Yes, Father. Tributes. When we find the location of his offering of the last tributes, we'll still only be finding where he was, not where he presently is."

"It's a delay we've always faced. We may not catch this wraith this year. After I'm gone, you may not catch him fifty years later. Nobody guarantees success, and the odds are dreadfully against us, but this is our noble purpose."

Liam expected a better reward for rapid and decisive success against Diane's wraith. A champion deserved better. But looking inward, he tapped lessons in humility and kept his ego in check.

But he wasn't sure how long he could suppress it.

Being a hunter, a knight, and a man of virtue was difficult. "What do we do now, Father?"

"It's quite simple. We follow our first clue. We travel."

CHAPTER 7

Edric clicked the remote controller to the warehouse's only automated door, waited for its rise, and then aimed the van into his home's ground level.

After clicking shut the portal behind him, he parked the vehicle on the concrete, turned off the engine, and stepped into the air-conditioned coolness. Reconsidering his tactics for deploying his four purchases into their jail cells, he climbed back into the driver's seat and then cut a tight semicircle to reorient the van.

With the cargo space and his four new prizes aimed towards the vast expanse of the warehouse's former storage floor, his women would see a small swath of their depressing confines. More importantly, the three tributes would see him discipline the fourth woman–his toy to enjoy as he wished.

He walked to the back of the van and opened its doors. Four restrained and distressed women looked at him. Having forgotten a blindfold to prevent the captives from seeing too much of their confines, he marched to a workbench and grabbed a rag. When he returned to the vehicle, he pointed to the closest prisoner and waved her forward.

She cowered and crawled from him.

He gestured again, and using the broken Arabic he'd learned over a century of exposure to multiple languages, he ordered her. "Come, or I will hurt you."

Obeying, she moved to the edge of the van.

He tied the rag around her eyes and then reached into his back pocket. After grasping his keys, he raised them and found the one for the vehicle's shackles. Reaching, he stuck the key into the irons and disconnected the nearest captive from the leg cuff.

Unwilling to coddle her, he yanked her and tossed her over his shoulder. As he walked towards the nearest cell's entrance, a thick exterior door he'd installed upon renting the structure, became visible through a set of metal shelves.

She wiggled and kicked in protest.

He angled her face for the others to see, formed a fist with his free hand, and thrust it into her jaw. She cried, and he repeated punching her until she collapsed.

Carrying her unconscious bulk required more of his attention since she'd stopped shifting her weight to balance herself. He adjusted her three times as he took her down a corridor of empty storage shelves and then past the universal gym he used to keep up his strength.

At the entrance to her cell, he dropped her on the concrete. Her slow breathing indicated she'd survived her blows, leaving her available for his needs.

Again lifting his key chain, he found the appropriate cut of brass. Sliding the teeth into the hole and twisting his wrist, he unlocked the bolt he'd installed with his own craftsmanship and slid it sideways. Pulling the door, he exposed one of many multipurpose enclosures that could serve as storage, a conference room, or an office. He prided himself on making this cell an exact replica of the other three, perfect for his needs and those of his overseeing spirit.

With his bare hands, he'd customized the windowless spaces with toilets. The effort prevented lingering stenches he would find offensive, and any dignity it imparted to the captives was secondary.

Expecting short stays from his inmates, he left other sanitary needs to moist wipes and garbage bags. For sleeping, he provided a cot, and since he deprived each prisoner of a chair, the cot allowed for seating as well. A switch beside the door controlled the solitary LED bulb in the ceiling of each confined space. It was generous by his reckoning.

In the center of the room jutted Edric's masterpiece. He'd broken into the floor and had embedded links of chain into new pours of concrete. He lifted his unconscious inmate's shoulders from the hard surface and dragged her into her confines. Using a third key, he shackled her ankle to the room's central anchor.

He visually checked her restraints. Handcuffs around her wrists, leg irons at her ankles, and the tether to the concrete assured her bondage. He considered keeping her blindfolded, but he needed the rag for the next victim.

When he appeared at the van's rear, he found compliance. The first tribute for his Master, the tall and thin one he'd won in the first auction, accepted the blindfold and remained stationary while he unshackled her from the cargo hold. On his shoulder, she remained silent and adjusted her weight to avoid falling.

Securing her to her cell's shackles proved easier than he'd hoped. A little defiance might have allowed a dose of discipline.

The final two tributes behaved as compliantly as the first, until he locked the last one into her jail shackle and removed her blindfold.

She scanned her room and then looked at him. "What kind of monster does this?"

He marched towards her, and she cowered as he lifted his arm to backhand her. But his domineering spirit stayed his strike.

The wraith obeyed one entity other than himself–the deity who enlivened his dagger, his Master. Commands came in rare and quick bursts of silence. In a flash, he received one. Leave her unharmed until instructed otherwise. She belonged to his domineering spirit, reducing Edric to a mere steward.

He grunted, stormed out of the cell, and locked it behind him. His captives secured, he rounded the corner to a stairway leading to the warehouse's second floor. After a brisk climb, he turned down a hallway leading to his quarters.

The former supervisory office was spacious and gave a panoramic view of the building's insides. Walking across the worn carpet brought him to the clear acrylic windows and gave him a panoramic view of his home.

Across from him, sunlight shone through the upper level windows. Inaccessible to street-level onlookers, the high glass squares allowed for secrecy. The lower level windows, however, were few and too small to allow human entry, and he'd painted over them with black paint.

Below him, empty metal shelves covered the area of a football field. A broken and scavenged forklift hinted at an abandoned inventory management system. Turning his back on the dormant work area, he examined his makeshift lair.

With forethought to entertaining clients and for supporting twenty-four-hour occupancy, the office displayed a measure of comfort and hominess. A wet bar with a semicircular booth lined one side, and a kitchen spanned the other. In the back corner, a sunken lounge provided seating in front of a television, and a door beside the refrigerator opened to the wraith's small bedroom.

He strode into his chambers and then reached into the top drawer of a wooden dresser with faded stain. After he grabbed a leather belt, he darted down the stairs.

On the abandoned inventory floor, he walked to the workbench that held various tools. He'd been fantasizing about a boxcutter and a claw hammer, in addition to the belt he gripped. Within a plastic box he found the blade, and the hammer was lying on the wooden table. With all three items in his hand, he marched to his toy's cell.

When he entered, he saw the groggy woman. She'd awoken, but she appeared dazed and unready for further torment. As she lay shackled, he noticed her enticing physique. Though she was of short stature, accounting for her lower bid price at auction, her curves formed where he wanted them, kindling his lust.

For a moment, he considered forced gratification of his desire, but he sensed his Master would disapprove. The deity of the dagger had gifted her for a specific purpose, for snuffing her life, and using her for sexual relief would be sacrilege.

He closed the door and moved to the next cell. After opening the latch, he gazed inside and saw the thin tribute sitting on the cot.

She seemed overwhelmed by the circumstances which had brought her to the auction block and then to the warehouse prison.

Adding to her psychological torment pleased Edric as he lifted the three objects–the belt, the hammer, and the boxcutter. "Choose."

She frowned. "Why?"

He snorted. "I told you to choose."

"I don't want to."

"If you don't choose, I will choose for you."

She became resigned. "What am I choosing for?"

"I told you to choose."

"How can I choose if I don't know what the purpose is?"

He turned away. "I will choose for you."

"Wait! The belt. I choose the belt."

As he'd expected. "Very well."

"What did I choose it for? You have to tell me!"

He closed the door and moved to the adjacent cell where he tormented the next captive with the same unanswered riddle.

She chose the belt, the least threatening of the three.

The third prisoner suffered through the same enigma to the same conclusion.

He returned the tools to the workbench and kept the belt, snapping it between his hands loudly enough for the inmates to hear. Walking to the first detainee's prison, he hoped to find her lucid as he unlocked the latch and peered inside.

She remained groggy.

His extended life allowed his patience, and he considered waiting for her recovery. But then he glanced at his watch and noted lunchtime approaching, and killing whetted his appetite.

He strode across the concrete floor to his workbench and exchanged his belt for a roll of duct tape. Then, lifting a nearby chair, he returned to the jail cell and set it beside her. "Sit."

She looked away. "I can't."

"Sit, or I will hurt you again."

Clutching the chair for support, she pulled her torso over the seat. Leveraging the back, she muscled herself upright, revealing the abrasions and bruises on her face.

He marched behind her and wrapped her torso and arms to the chair's back, leaving her handcuffed arms in her lap. After resting the tape roll on her cot, he withdrew his keychain from his pocket, found the proper cut, and unshackled her ankles from the concrete floor. A final wrap of tape bound her shins against the chair's legs.

"What are you doing?"

He backhanded her head. "Shut up."

She whimpered.

Bending at the knees, he wrapped his arms around her and lifted the combined weight of the woman and the chair. Stepping with short and deliberate strides, he carried her to the stairs.

Although a freight elevator provided an easier route, he wanted to carry her mass. The tug against his shoulders foreshadowed the gravity of her pending death.

Within his chambers, he carried her across the living space and then lowered her. He faced her towards the panoramic window.

Leaving his victim in anxious silence, he backtracked his way out his chambers and down the stairs to the warehouse floor. He moved to his workbench where he'd left his belt, and then he returned upstairs to his seated victim.

"Your companions chose this. This is their doing." He brushed aside his seated possession's hair, strapped the belt around her neck, and yanked the length through the buckle. One hand held the leather taut while the other pressed the enclosed loop against her nape.

But recognizing strangulation as an undesirable technique, he abandoned his charade of deviating from his modus operandi. He released the belt and reached into his pocket for a utility knife. With a swift motion, he mimicked the act of tribute.

A rush of satisfaction soothed him as he held the knife's handle against her stabbed chest to assure her demise. To become as God is, one must do as God does, and doling out death was the godliest act he could conceive.

And it felt good.

CHAPTER 8

Diane dreamt of a young woman burning on a cross, blood pouring from her heart's puncture wound.

Time stopped, accelerated, and slowed again as the nightmarish scene unfolded. The victim seemed distant, and then Diane was the victim. One moment, she was a sacrifice, then the next she was the savior.

Then a vision appeared in which an unseen wind flapped a milky gown over a female frame. The young woman, exposed and pierced during her death but now clothed in dignity and unblemished in the afterlife, called out in Hebrew. "Avenge me."

Diane understood the foreign words and responded in English. "Who are you?"

"We descend from the same line, the line of Nineveh."

"You're an empath, too?"

The ghost seemed to wrestle with the question, the black pools of her eyes narrowing as her misty brow furrowed. "I was, but I lacked your power."

"Why me? Why do I have all this supposed power?"

"You are an empath. You know."

She hated that answer when the francophone ghost had said it. Though this apparition was the twin of the maiden of the French millhouse, Diane knew she was a different spirit.

"How do I know you're trying to help me? How do I even know you're real?"

"You are an empath. You know."

Lacking a body, Diane imagined herself slapping her palm against her forehead. "Can you at least tell me your name? I never got the name of the last one."

"She was the Maiden of Anduze. I am the Maiden of Beit She'an."

Diane recognized the name's geographical reference to the new wraith's work fifty years earlier. "You're the last one he sacrificed?"

"Yes, his second. He sacrificed a sister in Urmia fifty years before me."

For an unmeasured moment in her timeless world, Diane enjoyed the concept of belonging to a sisterhood. She also found her mind running on steroids in her dreamlike trance, her memory perfect, and her quantitative skills impeccable. "He's killed twenty women, eighteen as tributes to the spirit of his dagger and two sacrifices to extend his life."

"No, he's murdered many more. This one is terrible."

"As opposed to the one in Michigan? He had sex slaves and murdered thirteen women every fifty years for five centuries."

"The one you destroyed killed only by necessity. The one you seek kills for sport. He's killed thousands, by his hand and by the orders he's uttered. He is far more dangerous."

"Does that change anything I'm doing?"

"You are an empath. You know."

The default answer annoyed Diane. "If you say so, but what am I doing here? Am I stopping this wraith just like last time?"

The apparition's face became pleased, almost smug. "Just like last time."

Knowing an exact repeat of her prior predicament was impossible, Diane doubted the maiden's response. The details would be different, but something important would be the same. She wanted to ask her spiritual adviser about it, but the ghost's smug visage suggested a dead end in the interrogation. So, she shifted her line of questioning. "How long have I been asleep?"

"Three hours."

That was a relief. She'd lost eleven days during her worst episode in the past. "Why did I fall asleep?"

"You tried to impart your will upon the daggers."

"I thought my dagger was mine?"

"It is a living entity. It will not obey orders it does not wish to obey."

"I commanded it to give up its energy to another dagger, and it didn't like that, did it?"

"Correct."

Diane assumed the ghost's terse answer and blunt tone included a tacit message about her realization having been obvious. A mortal woman doesn't tell an immortal dagger to give up its energy. She likened the relationship to a lion and its tamer in which the human so-called master elicits from the lion only what it's willing to give. "Got it. What about Liam's dagger?"

The ghost cocked her head. "The dagger belongs to both hunters, predominantly to the elder. How curious that you attribute its ownership to the younger."

Diane wondered if the maiden had just reversed the inquiry. "Right, the hunters' dagger. Did I try to force-feed it too much energy all at once?"

"It was wounded by the loss of its two hunters. Rarely does a wraith kill a hunter. Even more rarely do both hunters die. The dagger was traumatized."

Allowing for the feelings of enchanted bronze items, Diane conceded her failing. "I understand. I'll be more careful next time. There will be a next time, right? I still need to fix Liam's, I mean their dagger?"

The ghost kept her unearthly composure while leaving the question unanswered.

Thinking herself in a standoff of wills with her advising apparition, Diane confessed. "Fine, I have feelings for Liam."

Translucent lids formed like thin films over the maiden's black eyes while she seemed trapped in thought.

Expecting her ghost advisor to process and access information in an instant, the eye-closing gesture perplexed Diane.

Then the lids opened. "Feelings, yes. Of course. It is good that you admit them, for they are dangerous."

"How can they be dangerous? Isn't love the tool of the empath?" Diane thought she had her ghost in a logical bind.

"Love is the tool of an empath, but beware of infatuation."

Disliking her spirit guide's tone, Diane withheld the curse welling within her. "I'll work on it."

"Be sure that you do."

The warning seemed somehow given out of kindness, quelling Diane's urge to tell the ghost to remain silent. "I will."

"Above all, remember what your dagger is."

"I know. It's a weapon."

"Yes, but a dagger can be used as a weapon in multiple ways."

The concept of breaking one of her multi-colored manicured fingernails crossed Diane's mind, reminding her of the absurdity of her mastering a handheld weapon. "I guess so."

"He will kill again soon, and he will continue until you stop him."

"You mean, until I help the hunters stop him, right?"

Again, the ghost closed her eyes and withdrew from the conversation to tap some distant source of knowledge. "They cannot succeed without you."

Diane awoke in the hunters' home and gasped.

The elder hunter helped her sit. "Easy, young lady."

She coughed, and her throat felt dry and scratched.

"Can I get you some water? Perhaps some cough syrup?"

She shook her head. The coughing subsided, and she tried to speak. Her vocal cords failed, and her attempt to form words issued a squeak.

"Water, then." He stood, turned, and darted to the kitchen. When he returned, he held out a tall glass.

She grabbed it and sipped, and the cool liquid quenched a fire. Desiring more of the soothing sensation, she gulped the container's contents.

"I guess you were thirsty."

Nodding, she handed him the cup. Then she realized she'd quenched her thirst with one hand, keeping her dagger clutched in her other. "What happened?"

"Liam took our dagger back while you were sleeping. We have a bearing now. You did very well, I must say."

"But…" Her voice was regaining power but remained weakened.

"Slowly now. There's no hurry."

Having spent hours in a seemingly timeless trance, she agreed. As her memory fed her snapshots of her ethereal journey, she recalled images and sensations as if invoking a forgotten dream.

"Are you okay?"

"I think so." Her voice sounded better.

"You appear as if you'd seen a ghost. Given your history, I can only wonder."

She looked away to probe her memory. "Yeah, I did."

"Well, my dear empath and receiver of ghosts, did it tell you anything useful?"

She gathered her thoughts… Try not to fall in love with Liam. Use the dagger like a weapon but differently than she used it in Michigan. The wraith kills for sport. Treat every dagger like a temperamental feline. She groped to put the clues together, and then a conclusion struck her. "I think she told me that he just killed someone for fun."

"Really? Wouldn't we see some evidence on our dagger?"

There was much to explain. "I don't think he used his dagger. Help me to the observatory, and I'll tell you what I know."

CHAPTER 9

Liam sprang from the chair as his father escorted Diane into the cylindrical stone room. He couldn't restrain his elation in seeing her ambulatory. "Diane!"

"She's quite alright, I assure you."

In her right hand, her dagger reflected the room's lighting off its natural bronze surface. "Yeah, I'm fine."

"What happened? You were out for hours."

"Apparently, I was too demanding with both daggers."

Liam found the answer incomplete. "And?"

"And that led to a battle of wills, and I was outnumbered two to one against enchanted items."

Hesitant to accept the concept of cast bronze items with overpowering wills, he was dubious, but he'd delay any protest to an appropriate time. "Well, I guess those are tough odds."

Connor moved against the wall, giving Diane space to explore the fruits of her labor. She stepped to the central table and looked down at the dagger. "Its color's fading."

Any degradation in the knife's luminous flux had escaped Liam. "I hadn't noticed."

"It's obvious to me, maybe because I haven't seen it in a while."

Liam silently chastised himself. "If I'd been more vigilant, I would've noticed by playing the video with time compression."

His father rescued him from his defeatism. "Don't be too hard on yourself. There's no hurry. There's nothing else we can do today."

Liam agreed and stepped to the computer where he manipulated the footage of the blade. "Let me check the video anyway."

Diane stepped from the table. "What color should it be?"

"Father, can you answer while I'm working here?"

"Of course. I believe you know already that all unnatural phenomenon with our dagger occurs only when Liam or I are watching it."

"Yes."

"Well, the first but least frequent phenomenon is when a wraith moves at the beginning of his killing cycle. History has proven that they live the majority of their lives somewhere different than the location of their sacrifices."

"Like Traverse City in my case?"

"Precisely. When your wraith moved from Europe to Michigan before his killing cycle, our dagger glowed its natural color. This doesn't give us much tactical information, but it marks the beginning of a wraith's killing season."

From the corner of his eye, Liam watched Diane sit in a chair while the accelerated video on his computer showed his beacon's reddish hue waning. "Diane was right. The color's fading."

Connor shifted into story-telling mode. "Good. That means its slowly tending towards its healthier state. It should only glow red while there's blood on the wraith's twin blade. Unless this wraith's a complete dolt, he cleaned his dagger three weeks ago."

"How does your dagger know to respond to a given wraith's dagger and not to some other dagger?"

"The legends say our order has had every cursed dagger in our possession at one point in time. Whenever we caught a dagger, we had a twin cast with the same engravings, and our forefathers blessed ours to bind it to its cursed antithesis."

"Why didn't you hide the cursed ones from the bad guys?"

Leaning against the wall, Liam enjoyed hearing the exchange. It was a refresher course in his history, and given his father's habit of sharing secrets in random snippets, he hoped to learn something.

"If only it were that easy. We tried that early on, a thousand years ago. Unfortunately, the cursed daggers are drawn to the wraiths, and the wraiths are drawn to the daggers. Our security measures were sound, but the slightest mistakes were exploited."

"Daggers were stolen?"

"Stolen or mysteriously disappeared. The paired dagger is a sort of insurance policy."

Diane's eyes narrowed. "Where's the cursed dagger I took from my wraith?"

"Hidden and guarded. The priest took it back to the order, and from there, we'll trust people who dedicate their lives to protecting cursed objects from those who would steal them."

"What about the pointing?"

Liam considered interjecting his answers into the conversation, but with Diane seated by him, he instead stole glances at her beauty.

Connor sank into a chair and continued his lesson. "The pointing is the most useful aspect. Our dagger will point towards the wraith's latest ritualistic killing, be it a tribute to his demon lord or a sacrifice that gives him new life."

"But not a killing for sport?"

The comment caught Liam off guard, and he glanced at his father for guidance.

The elder hunter furrowed his brow. "You mentioned something about that in your vision. Can you expound upon that?"

"I'm not sure what I believe anymore. I'm having trouble telling reality from dreams."

"You've been through a lot." Liam felt like a dolt for saying it but hoped she'd find his sentiment compassionate.

"Tell us what you can, and we'll try to make sense of it. Remember, we've seen things that most people consider impossible."

"You remember how the sacrifice from France kept visiting me? Well, I think she's free and has moved on, along with the others my wraith killed."

Liam nodded. "That makes sense."

"While I was dreaming, the last sacrifice our new wraith killed showed up. We're calling him 'our wraith', right?"

Again, Liam nodded. "I like it. Father?"

"So be it. In fact, to avoid confusion, let's refer to the one Diane killed as something else."

Wanting to impress the beautiful empath, Liam sought a concise phrase. "Let's call him 'Diane's wraith'. He was targeting her, and she killed him. So, I consider it accurate."

Diane shrugged. "If you believe I haven't killed anyone else."

Connor raised an eyebrow.

"Just kidding, of course. I haven't killed anyone else."

Liam wanted to probe deeper into her latest dream, half-hoping to learn that he'd starred in it. "What about the new ghost?"

"She called herself the Maiden of Beit She'an."

The younger hunter grunted. "Huh. Interesting. Was the last one the Maiden of Anduze?"

"That's what the new maiden said. I guess I'm getting more confident with their kind. It seems like they need me more than I need them."

"Careful, young lady. Fate has a way to humble us all. We all need someone in the end."

Liam took the advice aimed for Diane as his own. For a moment, he realized his unparalleled success in killing Diane's wraith placed him at risk of conceit.

Diane frowned. "You have a point. The maiden warned me that this guy, our wraith, is an expert at killing. He's killed thousands."

Disbelief burst from Liam's lips. "Thousands? He's only been alive for at most a hundred and fifty years."

"She said by his hands or by orders he uttered."

Connor stood. "This could be a clue. It sounds like he's had a military background. Given that his first sacrifice was in Urmia, Iran–Persia at the time–I'd venture a guess that he was in the Ottoman Empire's military. There was rampant genocide in that area a hundred years ago."

Liam shrugged. "Agreed, but that doesn't help much."

"Not yet, lad, but it may."

For losing Diane for three hours, Liam expected better insights than an introduction to a new ghost and a warning about their wraith's military career. "Did the maiden say anything else?"

"I need to be careful with my dagger and yours. I've been pushing too hard, even when I thought I wasn't. I think the best analogy is dealing with cats. I can make them do what I want, but only if they're willing. I need to coax them."

Liam scratched the back of his head. "Bloody hell. Better you than me. I guess it's pretty cool that you're an empath."

"Thanks, I guess."

Feeling like a dolt for the failed compliment, Liam shifted to tactical mode. "Our dagger's still in need of healing, isn't it?"

"Yes. I think so. She said it was traumatized. I need to feed more energy into it from my dagger." She looked at the knife in her hand. "Whenever it's ready to give."

The answer frustrated Liam. "We can't circle in on the wraith until we know our dagger works. This leaves us stuck here."

"It's okay, lad. Our dagger will support us when we need. Diane's will do its part as well."

Liam wanted to press further into the inquiry, but the empath seemed content to hold her weapon in silence. After a moment, a new topic came to him. "Did the ghost give you any insight into your new weapon? You haven't had much time with it yet, but you're quite attached to it."

She seemed enraptured by the bronze in her hand as she stroked it with her fingers. "What?"

Becoming jealous of her dagger, Liam reiterated his question. "Your dagger? Did she reveal anything about it?"

"She said that a dagger can be used in combat in multiple ways. I suppose that means I'm not using it right."

Liam had watched her in a knife fight outmaneuver a wraith with five hundred years of combat training. He conceded she could benefit by strengthening her muscles and raising her cardiovascular conditioning, but nobody in the world could improve the technique she'd displayed with the weapon's enchantment guiding her. The concept of her using the weapon incorrectly muted him.

But his father posed a good leading question. "Did she say you were doing anything wrong?"

"No. It was more like there was something I was missing. Multiple ways to use a knife."

Liam considered the motions. Slash, stab, sweep, parry… like an expert, she'd demonstrated each move in her fledging fight.

Connor looked at him. "This is perplexing. You're sure she showed all the skills in her fight?"

He'd mentally replayed her amazing display. "Yes. I think."

"That leaves us with a riddle, doesn't it?"

Liam looked at the curved stone wall and pondered the mystery. The overlooked answer had to be obvious.

Diane stood, walked to Connor, and lowered her dagger into its wooden box. Then she returned to her chair. "That's all I got from my dream."

Relieved the charmed dagger had relinquished its hold over her, Liam focused on the problem. Within moments, a solution jumped into his mind. "I've got it."

"What I'm missing with my dagger?"

"Yes. It can be used at distance if you learn how to throw it."

"I don't want to throw my dagger. What if I never get it back?"

"I have a feeling it will always find you." He stepped to the door.

She looked up. "Where are you going?"

"Come on, and bring your dagger. We have enough daylight left to begin your knife-throwing training."

CHAPTER 10

Diane smelled the sweet cut grass and the distant boggy scent of peat moss while trailing Liam to the gun range.

Although the young hunter carried the heavy bag of weapons over his shoulder, he outpaced her along the dirt path. "Come on. Can't you keep up? The sun's going to set in a couple hours."

"If I go any faster, I'll break something." On cue, she tripped over her undersized foot, rolled her ankle, and planted her hip in the soft lawn.

In an instant, he appeared beside her. "Are you okay?"

She enjoyed the attention and let him tend to her. "Damn it. I twisted my ankle."

He cupped her shin, pinched the tip of her shoe, and rotated her foot in gentle circles. "How bad?"

"Not that bad. Help me up."

He grabbed her shoulders, and his arms became steel rods lifting her to her feet.

"Thanks. I'm such a klutz."

"I see that. What did you trip over?"

She looked away. "Myself."

"This could be more challenging than I thought." Hiding any pain in his fractured right arm, he hoisted the bag of weapons over his shoulder and headed down the path.

"Aren't you going to wait and see if I'm okay?"

"No."

"What?"

"No, you're fine. Come on."

"Ugh." She trotted to catch him. "How'd you know I was okay? How'd you know that my ankle didn't hurt?"

"I had faith that you'd manage."

"That's mean!"

"It's not mean. I checked you out. You're fine."

"Do you get a rush out of being a knuckle-dragging he-man?"

As he walked towards the low sun, a smirk spread across his face. "This knuckle-dragger saved your life."

"And don't forget that I saved yours, too, buddy."

He looked over his shoulder and winked. "I'll never forget. I promise."

She disliked him belittling her knife fight victory, but she agreed making light of it helped in moving on from the past. "Great. At least we've got that straight."

He led her through two hundred more meters of hiking and then stopped at a high wooden table. With a clank, he tossed the bag from his shoulder onto the platform. "Let's start with something easy."

Standing at the table, she saw a small field of grass with a matted path disappearing between distant berms she assumed were used to stop bullets. She then looked to her left, over Liam's shoulder, and saw a small wooden shed. "Is that where you keep the targets?"

"I'll get you a target soon, but first, let's practice the motion." He pulled a small knife from the bag and pinched its tip. Twisting at his waist, he raised the blade beside his ear. "See how I'm holding it?"

"Yeah."

"The power comes from your hips and from here." He tapped the wide muscles under his arm.

"Got it."

"Keep your wrist steady. Aiming comes from the arm, not the wrist like you might think."

Although she heard him, she was thinking about the rainbow-colored zigzag patterns she'd spent hours painting on her nails last weekend while trying to recover psychologically from imprisonment and mortal combat. "Okay."

"Watch me do it, nice and easy. A simple arcing throw, not trying to overpower it. Just let it fly." Despite his cast, he released the blade into an end-over-end ballistic trajectory, and it landed with a silent stab into the soft dirt.

"That looked easy."

He winced. "Actually, that hurt a bit."

"Your broken arm?"

"Yeah, I should've thought that through better, but I was trying to make the point of keeping it easy, as opposed to forcing it. Now you try and see how close you can get to mine." He handed her a knife.

She pressed its tip between her thumb and index finger, and then she lifted it over her shoulder. Momentum carried the knife backwards, and it slipped from her hand. Squealing, she danced from the falling blade, which thumped the dirt behind her.

Wide-eyed, Liam appeared stunned. "Wow. That was spastic."

"That doesn't count. I was nervous."

"Count as what? Nobody's keeping score."

"Well, I was. Let's start over."

He knelt, lifted the knife, and placed it on the table. "Take it back slower. You're developing your form now. You can learn speed and power later."

She pinched the knife again and held it by her ear.

"Hey, it's still in your hand. You're doing better already."

"Shut up!"

"I'm trying to encourage you."

"No, you're mocking me. Should I throw it now?"

"Very slowly, yes."

Gravity pulled her arm downward in a tighter arc than she'd anticipated. Adjusting to her toss, she kicked her leg up, lost her balance, and slapped her weak hand into the table to break her fall. The knife bounced, cartwheeled, and fell to its side.

"That was hideous."

"You act like this is so easy, but you grew up doing this."

"That's true, but I've got to be honest. You're terrible."

She flicked her wrist at him. "This whole thing was your idea."

"I'm pretty sure your ghost meant for you to throw your dagger."

She sighed. "Fine. Let me try again."

"After I put on a suit of armor."

She shoved him, and his chest felt like stone. "That's not funny."

He chuckled. "Do you have any idea how hard it is not to laugh? You may be the most hopeless person to ever try this."

She shoved him harder, and he didn't budge. It was like pushing a bull. "Just give me another knife."

Rolling his eyes, he obliged with another dull blade that appeared weathered. "God help us all."

She silenced him with another flick of her wrist and then lifted the weapon with her throwing hand. With deliberate slowness, she cocked her arm and then flipped the knife forward. It toppled and landed in front of her.

"That's a little better."

"A little? I threw it perfectly straight."

"Um. Not really. But it wasn't abysmal."

"This isn't fair. I need a target to aim for."

"That would do more harm than good."

"How?"

His shoulders slumped in defeat. "I was going to say that you'll ruin your morale when you keep missing it, but I won't win that argument, will I?"

"No. Get me a target!"

He bowed. "If the Lady of the Dagger desires a target, a target she shall have."

She wanted to chide him for his sarcasm, but she liked the title and hoped he'd use it again.

He jogged to the shed and opened its door. Moments after disappearing into its darkness, he emerged hugging a three-colored circular target mounted to a tripod of thick wood. Lumbering into the field, he carried it ten paces from her and then plopped it onto the ground.

"Isn't that kind of close?"

He stepped to her, ducked under the table, and appeared beside her. "I'll move it back if necessary."

"Can I have a knife?"

"Sure." He reached into the bag and handed her the next dull blade, which had spots of rust.

She cocked her arm and lobbed the projectile two meters over the target. "Woo-hoo! Did you see that?"

"I'm not sure we're watching the same spectacle."

"Didn't you see how far it went?"

"You do understand that the idea is to embed the knife into the middle of the roundy thingy?"

"Why don't you show me how it's done, smartass?"

He pulled out a knife, raised it to his ear and threw it into the edge of the bullseye. "Not bad for wearing a cast."

"Showoff. Give me another one."

He handed her another training blade.

The motion was becoming familiar, and she managed to bounce the knife off the target's edge. "Sweet!"

"Actually, that is showing some progress."

"Another!"

"Here you go."

Her confidence building, she put power behind her throw, but the knife veered into the ground.

"That's a common mistake. When you try too hard, you end up throwing it downward. Try it again with less power." He handed her another practice weapon.

Her lobbed knife pierced the bottom of the target, rotated down, and then lost its battle with gravity. "That counts, right?"

"You're definitely getting better. That's all the knives, though. Wait here while I gather them for another round."

"Let me try my dagger first."

"Maybe later. Let's not interrupt our momentum. You're making good progress."

With her knife hanging from the belt on the hip that had escaped grass stains during her tumble, she questioned his assumption. "I don't get it. What interruption?"

"I don't want to make the roundtrip back to house."

"What are you talking about? It's right here." She looked at her hip, but her dagger had transformed into a transparent outline showing distorted blurs of brown dirt by her foot and hazy blue denim threads by her thigh.

Crouching, he stared at her hip. "Fascinating. I see it, but barely, and only if I stare."

"It looks weird to me, too, like a big block of thick glass."

"I wonder if we're seeing the same thing. It's almost perfectly invisible to me, but not quite."

"Should I touch it?"

"Yeah. Go ahead."

Tapping its handle, she felt its cool hard metal, which assumed an azure glow with her skin's stimulus.

"You see the light blue, right?"

"Yeah." With the demonstration complete, it became clear ice again, and she released it.

He stood. "Here endeth the lesson."

"Why? You said I was getting good."

"More like, here endeth the riddle. The combat usage your ghost was referring to was camouflage. Your throwing is awful, but you can somehow turn your dagger invisible. We need to figure out how you control it." He ducked under the table and moved to the left to retrieve her first knife.

Considering his assessment incomplete, she reached for her dagger, pulled it to her ear, and hurled it. It glowed azure while it flew and then assumed its natural bronze appearance upon stopping–dead center in the bullseye.

Liam stared at the target, looked at Diane with awe, and then marched to her dagger. He pulled it from the bullseye, turned to her, and threw the knife.

Her brief fear of being impaled vanished as she sensed her weapon's obedience and extended her right hand. The dagger glowed azure, curved its flight trajectory, and then pressed its handle into her palm.

He gazed upon her like a goddess and spoke with reverence. "Lady of the Dagger, indeed."

CHAPTER 11

Liam reached the house and opened the exterior door.

"Thanks." Diane slipped into the laundry room ahead of him.

He closed the door and accepted the intertwining of their fates. The discoveries on the weapons range had proven she belonged with him and his father hunting the new wraith. But he knew convincing the elder hunter of their conjoined destinies presented a challenge.

"Do you want help putting things away?"

"I'll manage, thanks. Why don't you clean up and get ready for supper?"

She stepped into the living room and out of sight.

Free of her captivating awe, he exhaled a long sigh. Her powers extended beyond her awareness, and the unknown made him anxious. Seeking his father's advice, he dropped the sack of knives and strode to the study.

Seated behind his desk with a hardcover book in his hands, the elder hunter looked up. "How was her training?"

"You wouldn't believe the ending. You wouldn't believe the beginning either."

"I'm all ears."

Liam explained her clumsiness, her slow learning, and her supernatural control of her dagger.

"You didn't throw it directly at her, did you?"

"Of course not. It was well wide, but she caught it like a cricket ball. And I swear it swerved in mid-flight for her."

"Like the first time you threw it to her in Michigan."

"Exactly. There's more to her power, her dagger's power, or both, that we're not seeing."

"You can't expect it all to be predictable."

The comment seemed like an opening. "Life isn't predictable. That may be a good reason to have an insurance policy like Diane on our mission."

His father swiveled in his chair and closed his book. "You know I have reservations about that."

"So do I. But she's a strong woman, and I believe it's her destiny to join us."

"I couldn't live with myself if something were to happen to her."

"I'm pretty sure she intends to join us, and I don't think you'll be able to stop her."

His father frowned and grunted. "I don't like it. What about her responsibilities to her family? I suspect that her grandmother can tend to her brother for only a limited time."

Liam had thought it through. Money and hospitality could solve everything. "We can fly Nana and Josh out here and let them stay with us."

"We're not going to be here. We'll be traveling, hunting after the new wraith."

"We could rent a large motorhome like last time."

"That was a stress they both endured thanks to their love for Diane. I don't see either of them enduring it for strangers."

"She's an empath. She probably has divine powers of influence to make them join her, if she wants."

"If she's that powerful, she could just as easily convince me with her mental prowess and save you the trouble."

Liam considered asking her to oblige his father's challenge, but it would be a last resort. "I don't think any of us want to test our abilities against each other."

"Yet you threw a knife at her."

"Not at her. Near her."

"With your aim, that could just be semantics." His father held a stern look for two seconds, but then a smile appeared on his face.

"Not funny, Father. Okay, it's a little bit funny. But it's not true. I've been practicing."

"Oh, I don't doubt it. You've got great skills, which is precisely why I think we should tackle this mission ourselves. It's our heritage to hunt as a pair, succeeding by our own means as father and son."

A question crept into Liam's mind. "Did the order give you a copy of the prophecy book from the hunters we're replacing? Maybe there's guidance in there."

"I was wondering when you'd ask." He reached into his top drawer and withdrew printed sheets.

"You had their book, and you didn't share?"

"Some things are best shared only when requested. You've been digesting a lot of information, and I didn't want to burden you."

"I could've been studying that!"

"I assure you, the order already has. The first chapter is a complete match with our book. The history of hunts and lessons to be gleaned from them align with ours as well, although the narrative is much shorter. The only major difference is the compressed timing of the lunar cycle, which you already know about."

"Yeah, three tributes per full moon over three full moons. You're saying that's the only difference between our book and the one we inherited?"

"Not me. Historians and cryptographers at the order. But yes, I read the translations and agree with the experts."

Remembering the connection between the book of his lineage and that of Diane's, the younger hunter saw a peculiarity. "We have different hunter lines who hardly communicate with each other over centuries, right?"

"It's more restrictive than that. We never communicate. All our communication is hierarchical through the order."

"Diane's line has a book for empaths, and her first chapter was tied to our first chapter with a shared encoding scheme. Don't you see the significance? Doesn't that mean that all hunter lines are connected to Diane's line somehow?"

The elder hunter's brow furrowed. "All hunter lines are interconnected to each other, as are all empath lines. I don't think you can draw any special conclusions from that."

Fearing he'd have to send the beautiful empath back across the ocean, the younger hunter admitted defeat. "I guess you're right. Where does this leave us?"

Connor scowled and reached for his chest.

Liam thought his father was suffering a critical internal loss of blood flow until he felt the tingling sensation, too.

The elder hunter looked up from his seat. "I'm feeling something bizarre, but it's not life threatening."

"I feel it too, I think. It's weird, like… tingling, distress."

"A distress signal."

"Our dagger!" Liam darted for the observatory. Then he stopped and waited for his father, who had the combination to the latch.

Connor trotted ahead, fumbled for the latch, but found the door unlocked. He entered the room.

Liam followed and saw Diane standing with both enchanted daggers pressed together in her hands. One emitted azure light while the other turned black. Then the second knife glowed red as its energy source went dark.

"Hi guys. Hey look, they're friends."

The elder hunter sounded shocked. "How did you get in here?"

"I used the combination."

"I didn't give it to you."

"Yeah, he hasn't even given it to me yet, and I live here."

"You must have. How else would I have known it? Anyway, your dagger was ready for full healing, and mine was ready to heal it. So, I brought them together. Turns out, I hardly need to be involved at all. I can hold them like this and let them take care of it."

His father sounded incredulous. "How long have you been here?"

"About a minute, I guess. Why?"

"That's when I received a tingling sensation in my chest. I can only assume that's a distress call from our dagger."

Liam stepped towards her to get a better view of the weapons, which continued their oscillating exchange of light and energy. "What's done is done. May as well let her finish."

Consumed in a piercing analysis, his father squinted. "Diane, can you put down our dagger?"

Diane seemed happy, like her knife was a source of joy and nothing else mattered. "It's not ready yet."

Connor dug deeper. "But could you put it down if you tried?"

She frowned. "Oh, I don't want to hurt the poor thing like that. It's been through so much already."

Liam thought she behaved like a mother with her child. "How long until it's ready?"

"A little patience, a little love. Not long now."

The younger hunter watched the dark sanguine of his inherited blade shift to a lighter red and then towards a coppery pink. "Do you see that, Father?"

"Indeed I do, if you mean the softening of the red light."

"Yeah. It's taking in less energy with each pulse."

Diane admired the healing activity in her hands. "Because it's almost all better."

The flashing lights stopped, leaving the empath's weapon glowing a steady light blue in her grasp while the hunters' dagger assumed its natural bronze.

Diane separated the weapons, one into each hand, and then she placed the healed knife onto the table. "Your dagger's ready."

Liam noticed the blade's orientation holding firm where she'd put it. "It should be pointing towards the wraith's last kill." He glared at her. "Did you break our dagger?"

"No, it's fine."

Liam was getting frustrated. "It's lying there limp instead of doing its job."

She furrowed her brow. "I know it's fine. What's it supposed to be doing again?"

"It points towards the killing site where he last stabbed a woman in the heart."

"Isn't that old news?"

He'd explained it to her once, but she seemed mesmerized, her focus elsewhere, while holding her azure knife. So, he tried again. "He's drawn to the location of the sacrificial ritual–the final kill. As the final kill approaches, he becomes more restricted within a radius of the ritual's location, and we can get closer to him with each kill."

"Oh, I get it. Sorry. I think I was blocking your dagger's energy."

Liam scowled. "Huh?"

"It's still scared."

The young hunter pointed to himself. "Of me?"

"Sort of, you and Connor. It's like stage fright. A little nudge should fix it." She stuck her bluish dagger over the table and clanked it against the bronze weapon. The hunters' dagger wobbled, rotated, and steadied.

Leaning, Liam aligned his eye with the straightedge over the blade and noted the orientation. "Bearing zero-nine-seven. Right where it steadied last time."

Caressing her dagger as she walked, Diane departed. "Is dinner going to be ready soon? I'm hungry."

Lowering his voice, the young hunter announced his assessment. "There goes the Lady of the Dagger."

"A fitting title, indeed. So be it, then. I'll call the order and make the arrangements. Diane's going to be working with us for a while."

CHAPTER 12

Diane hung up her phone and placed it on the nightstand. In the hunters' house guestroom, she lay back on her bed and tried repeating the trick that had helped save her in Michigan.

Her brother, Josh, was her ideal supernatural receiver, and she hailed him with her emotions. Assuming him lonely without her, she attempted love, loneliness, and anxiety. Reclining with her head on the pillow, she closed her eyes and meditated.

"Josh?"

In their shared spirit, his voice was distant. "Diane?"

"I'm here. Can you hear me?"

No response.

She realized the strongest links occurred when danger drove up her emotions. Today, she was calm, weakening their connection. "Josh? Are you there?"

Nothing.

"If you can hear me, pick up your phone. We need to talk."

The link died, and her awareness returned to the view of an old crossbeam timber holding up the attic.

Rolled to her side, she grabbed the phone from her nightstand, and then stood. She lifted her phone and called him.

He answered. "Hello."

"Where've you been?"

"My phone was on silent."

"You heard me asking for you to answer, right? Telepathically?"

"Yeah."

She wanted to review the strength of their supernatural connection, but logistical concerns were more pressing. "Did you and Nana get your plane tickets to Ireland?"

"Nana says she did."

"So the credit card number I texted you worked?" The elder hunter had given her the number, which she assumed came from his secret order.

"Yeah."

"When do you get here?"

"Not tomorrow but the next day. In the morning."

"Okay, great. Can you send me the information?"

"I don't know."

She heard his tension and knew that a deeper probing would frustrate him. She backed off. "That's okay, Josh. Is Nana there?"

"No."

"Can you remember to ask Nana to send me an email?"

"Yes."

"Please."

"I said 'yes'."

"Okay, Josh. May I text you a reminder, too?"

"Okay."

"Thanks, Josh. I love you."

"I love you, too. Bye."

She hung up and walked to the dining room where the housekeeper placed meatloaf and gravy in front of the hunters. "Is there anything for dinner that doesn't cause a heart attack?"

Connor pointed to a bowl of greens. "There's a salad, and we have plenty of mashed potatoes."

She sat next to Liam and covered her plate with romaine lettuce, cherry tomatoes, and a heap of potatoes. Then she shared the news from her phone call. "Josh and Nana bought their plane tickets."

Connor swallowed a bite of meatloaf. "The credit card number worked?"

"Just fine, thanks. I need to verify with Nana, but Josh says they'll be here the morning after tomorrow."

"Excellent. I look forward to seeing them again."

Beside Diane, the younger hunter consumed a mouthful that would have choked her. "Does that mean Diane and I are traveling without you?"

"Much as I'd prefer to chaperone you two, I'd like Nana and Josh to see a familiar face when they arrive."

The comment irked Diane. "We don't need a babysitter."

"Yeah, Father. We'll get along smashingly without you."

Though she wanted to be alone with Liam, the idea of traveling with him made her nervous. "It should be productive, but it could be fun, too. I've hardly set foot in any European countries."

The young hunter swallowed another herculean bite. "Where have you been already?"

"I've got cousins I've visited in Denmark, and I did a study abroad in Italy, you know, to keep up with fashions."

"Well, then. I'll have to take you to new places."

It sounded exciting. "Where do we start?"

"We'll start in the crossroads of Europe. I'm taking you to France."

The next evening, Diane and Liam arrived at Charles de Gaulle Airport and registered at the Sheraton. For an upscale airport hotel, its carpets were worn.

She entered her room and tossed her luggage onto the queen bed. Seeking a change from her hosts' Irish home cooking, she thumbed through a list of dining opportunities, and the lobby restaurant offered a good menu. She picked up her phone and called the hunter. "Let's go to the hotel restaurant."

"Fine with me. Just let me finish something here."

She was curious, but she also wanted to keep him from disappearing for an hour in his work. "Can I see what you're doing?"

"Sure, I guess. Come on over."

After a quick check in the mirror and a swig of mouthwash, she walked to his room and knocked on the door.

With a stern face, he opened the door and let her in.

"Why do you look so serious?"

"This is serious work."

She followed him to a desk he'd cleared for his dagger but tripped on the carpet. "Ouch!"

"Are you okay?"

Her arm against the wall, she'd caught herself before breaking or spraining anything. "I'm fine. Just my usual clumsiness." As she regained her orientation, she looked at the desk. The bronze weapon appeared steady on a bearing, next to a handheld electronic device. "What's that?"

"It's a GPS compass. That's how I can tell what direction it's pointing."

"What's it say?"

"It's pointing on bearing one-zero-three."

Forgetting her hunger, she became curious. "What can you tell from that?"

"In theory, it geolocates the spot where he killed his last tribute."

"Why only in theory?"

He leaned into his laptop and tapped its keys. "The answer's only as good as the accuracy. The two bearings are too close together to be useful."

"Which two bearings?"

"The one from home and the one from here. They're almost on top of each other. Take a look."

She stooped towards the screen. The lines looked thick and touched each other all the way from Serbia to Syria. "I see what you mean. Stopping here didn't help much."

"Unfortunately not. We need to change our geometry and come at this from the side. Looks like Athens or Sevastopol would work best for our next measurement. We could also do Sicily, Malta, Bucharest… you see the pattern?"

"You had me at 'Athens'."

He rotated the laptop back towards his face. "Alright, I'll book the tickets."

"Not now. I'm hungry."

"We need to leave tomorrow. This won't take long."

She glared at him.

He got the point. "Dinner, it is. Let's get moving, then."

Exercising her prerogative, she changed her mind. "If this is my only night in Paris, let's forget the hotel restaurant and head out and explore a little."

"Well, I suppose that's okay. Where do you want to go?"

"No idea. I'll know when I see it. I want to see the city."

"All the tourist sites are closed."

"I don't care about that. Let's just walk around."

"Is there anything in particular you want to see?"

"No."

"Fine. I've been to this city a few times. I'll show you around."

After a ride on the Metro, she climbed into the warm evening air. The underground scents of musk and burned rubber gave way to the stench of dry urine, which seemed to rise from the sewer system and the bricks of the city. Hoping to acclimate herself to the smells, she kept her observations silent.

"Follow me. I'll give you a walking tour before dinner."

She followed him over a bridge, and as she looked to her right, she saw the back of a Gothic structure. Flying buttresses, thin spires, and two front towers caught her eye.

"That's Notre Dame."

"Cool."

He played tour guide while they walked along its north wall. "It took about a hundred years to build the bulk of it and then another hundred years for the finishing touches. They didn't finish most of it all until about eight hundred years ago."

The famous north rose window showed a rainbow of colors. Then, as she rounded the building, its western front came into view. Between its twin rectangular towers, a smaller stained glass window reflected the setting sun's rays.

He led her over the plaza in front of the cathedral, towards another bridge. "We'll cross the Pont Neuf. It's famous."

The sun painted the stone arches a golden beige. Cars and foot traffic covered the bridge, and below the structure, scattered individuals stood by the river's shore.

"Now you can say you've walked on the oldest standing bridge in Paris."

For the first time since meeting the young hunter in person, she saw the opportunity to probe his personal life. To start, she picked a simple subject. "You know a lot about France. Do you speak French?"

"Yeah, Father made me learn French, Spanish, German, and Italian. I wouldn't call myself fluent in any of them, but I can get by in each."

"That's still impressive. Why'd he make you learn them all?"

He shrugged. "The same reason he made me do anything."

"Hunting a maniac."

"Since I was old enough to aim a toy pistol, he told me I was going to be a hunter. Over the years, I realized I was called for a special purpose, not that I'm sure I liked it."

She enjoyed hearing him share about himself. "What's it like when you realize your future's been planned out for you?"

He raised his eyebrows. "Great question. I don't think anyone's ever asked me before."

"Not even your friends?"

"I had friends in school, you know. I was a very good athlete. So that made it easy to have blokes to hang out with. But I had to keep the whole wraith thing a secret."

"That must have been tough. You're kind of like batman."

He chuckled. "Looking back, I would've thought it impossible for me to keep the secret, but there must've been divine intervention. It wasn't always easy, but I managed."

A few emotions rolled through her. Gratitude, for him saving her life. Sadness, for his lack of choice. Envy, for his certainty of purpose. "You still didn't answer my question."

"Which one?"

She followed him onto the street that curved with the Seine. "What's it like having your future planned out for you?"

"I don't know any different. What's it like having a choice?"

Unsure if he tried to deflect the question or just needed guidance on how to share about himself, she took the lead and risked a verbalized stream of consciousness. "Choice is tough. I feel turned around. I have to take care of Josh, I'm trying to get a degree, and I'm trying to pay the rent. Then, well, you know the rest. Having a choice means I need to set the priorities, make decisions, and give something up when there's not enough time or money."

"I have no idea what it's like having to earn money. That's always been covered for me."

"I'm so jealous." She felt silly for blurting out the comment.

"Understandable. I've never felt the pressure, but I knew schoolmates who had to work from young ages. Some families suffered every problem you could think of from financial stress."

"We were never poor. I've seen poor. We had food and a roof over our heads."

He walked in silence and led her around the side of a building with the squared and expansive architecture of a Middle Age castle. Around a corner, he pointed towards a glass pyramid she'd seen in countless photographs. "That's the entrance to the Louvre. This entire castle used to be a garrison, but it evolved into the largest museum in the world."

"Nice." She took in the Louvre and then turned. Against the setting sun, she raised her hand. Beyond a fountain she saw a narrow tapering column of stone that reminded her of a miniature version of the Washington Monument. "What's that?"

"That's the Obelisk of Luxor. And that huge arch over there is the Arc de Triomphe."

She stopped. "Hey."

He halted his strides and faced her. "Why are you stopping? I thought you were hungry."

"What about your vow of chastity?" Though her direct question felt awkward, she had to know.

"What about it?"

"It hasn't been easy for me, but it's about choice. I had a choice in my belief system, and I'm saving myself until marriage. I want to know what it was like for you, having no choice."

"It's different for me because it's permanent. No sex, ever. No children. No bloodline. No family other than my father until he dies, and then I'll wait until I'm fifty years old to inherit a baby boy that a mysterious order will place on my doorstep. And then I'll teach him to help me kill a savage."

She considered it ten to twenty years of loneliness followed by a bizarre fatherhood, but it beat a sentence of permanent solitude. "And there's nothing you can do to change it?"

"I would if I could, at least I think I would. But who am I to challenge a thousand years of tradition?"

She saw herself as a living reason to challenge it. "But you're the first hunter to save a wraith's victim in a thousand years."

He shrugged. "So?"

"What do you mean? Have you been brainwashed? You don't have to follow anyone's rules anymore. When you saved my life, you did something nobody had done in a thousand years, and you did it so fast that you saved a half dozen extra lives."

"Yeah, I feel great about that, but why would that change anything? We're dealing with supernatural divine forces that we barely understand. The last thing any of us should do is make up the rules as we go."

Recognizing the limitations of his paramilitary upbringing, she attacked it from the flank. "I don't think I ever thanked you properly for saving my life."

He gave a dismissive wave. "No need. I never thanked you properly either. I was a bullet away from death until you saved me."

She stepped into him, moved quickly, and pressed her lips against his. A jolt of electricity ran through her before he recoiled.

"Why'd you do that? You know I'm sworn to chastity."

"Nothing wrong with thanking you properly."

He turned and started walking. "Please don't do it again."

Behind her back, she crossed her fingers. "I won't. I promise."

CHAPTER 13

Liam opened the door to the airport hotel room in Athens, Greece. Having accepted the empath's insatiable curiosity in France, he escorted her into his work area.

"Can I help you set up?"

"Clear the desk, please." While he heard her decluttering the surface, he withdrew his GPS compass from his pocket and handed it to her. "Here. Just set it down."

The compass clinked against the desk as she lowered it.

Liam lifted the weapons case from under his arm and set it on the bed. Facing it away from his body, he opened it, closed his eyes, and reached around the lid. He ran his fingers over the crossguard, grabbed the handle, and raised the weapon. Aiming it to the northeast, he opened his eyes, and the dagger adjusted its orientation as he clutched it.

"Is it pointing itself or are you pointing it?"

"I'm only helping it overcome gravity to keep it off the floor. It's doing the rest by itself." He stepped to the desk and set the dagger beside the electronics. It oscillated through several wobbles while settling. Eyeballing its orientation to the compass, he announced the bearing as he committed it to memory. "Zero-five-two."

"Is that good?"

The sections of the globe he'd committed to memory gave him the answer. "Good or bad, that's Istanbul, or real close to it."

"Is that where we're going next?"

"Don't bother unpacking. It's where we're going now."

"You know, you could save time and money by avoiding hotels and doing this somewhere easier, like in an airport."

Of course, he'd thought about it. "Have you ever seen someplace with guaranteed privacy in an airport?"

"Yeah, a bathroom stall."

He conceded her point. "I can't say that you're wrong, but I like having space to move about and think without people watching me."

"And you're thinking about giving up this nice hotel room and catching the next plane to Istanbul?"

He grabbed his knife and put it back in its case. "Now that the dagger has spoken, there's nothing left for us here."

For lack of precise tactical knowledge, Liam had selected a four-star hotel near a park that curved down a hill towards the Bosporus. His Turkish being terrible, he appreciated the taxi driver's rudimentary English skills.

"You have an easy walk to the strait and to Blue Mosque. You walk further along the water, and you can find the Hagia Sophia. There's lots of good food, too, especially over there on the Asian side. Many ferries run all day."

Liam glanced out the window at the passing buildings. Standing four to five stories tall, they lined the curved and hilly street "Sounds great. Are you sure you know which hotel is ours?"

"Of course, just one more block." After the driver continued in silence to fulfill his promise, he double-parked and hurried to help his passengers with their bags.

Appreciating the safe drive and the helpful English advice, Liam pressed a large tip into the driver's hand and then led Diane into the hotel. Being within walking distance of the latest kill tested his patience, but he reminded himself that his working timetables spanned weeks and months, and he could remain calm when waiting minutes.

As he checked in, Diane joined him. "There's a lot to see in this city. I hear Istanbul's really cool." Somehow, being imprisoned and seconds from death in Michigan and then joining a hunt for a monster worse than the one she'd escaped boosted her energy.

He liked her enthusiasm. "Sure. We may be here for a while."

The clerk reached across the desk and handed both room keys to Diane. She darted around a corner and towards a stairwell while leaving the baggage by Liam's feet.

"Diane!"

She stopped. "What?"

He referred to the dagger by its public pronoun. "If you're going to leave me with all the luggage, can you at least take the artifact with you?"

Surprising him, she shifted the weapons case that had been hidden around the corner. "You mean this?"

"Yeah. Good work. Set it up for me, please."

Unable to match her pace, he trailed her as he carried two suitcases up three flights of stairs. He found her door and yelled through it. "Diane!"

The latch unlocked, and her big, beautiful, brown eyes appeared. "Hi."

"Hi. Can we get started?"

"Sure. How do we do this?"

"Take the bags and put them out of the way." He extended hers, which was by far the heavier one, and then he gave her his lighter suitcase.

"Okay. The bags are on the bed, and everything's set up on the table."

"Not everything." He reached into his pocket and pulled out the GPS compass.

Grabbing the electronic direction-finder, she smiled. "Oops. Forgot that minor detail."

"Put it on the table out of the way of our artifact. I don't want them touching each other."

"Got it." She disappeared and then returned.

"Now. Just make sure our artifact's free to rotate."

"I did. I'm not an idiot."

He found her playful, but her forced kiss in Paris–the first kiss for the young hunter who'd sworn himself to chastity–made him doubt her judgment. "Agreed, you're not an idiot, but I had to verify."

"Fine. You verified."

"Okay, this one's worth recording. Get your phone ready and let me know when it's capturing a video of our artifact."

She stepped back from the door, raised her phone to her face, and pressed her thumbs into the touchscreen. "Okay, I'm recording."

"Here I go." He reconsidered. "No, wait. Did you close the curtains?"

"Oh, shit. Sorry." She made noises as she trod about the room closing curtains. "Okay, now we're ready, and I'm recording again."

"For real, this time. Here I come." Closing his eyes, he squeezed through the doorframe and sealed the chamber behind him. Feeling the flat wooden panels for reference, he faced the room and opened his eyes.

Diane stood over a table and aimed her phone at the moving dagger. Beside the GPS compass, the blade rotated clockwise. "It moves so slow."

"It's not that slow. Remember how slow it was before you healed it?"

"I guess it's all relative."

"Look, it's already slowing… and it's stopped."

"Should I line the compass up with it?"

"Yeah, go ahead." As she shifted the electronic device about the table, he knew it would reveal a northwesterly number based upon his observation of the room's position.

"It says three hundred and forty-one."

"That's three-four-one when speaking it, but yes, that sounds about right." He stepped to the bed and withdrew a laptop computer from its bag. Tapping in the new bearing using the hotel's coordinates as the line's origin, he saw a locus of diverging lines.

"Did you find the spot?"

"Not quite. The lines of bearing from far away are spread apart too much."

"Huh?"

"The lines from home, Paris, and Athens were good enough to get us to Istanbul, but they're too far away to be meaningful within several miles."

"Got it. So, what's next?"

"We move around the city and get more bearings."

"I thought you liked having room to move and think."

She was right, but he saw few options. "True, but we'll have to make do. I've got an idea."

In his best Turkish, Liam ordered dinner for himself and Diane. Pointing at the menu spared him from a communications breakdown, and as the waiter departed, he looked across the table at his companion. "Thanks for your help."

"No problem. I know the cuisine, sort of. It's a lot like Nana's."

"I'm sure it'll be good since you picked it." He scanned the restaurant and noticed patrons at three other booths. Judging his secrecy sufficient, he lifted the plastic case and pushed it across the table.

She pulled the case beside her glass of water. "Close your eyes."

He complied and heard the weapon clunk against the dining surface. "Is anyone looking?"

"Nope. Open your eyes."

When he saw the dagger, it rotated towards his stomach and stopped. He withdrew his GPS compass from his pocket and aligned it next to the blade. After he memorized the bearing, he shut his eyes again. "Got it. Put it away, quick."

"Done."

He opened his eyes, stowed the weapons case on the seat, and lifted his laptop from its bag by his hip. The new line from the restaurant crossed the one from the hotel in an industrial district outside the city's limits. The information was good enough to place him within a few hundred meters, and he needed to rent a car to give them secrecy in their final measurements.

"Where's it pointing?"

"Real close. We'll finish this with a drive around the area tomorrow. We'll need a car and daylight."

"So, we can chill and enjoy dinner?"

"Maybe. I need to call my father so that he can plan."

"Why do you have to be so intense all the time?"

What she considered intense, he considered normal. "I hadn't thought about it. Probably because I'm always at war, at least in my head. My purpose in this world is hunting, killing, and protecting."

"Well, you need to relax."

"I don't think I can. There's always something else I need to be doing. And when I do succeed in my life's calling, they give me another job that's even harder." The words sounded like whining as he said them, but sharing with her felt safe.

She seemed understanding. "Share the load. Let me call your father."

The offer was an invasion of his routine, but he welcomed her intrusions into his habits. "I guess so. Do you know what to say?"

"It can't be that hard. Come to Istanbul and don't forget Josh and Nana."

Something seemed incomplete. "I don't know how close the wraith is to Istanbul now. I get the sense that he won't travel as far as your wraith did."

"Me too."

He doubted his intuition but trusted hers. "Really?"

"Yeah. I think he's going to kill all his tributes in this city and do his final sacrifice here."

"It's a big city. He could get away with it. And God only knows how in tune a young wraith like him is with the concept of how he's hunted."

The waiter brought crispy disks of hot bread and a plate of raw vegetables as an appetizer. She rolled pickled cabbage into a small wrap, bit into her creation, and swallowed. "That makes sense. He's already nearby. I sense him."

CHAPTER 14

Diane dreamt of a young woman burning on a cross, blood pouring from her heart's puncture wound.

Time stopped, accelerated, and slowed again as the nightmare unfolded. The victim seemed distant, and then Diane was the victim. One moment, she was a sacrifice, then the next she was the savior.

A familiar ghost appeared, an unseen wind flapping a milky gown over a female frame as she called out in Hebrew. "Avenge me."

Diane responded in English. "Are you the Maiden of Beit She'an?"

"I am your sister in the line of Nineveh."

"You all look the same. Seriously. So, is that a 'yes'?"

The black pools of the maiden's eyes narrowed as her misty brow furrowed. "Why must you know?"

Diane reversed the cryptic inquisition. "You're the ghost. Don't you know?"

"Yours is not to question."

"Why not? I just asked who you are. Aren't we a team?"

The apparition's face darkened, and her mouth widened as she screamed with the anger of a dozen victims. "You will help us, or you will suffer!"

For a timeless moment in an ageless world, Diane locked her so-called sister in a stalemate in the battle of wills. Her growing powers giving her special insights, she held her ground. "If I don't help you, you'll suffer, too."

The maiden's expression softened. "We need your help."

"So, you need my help, and there's a bunch of you? I've been through this before, and I bet I have some sort of choice about doing this again. So, if you need me, you might want to back off with the scare tactics."

The maiden closed her eyes to tap some distant source of knowledge. "I am the Maiden of Beit She'an. I agree that you have a choice in helping me and the other sisters."

"You're awful testy for a ghost."

"I retain my human frailties until I pass."

"Pass where?"

"You are an empath. You know."

She had a few good guesses, but she had more pressing avenues of questioning. "And you want my help to pass?"

"Yes."

"By killing the wraith that killed you?"

"Yes."

"You already told me that I need to kill him. Why are you telling me again?"

"You must uphold virtue while defeating him."

That was a new wrinkle to Diane. "I thought this guy was horrible and needed to die by any means possible. Are there rules I need to know about?"

"You're an empath. You know."

"Ugh! Again with that. What are you trying to tell me that I don't already know?"

"You love the young hunter."

The accusation resonated as a possible insight. "You warned me about infatuation last time."

"When you kissed him, you discerned the difference."

The truth hit hard, but Diane fought it. "I have lots of love for many people. It's the way I am. I suppose it's part of being an empath."

"You love him as a desired mate."

Diane found this ghost far more annoying than the French maiden, and any suspicion about the Israeli maiden being a paranormal rehash of her francophone twin evaporated. Though she found the ghost testy, she appreciated her directness. "He's sworn to a life of chastity. That's one of his life's rules."

"Love ignores rules."

"Ugh. You're right. This is going to be hopeless. Am I giving myself a guaranteed heartbreak?"

"You are an empath. You know."

"Not that again!"

"You were wise to advise him to challenge the rules."

"My God, do you spy on me twenty-four-seven?"

"You are an empath. You know."

She knew, and her nonverbal dreamlike tone was cynical. "Sorry I asked, but he didn't budge when I suggested he'd earned the right to break the rules."

Again, the maiden closed her eyes and fell silent. "Remember what love is."

"I know, I know. It's a bunch of emotions I need to conjure when I link with the wraith. It's the tool of the empath."

"It's a more powerful tool than you know."

"Of course, it is. Can you be less cryptic without telling me that I should know what you mean because I'm an empath?"

The apparition smiled. "The greatest power of love is surrendering oneself."

Diane's memory with her paranormal sisters amazed her with its accurate vividness. "Your French twin sister already told me it includes selflessness."

The maiden gave a slow, reverent nod. "Our sister is correct."

"Right. Our sister. What's the difference between selflessness and surrender?"

"One causes the other."

Diane mulled it over. "Are we talking about Liam, the women I'm trying to save, our victimized sisters, or the wraith I'm trying to kill?"

"Your selfless surrender is required to resolve all these challenges before you."

Liam was a challenge? She liked that. It was better than seeing him as a lost cause and another stillborn romance. "What are you talking about? How selfless? Am I going to die?"

"You are an empath. You know."

Lacking any intuition of the answer, Diane disagreed. "Do you say that to protect me, to piss me off, or to hide the fact that you have no idea yourself?"

"I gain nothing by angering you. I gain everything by helping you."

"Sounds cliché."

"I am limited in what I can tell you."

"Sounds cliché again."

"But true."

"Okay, let's say I believe you want to help me, but you're limited in what you can tell me. Are you limited because you don't know or because some godlike power is holding you back? I just want to know who my teammate is."

"The future is never certain. Free will keeps possibilities alive."

Diane found the answer incomplete and evasive. "Now you sound like Liam and his double-slit experiment." Her memory continued to impress her.

"The young hunter is correct. The daggers react to their observers."

"Mine, too?"

"All enchanted daggers."

"Was Liam right to make me throw it? And what about when he noticed it was almost invisible? Should I use that knowledge to defeat the wraith?"

"You are an empath. You know."

Diane cursed in Aramaic. "*Babus ganug, dewaneetha.*"

"I understand all languages."

"Right. Shit. Sorry about that."

"You will wake soon. Ask the right question."

"Is this some sort of game to you? No, wait! Don't answer that. I don't want to hear it again. Let me think it over."

The translucent lids slid over the maiden's black pools, but as she became quiet, she emanated an edgy vibration. Her eyes opened again. "I am being driven away. Please hurry."

The time pressure kicked Diane's ethereal mind into overdrive. "You said I'm facing a selfless surrender by helping pretty much everyone connected to hunting the wraith. But you also said I would suffer if I didn't help you and our sisters the wraith killed. Doesn't this mean that I just have to kill him, and everyone wins?"

"Yes, but that is not an insightful question. Please, hurry. I cannot advise you again before the next full moon."

Diane found the first scheduling information about her ghostly visits stressful. Selflessness. Surrender. Unknown life or death outcome.

The misty white figure began to fade. "Please hurry."

"When you say I'm an empath and I know, you don't mean I know everything. Instead, do you mean I know what I don't know?"

"Correct. Please hurry."

"I have to be selfless, but I don't know if I'm going to die by hunting the wraith?"

"Correct. Please hurry."

"Does that mean that I need to be willing to die to save everyone else?"

As she became a phantom of milky dots, the maiden sounded hopeful and relieved. "Yes. And now I can reveal what I wished."

"*Yulla!* Tell me."

"If you fail to risk everything, you will fail to redeem us all, and a dagger will pierce your soul."

"What? Metal can't pierce spirit."

Disappearing, the ghost uttered her final phrase. "If you fail to risk everything, the young hunter will die."

CHAPTER 15

The next afternoon, Liam scanned the rural road for signs of industry from the passenger seat of the rented Fiat 500X. In his lap, the dagger rested on a plastic cutting board next to his phone which ran a navigation application in its foreground.

From the driver's seat, Diane aimed the wheel along the short dirt and gravel car path that cut through hills and paralleled a lifeless lake connecting Istanbul to its suburbs. "Anything yet?"

His dagger pointed ahead. "No. Give it another five hundred meters. That's where it should be, if I trust the measurements."

"I don't see anything out there, other than some sheep behind a rickety fence."

As the car rounded a curve, Liam expected the blade to move. "My coordinates say we're coming up on it. It should be right near the road."

"If your measurements are accurate, right?"

"Right. A lot of this has been rather blunt, so far. But we've got to be close."

"You said you were expecting a building, though."

With the compressed lunar cycle, the young hunter expected his new wraith to suffer from a tight geographical constraint, and he expected the victims to be local. Although his laptop's map and navigational program excluded signs of a nearby structure, he'd hoped to see a shed by the roadside. "Yeah. I did."

"We'll know soon. I feel it."

On a straight section of road, the dagger whirled towards Diane's midriff, continued its rotations, and then steadied at Liam's side. "Whoa! That's it. Turn back."

"Turn back where? There was nothing there."

As he closed his eyes and wedged the knife between his back and the seat, he questioned the weapon's health. "Right, but the dagger has spoken."

She whipped the sedan back towards the city's center and drove at a crawl.

"That's good." As the vehicle stopped on the roadside, Liam stepped onto the gravel and extended the dagger before him, like a divining rod. Ahead of him, a lush field of grass led to pine trees covering the looming hill.

The curious empath nestled herself beside him. "Let me try it." She grabbed the weapon.

"Hey! This thing's sharp. Magically sharp. And why you?"

"Because I want all my senses in tune with this… what do we call this situation?"

Against her iron will, he relinquished the blade and kept pace beside her with his gaze upon the weapon. "I'd call it a tragedy, since you had to ask."

The enchanted weapon satiating her seemingly infinite curiosity, she crept forward. "No, I mean what we're doing about it."

"You mean our response. We just call it a mission."

"Yeah. I want to get completely in tune with our mission." The dagger led her two steps onto the grass, aimed her towards the road, and then reversed her direction towards their parked car.

As a truck carrying sheep approached, Liam stepped between it and the dagger and pushed the weapon behind his back. "No need to advertise our abnormal behavior to onlookers." When the vehicle showed him livestock tails, he watched Diane.

She walked in a tight circle. "It happened right here. He stopped on the side of the road and killed them right here."

Liam considered the logistics. "At least we know he has or had a large passenger vehicle–or something bigger."

"That doesn't help much, does it?"

"Maybe. We need to use clues when we find them." His words of encouragement failed to motivate him as the search seemed to flounder. "Why don't you take a video of this place, a full three-sixty in case we missed something?"

Enthusiastically wiggling her dexterous thumbs over her phone's touchscreen, she completed the task before he could connect with Ireland through his own device.

Holding the speaker to his ear, he listened to the ringtone, followed by his father's voice.

"Liam? What news, lad?"

"We're at the site. It's in the middle of nowhere, between unpopulated hills on the side of a dirt road."

"Oh, dear. That's odd."

"Yeah, it is. Diane's taking a video so that you can see it, but there's nothing normal about it." As his words replayed in his head, he questioned what could be normal about a man stabbing three women in the heart.

"You saw no publicized evidence of stabbings in the area?"

It was one of the first things he'd researched. "I checked the Internet archives for stories about heart stabbings, but there weren't any."

"Perplexing. But it's consistent with what you're finding."

"I think this means he had a large vehicle, like a van or a truck, and he killed them inside it."

"But consider his exposure to the moon. He needs to be in moonlight to offer his tributes."

Liam reached for a speculative answer. "Maybe he had a sunroof. Or maybe he just waited until there were no other cars on the road and dragged his victims outside the vehicle one by one, killed them, and put their bodies back in."

His father's sigh was loud enough to give the young hunter his negative feedback. "I doubt it, but it may not be necessary to understand. Act upon the evidence you have, then you can consider the more complex issues later."

Liam wanted to use knowledge of the wraith's vehicle to pursue him, but he found the elder hunter's advice sound. "Okay, Father. Let's act upon what we've confirmed today. He killed right here, a stone's throw from Istanbul."

"This wraith's history is far less documented than Diane's wraith, but it's logical to assume him less mobile based upon his tighter lunar cycle. Istanbul's a large enough city for him to hide throughout his entire cycle."

"Then I'll see you soon, with Josh and Nana?"

"We'll be there tomorrow. Good bye, for now."

Liam hung up and slid the phone into his pocket. Returning his thoughts to his immediate location, he turned towards Diane.

Her eyes closed, she stood on the exact spot of the homicide, holding a dagger in her hands. But the weapon's identity surprised him when it appeared translucent.

"Where's my..." His voice tapered as he saw her entranced, ignoring him. He concluded she'd returned his knife to its case and had grabbed her own weapon from wherever she'd hidden it.

Peaceful, she seemed captivated in a trance.

Enticed to gaze upon her beauty, he risked stepping close to her, but as he approached, he felt warm metal against his neck. Halting in his tracks, he glanced at her arm and gasped at how fast she'd raised her blade to his throat–with her eyes closed. "Bloody hell. What's wrong with you?"

She remained in her silent trance.

He stepped back, and as his adrenaline subsided, he pulled out his phone, aimed it at his spellbound companion, and captured a video.

Supernatural forces seeming to guide her slow, deliberate movement, she drew the knife back to her chest and clutched it with both hands.

"What the hell's going on in your head?"

As if his quip had prompted her, she lowered the dagger and opened her eyes. "Oh my God, you won't believe it."

"Try me."

"I just had a flashback through his eyes."

His adrenaline kicked in again. "The wraith's eyes?"

She nodded several times.

"This is new. This has never happened."

"Tell me about it!"

Since she seemed flustered, he tried to calm her. "You're going to be fine, I'm sure.

"How long was I out?"

"Just a couple minutes. You were taking a video of the area when I turned away to call Father, and by the time I hung up, you were in la la land."

She slid the dagger between her hip and her belt.

"Where were you hiding that?"

"I wasn't. It was right here against my jeans the whole time."

He doubted her. "While you were driving and walking?"

"Yes! What's wrong with you?"

He reminded himself to avoid agitating the empath and also to concoct a tactic that could capitalize upon her dagger's camouflage. "What did you see?"

"I was seeing, hearing, feeling, smelling… everything. It's like I was him. Oh my God, I was him."

He wanted to hug and reassure her, but he feared a knife to his throat. "Can you tell me about your experience?"

Her hands trembled. "I was killing women. It was sickening."

"That may explain why you almost sliced my neck open."

"What?"

"You don't remember?"

"No! Did I hurt you?"

Recalling the fear, he caressed his throat. "I'm fine. It was just a scare, but you moved like lightning and put your dagger against my neck with your eyes closed."

"Holy cow. I don't remember."

"No hard feelings, but I'll have to never forget that you carry an invisible and assertive knife."

Ignoring the comment, she began pacing. "I feel gross. Disgusting. He's a monster."

"I know, but you've faced a monster before and defeated him."

"No, you don't get it. This guy's ten times worse. He's getting a thrill out of killing. He's sick. He's a psychopath."

"Can you tell me about it? It might help you feel better. It might help us catch him."

She kept pacing. "I don't know."

A frightening possibility entered his mind. "Are you sure it's a flashback and not a premonition?"

"Yeah. I think so. Pretty sure."

"Try telling me about it. Let me see if I can help.

She stopped on the spot of the wraith's latest homicide. "It'll make me feel sick to relive it, but here goes." For a reason Liam considered too perfect to be random, she lowered her fingers to the invisible dagger at her hip and caressed it, restarting her trance.

"Diane?"

Her eyes closed, she ignored him. After she meditated in metaphysical silence, her eyes flitted open. "I was him again."

"I'm sorry."

"No, it wasn't as bad. I was seeing clues. I was seeing how he picks his women. It's disgusting. It's sad, but it wasn't as horrific as it could have been."

"Can you tell me?"

"Yeah, but let's sit down. This is wearing me out."

"Fine, let me help you." He extended the cast of his injured arm, rethought his strategy, and stepped to her other side.

She grabbed his forearm. "Thanks. This story's going to be long, and it's going to be nasty."

CHAPTER 16

Eight weeks earlier, Edric made the mistake of waiting to purchase his women the day of April's full moon.

After buying two women at the auction block, he grew anxious as a man with German accent, a tailored suit, sunglasses, and a ponytail latched onto his desired third victim.

The German raised his hand. "Two thousand."

From the stage, the long-haired minion projected his voice over the audience. "I have two thousand liras from the gentleman with the sunglasses. Can I get twenty-one hundred liras? Twenty-one hundred for this lovely Egyptian goddess?"

With two thousand liras remaining in his buyer's account, Edric had reached his limit. Desperate, he raised a finger.

"I have twenty-one hundred from… wait. I've got the signal from the back of the room. Sorry, sir, you'll have to deposit more funds into your account to bid further."

Terrified he would come up short on tributes, he nodded his understanding and lifted his cell phone to access his bank. The weak signal slowed his application to a crawl, and he left the room to improve his connection.

Outside the building, he fumbled through brightening his touchscreen, logging in, and typing in a sum of money to transfer from his main account to the one facing his peddler of human flesh. To his horror, he'd already maxed out his daily transfer limit in preparation for the auction.

"Damn!" He buried his phone into his pocket and reentered the building. Though he'd just left, the guards subjected him to the usual security process, slowing his return. When he reached the auction floor, a girl with a starting bid beyond his reach stood on the stage.

Frantic, he sought the seller in the back of the room.

Flanked by two husky bodyguards, the short, barrel-chested boss looked at Edric with a face of stone and spoke with a gravelly voice. "I know what you want. The answer is 'no'."

"But I've got the money."

"That's what they all say. I extend no credit to first-time bidders." The boss glanced at his guards, who seemed to double as his lackeys who laughed at his humor. "I extend no credit to my long-term customers either."

As he turned in defeat, the wraith smelled the sharp, spicy sweet scent of the seller's cologne. Desperate to find a third tribute, he scanned the audience and saw the victor of his failed bid watching the present auction.

He brushed by random shoulders to reach the German's side. "I will pay you twenty-five hundred for her."

The German man's ponytail wiggled as he scoffed. "I'm rather attached to her already."

"Three thousand."

"She's not that pretty. Why are you so desperate?"

The truth was impossible to share, and every lie running through his mind was weak. "I must have her. Thirty-five hundred."

Removing his sunglasses, the man looked at Edric with dark, penetrating eyes. "Four thousand. Cash. You have one hour, or I leave with her."

He could withdraw the cash from a local branch of his bank and return in time. "Agreed."

Two hours later, the relieved wraith drove his van of three Egyptian women through the city. Killing had been easy in his past, but operating to the deadline of a setting moon with minimal guidance from his Master was proving difficult.

His lording spirit had uttered a wordless warning–give tribute far from the warehouse to prevent the hunters from discovering it, and avoid witnesses since incompetence would be punished.

To prove his competence, he'd planned it out… the van, a secluded corner atop a parking garage, the back of the vehicle facing the rising moon. He'd even checked the spot last night, verifying he'd operate under the moon's light when it reached its predictable elevation in tonight's sky.

As he rolled the vehicle up the final ramp to the exposed fifth floor of the parking structure, adrenaline pumped through his veins. Relieved to see an empty expanse of parking spots in the late evening darkness, he drove to the lot's far corner.

After aiming the rear of the cargo bay at the low moon, he kept the engine running to preserve its rumbling, distracting noise. He stepped from the driver's seat, walked to the opposite side of the vehicle, and opened the passenger door. Under the glove box, his weapons case called to him. He opened it, withdrew his dagger, and slid it into his belt. He then yanked the painter's tarp from the passenger seat and carried it to the van's rear.

When he swung open the doors, three swarthy-skinned, shackled women remained uncertain of his presence until the fresh air cued them. Despite noise canceling headphones over their ears and blindfolds covering their eyes, they looked towards the draft Edric created when he unsealed their enclosed environment.

To avoid panicking them, he gently lowered the tarp over the cargo bay's floor and unfurled it. He ducked under the ceiling and crouched while approaching the closest woman. He pulled off her headphones and spoke in his best Arabic. "Sit on the edge of the van, and I will help you to the curb."

"Why won't you let me see?"

"I'm sorry, the clients demand it. They don't want their women knowing their surroundings. I promise they will treat you well, however."

"Anything to get out of this van."

"Yes." He reached for the keychain in his pocket, lifted it to his face, and examined it. Finding the correct key, he slid it into the latch and unshackled her from the floor. "Come. Stay low." He grabbed her arm and lifted her towards the moonlit back of the bay.

She made awkward, uncertain steps as she followed him towards the open air and under the moon's mystical light.

"Stop. Sit." He lowered her to her haunches. "Throw your legs out."

Contorting, she wiggled her leg irons over the cargo bay's lip.

Withdrawing his knife and holding it aligned with his forearm, he lied. "I will now help you down." He crouched behind her, slipped his hands under her arms, and reached forward.

"What are you doing?"

"I'm helping you down, like I said." He clutched the handle with both hands, aimed the tip at her heart, and pulled the knife into her chest. It glowed red, signaling acceptance of the tribute.

She gasped, shuddered, and collapsed to the tarp.

With her blood gushing, he unfurled the tarp deeper into the van and then rolled her to the side. He stood, avoided the forming pool of red fluid, and walked towards the next, unaware victim.

After killing the next two tributes, he drove away.

Three corpses bleeding in the cabin, the wraith backed the van into his warehouse. To simplify the final steps, he parked the vehicle near a sewer drain. After stopping the engine, he walked to the rear of the cargo bed, opened the doors, and watched the blood trickle to the floor.

As the crimson fluid flowed into the drain, he started his next gruesome task.

Hurried steps brought him to his workbench where he unlocked a drawer containing his stainless steel butcher's bone saw. He returned to the vehicle and climbed inside. Kneeling into the pool of blood on the tarp, he grabbed a foot and rested the tool's teeth on a shin.

He started cutting. With patience and effort, the lower leg came off. Cradling the removed partial limb against his chest, he carried it to the used animal incinerator that abutted a warehouse wall.

Standing twelve feet tall, the apparatus promised a clean burn. Having bought it from a retiring poultry farmer, the wraith had connected it to his building's natural gas line. He pushed the severed leg into its lower chamber, latched shut the heavy door, and turned on the machine.

Based upon advertised burn rates, he expected the bloodied limb to become ashes in less than an hour. During that time, he further dismembered the corpses for disposal in the incinerator, which would also consume his clothes and his tarp before he cleaned his floor and his van's cargo bed with water and oxidized bleach.

While he cut into body parts, he reminded himself to move more money into his bidding account and to buy his women ahead of time. That would require holding them until the next full moon, necessitating the addition of shackles and plumbing to the vacant offices.

He also needed a new killing location for May's full moon. It had to be distant from the warehouse and the parking garage.

Recalling the maps of Istanbul, he decided upon a dirt road populated by sheep between the forested hills to the west.

CHAPTER 17

Fatigued, Diane smelled sheep manure as she rolled forward from the passenger seat of the Fiat 500X.

The young hunter's strong arms stopped her. "Easy. What's wrong?"

"What's wrong? I just lived through his murders twice." She'd experienced it through the wraith's senses and had then recounted the story to Liam, sharing whatever details she could recall under his rigorous questioning.

"Sorry."

Living the past through a monster's body was an unnerving experience. "Do you think it helped?"

"I don't know how much yet, but yeah, you opened up a lot of possibilities. We know he bought the tributes at auction, he killed the first group on a parking garage, he killed the second group here, he's used a white van, and he's had access to a large building."

She swallowed to quell a rising nausea. "And he has a big saw and a cremation machine."

"Bloody hell. That's gruesome, but we knew it would be ugly."

"Not this ugly. He makes my victim in Michigan look like a boy scout."

"Are you sure this was a flashback and not a premonition?"

She knew she'd relived history. "Seriously? How many times are you going to ask?"

"I'm just trying to be certain."

"I'm certain. What more do you need?"

"I guess you have new power. You didn't have your dagger during the hunt last time. This time, it's acting like some sort of charm and helping you see clues."

"But you don't know how useful they are yet."

His face showed concern. "I'll need Father's help. This is a lot to deal with."

She recalled the hunters' rules precluding their requesting assistance. "I wish we could call a professional detective."

"What would we say? You saw the world through the killer's eyes?"

"Some police forces use mediums."

His smile put her at ease. "True, but we have the Lady of the Dagger and the two best wraith hunters ever, not to mention a couple volunteers from your family."

The thought of her family lifted her spirits. "Yeah. Brilliant Josh and Machinegun Nana."

He chuckled. "Machinegun Nana! I love it. How can we fail with Machinegun Nana on our side?"

"I don't know. I don't know if we're in too deep with this. It's happening so fast."

"It's been a fast few days. Let's get you out of here."

"Where are we going?"

"Wherever. You've done enough today. I'm giving you the evening off."

As she watched the evening's shoppers scurrying for their last street-side bargains, she dipped her rolled grape leaf into a cup of yogurt. The summer breeze carried the vibrant music from the central square to her ears. Looking up as she bit into the tangy tartness, she saw a man twirling in a dress. "How cool."

Across the wrought iron table, Liam shoved a roasted chicken leg into his mouth. "Huh?"

"You eat like a caveman."

Dropping the half-eaten limb onto a bed of bulgur wheat, he mumbled his retort. "Is that a compliment?"

"No!"

"Sorry?"

"Stop apologizing. And if you are apologizing, don't phrase it as a question."

"Um, sorry?"

"Ugh. Just look over there." She pointed at the dancing man whose dress twirled like a light blue disk under his raised arm and his fez.

"Wild. I'm getting dizzy just looking at him."

"See how he looks straight ahead half the time and straight behind half the time. That's how he keeps his bearings."

"I guess you'd know."

"Huh? What's that supposed to mean?"

"Don't all girls learn how to dance?"

She tried to sound sarcastic. "Yeah, and we play with dolls and paint our nails."

"But you do paint your nails. I've seen them."

"Ugh! Men. This is why I'm glad I don't have time to date."

"Well, they're pretty."

Inspecting her fingers, she noticed the multi-colored pattern's progression away from her quicks. Natural growth and trimming had trashed half the design, and she'd split a nail during her knife-throwing lessons. She aimed the busted one at him, which happened to be on her middle finger. "Really? You think this is pretty."

As if aggravating her had become sport, he smiled. "Um, sorry?"

She smirked and threw a chunk of flatbread at his face, but with her poor coordination, she pelted the shoulder of a woman seated at the table behind him.

The woman glanced over her shoulder and looked to Diane.

The empath shrugged and blushed. "Sorry!"

Liam shook his head. "Has a doctor ever checked you for a neurological disorder? I think some of your motor control nerves were cross-wired at birth."

"Shut up!" She hoped he was flirting, but it was hard to tell with his vow of chastity. At least the attention was nice.

The next morning after a continental breakfast, she read a book on her phone in the hotel lounge.

In the cloth chair beside her, the hunter glared at his laptop and grunted.

"Did you find something?"

"I'm not finding a bloody thing. The English translations of Istanbul's real estate archives are horrible, and hardly any of the sites are in English. Whatever's going on, I'm not finding much."

"It figures. You don't speak Turkish?"

"Maybe some basics, but I can't read it. But even looking at the pictures, it's obvious that very few listings end up on the Internet. A city of this size should have twenty times as many listings. It's got to be all word of mouth among real estate pros and their clients."

Diane returned her eyes to her book.

"Are you sure you didn't see anything that could identify the building?"

The sickening existence within the wraith replayed in her mind. It had been a tunnel vision view. "It was a concrete floor with indoor lighting. If I magically conjure up a license plate or the guy's Facebook account, I'll let you know."

"I had to ask."

"No, you didn't. That's the problem. I'm giving you good information that's painful to acquire, and you don't appreciate it."

Before the abashed hunter could annoy her with another apology, the impressive figure of his father walked into the lobby.

Though in his mid-seventies, Connor moved with the ease and vigor of a man half his age. With obvious attention to his posture, he stood straight. "Good morning everyone."

Liam lowered his computer to his chair, walked to the elder hunter, and embraced him.

In contrast to Connor, Nana lumbered into the hotel laboring against decades of injuries, surgeries, and stressful aging. Instead of moving with an easy grace like the hunter, she powered through her physical limits with an iron will.

Walking behind her, Josh read his tablet.

Diane squealed with joy and pranced to her family. Hugging them was like being home.

Imposing his presence as the elder, Connor addressed the team. "Shall we get our bags into our room and head out for coffee? I'm sure we have much to discuss."

CHAPTER 18

Nestled between Nana and Josh in the back seat of the 500X, Diane watched people strolling along the footpaths between manicured hedges and decorated trees in the Sultanahmet Meydani public square.

Driving, Connor pointed out the passenger window. "You can see the spires of the Blue Mosque's towers that way. If I'm not mistaken, there are six of them, and they are indeed blue at the very tops. Formally, it's known as the Sultan Ahmed Mosque."

She looked, and as the land dipped towards the water, the structure's towers rose into the sky. "Cool."

"Cool, indeed, young lady. It will definitely be on our vacationing agenda. I also insist that we see the Hagia Sophia."

"What's that?"

As Connor guided the Fiat around the street's corner, he pointed through the windshield. "That's an excellent question. The simple answer is that it's that huge old building over yonder that resembles a cathedral, which it was long ago. It's a museum now."

From the passenger seat, Liam uttered a clarification while keeping his face aimed at his laptop. "It was actually a Catholic church for a while, too."

"Indeed, it was, lad, during the crusades, the fourth, if I'm not mistaken."

"I'm sure you're right, Father, since you were there."

Connor launched a playful but quick punch into his son's shoulder. "Anyway, Mehmed the Conqueror overtook Istanbul, which was called Constantinople at the time, and claimed the city for the Ottoman Empire. It then became a mosque for approximately five hundred years. They destroyed or plastered over most of the Christian images and mosaics, but we'll see some remnants when we visit. It's quite worth seeing."

Excited about the onslaught of culture, Diane forgot her horrific visions. Her family's presence and the calming effect of the elder hunter ratcheted down the tension between herself and Liam. She wondered if he pushed her too hard and if he did so to avoid addressing the feelings developing between them. "I can't wait to see it. What do you think, Josh?"

Beside her, her autistic brother read an article on his laptop. "About what?"

"About seeing the Hagia Sophia."

"Sounds great."

"Do you even know what it is, Josh?"

"I was listening when Connor just told you. He's right. It says so right here on Wikipedia."

Diane was curious about the young hunter's interests. "What about you, Liam. What are you studying there?"

The young hunter kept his face aimed at the screen on his lap. "I'm looking for a way to capitalize upon your new ability to see historic visions."

She rolled her eyes. "Are you looking for a machine that can probe my head and replay my visions for you?"

"That would be nice, but I'm pretty sure they don't exist. I'm checking the specifications of the highest-flying drones, but nothing can maintain a good altitude or flying time to spy on a city the size of Istanbul."

"Spy on the city for what?"

"For the van you saw in your flashback through the wraith's eyes."

She groaned. "Do you really expect me to watch videos of a huge city's traffic to find a van I only saw pieces of?"

"Unless you have a better idea, I don't see what our next move is other than waiting for the next tributes to die."

"I don't have a better idea, but that doesn't mean we have to try something crazy."

Liam ignored her rebuttal. "Father, if we saw the wraith on video, would we see his true evil essence?"

"You mean if a camera saw him walking on the street?"

"Yeah."

"I'll check with the order. They should know, but my sense is that he'd look like a normal human."

"What if one of us were watching through a lens?"

"Then, yes, I imagine, as if we wore glasses or contact lenses. But at this point, you're bending my understanding. However, I would say that any video replayed from stored media would render him as normal, which makes sense. Per my understanding, electronics aren't designed to store spiritual effects."

The question piqued Diane's interest. "He looks abnormal to you?"

"According to Father's answer, it's only to our naked eyes or through a lens in real time."

"What does that mean? What does he look like?"

"I saw your victim in Michigan. Twice. It was like looking at Satan himself. A beast. Wretched, hairy, leathery, decaying, putrid… Words can't describe something so ugly."

Having seen the true essence of the savage in Michigan, she agreed. Words failed to describe such ugliness.

Ten minutes later, Diane tipped back the thick, mud-like fluid of her Turkish coffee. It tasted like bitter, flavorful sand. She returned the cup to the table, placed its saucer atop it, and then flipped them over.

Liam, a biscotti in his face, chewed and mumbled. "What are you doing?"

"This? It's fortune-telling. The grounds form patterns and shapes. Then people who are skilled at reading them can tell the future."

"Is it a skill, or is it a gift, like you have?"

"A little of both, I guess."

The young hunter gulped from his large cup, clanked it back to the saucer, and wiped his lips. "Are you sure you want to do that? Isn't it better to make our own destinies?"

The empath appreciated his boldness and coerced herself against her curiosity to push her inverted cup away. "Sure. We'll make our own destinies."

Lowering the espresso pinched between his thumb and index finger, Connor scoped out his approach to the investigative effort. "Liam's briefed me on what you've learned. It's quite helpful, but we can't act upon it until we get at least one breakthrough."

If he intended to ask her to relive the nightmarish scenes through the wraith's body one more time, she'd scream. "What sort of breakthrough?"

The elder hunter always seemed imbued with calming wisdom. "You've discovered several clues that outline a pattern. If we can identify one point in that pattern, we can start there and tighten our tracking. For example, if we can find the supplier of his trafficked women, we'll find his van when he arrives to purchase more victims. If we find his van, we can track him to his lair."

The younger hunter gulped again and lowered his cup. "Maybe. Since Diane was seeing the past, anything she saw may have already changed, but we'll make some educated assumptions. In Father's example, we assume that he goes to the same supplier for his women and is still driving the same van."

The approach sounded unreliable to her. "So, we need to find a way to track down something I saw in my visions, but even then, it's hit or miss?"

Connor's eyes tightened. "Our work is never certain. We work with what we know and forge ahead to save those we can."

The empath received intuitive signals revealing a better but more dangerous way. "It's not going to work."

The elder hunter angled his head in doubt. "How can you know? You sound certain. Please don't let Liam's frustration skew your perspective. He's young and often frustrated."

The young hunter shot his father a sideways glance.

Diane doubted Liam was skewing her perspective. She was an empath. She knew. "I just know. We have to do something else."

"Very well, young lady. I'm open to ideas. What do you have in mind?"

Fear rose within her as she shared her idea, but it issued from her throat as destiny. "You'll get me on the inside. You'll get me in front of the wraith and use me as bait."

CHAPTER 19

Liam coughed as coffee traveled down his trachea. "Bloody hell!" Hacking air from his lungs, he turned his head towards the floor to avoid shooting germs onto Josh, who sat beside him.

From his other side, his father tapped his back. "Breathe, lad."

The young hunter recovered. "She can't! Absolutely not!" He regained his posture and glanced at the faces around the table.

Connor fell into silent meditation before speaking. "I dislike the idea, too. If you remember, I protested her involvement in this mission originally, but now that she's here, we have an obligation to listen to our empath."

Liam refused. "No, we can use drones… other technology… our wits. Anything but risking Diane."

She frowned. "It's not your decision. It's Connor's."

"You're not going to seriously consider this, are you, Father?"

Shadows covered the elder hunter's eyes as he contemplated the idea. "I will indeed listen because she has insights we lack. She's tapped powers beyond our understanding."

Liam's heart pounded. "That's the problem. She's doing crazy shit beyond our understanding. That doesn't mean we can take it all as the gospel truth."

Raising his voice, the elder hunter declared his place in the hierarchy. "Watch yourself, lad. You're becoming emotional."

"Sorry, Father." He noticed himself having to apologize too much.

Diane appeared thoughtful. "I'm not exactly thrilled about being a prisoner again, but I'm getting the feeling that it's what I'm supposed to do."

Liam's feelings were opposed to hers. "We don't even know if your visions are true until we test them out. What if you're wrong?"

"I'm not."

Locking eyes with the beautiful empath was harder than he expected. Until the end of last month, he'd dedicated his entire life to protecting her, a stranger. Now, despite knowing her for two weeks, he knew she belonged in his life.

"But how can you know you're not wrong?"

Her brown irises became shrinking annuluses around her dark, dilating pupils.

"Diane?"

She'd fallen into the familiar trance.

The young hunter pushed his chair back and stood to examine her.

Her graceful arm ran down the side of her blouse and into the purse hanging on her chair's back.

Liam grunted. "Sneaky woman. She's got her dagger in her purse. She's getting herself another dose of mystical visions."

Except for Josh, who kept his face in his tablet, everyone leaned towards the empath. As her reverie ended, she blinked. "I know what to do. I saw a vision. A future vision."

Liam sank into his chair. "Now you're seeing the future?"

"It wasn't really a definite future. It was more like a guide about what I should do in the future."

There were limits to how far the young hunter would trust her. "In Michigan, you could only link to people in real time. Yesterday, you stumbled upon historical links with your new dagger. Now, all of a sudden, you can see forward?"

"If you don't like it, you can test me."

"How?"

"I know the place and time of what I just saw. If everything happens as I expect, you'll know I'm right. If not, then no harm done."

Liam found her approach intriguing but simplistic. "That would all depend on the details."

"I saw a bunch of young Iraqi women. There were five of them, and they were scared and huddled in the back of a big truck."

"How big?"

"I don't know."

He reached into the computer bag at his feet, grabbed a laptop, and placed it on the edge of the table. "I'll help you figure it out with some pictures. While I'm looking them up, why not explain how you know they were Iraqi?"

"By the way they looked. I know my heritage."

He'd expected more. "You concluded their country of origin by observation. No sixth sense?"

"Yes, I had that, too, but you're starting to doubt anything about my powers. So, I didn't add that part. I know they were Iraqi."

A waitress approached the table, cleared plates, and took orders for refills. Liam used the distraction to invoke a page of a transport company in Istanbul with a gallery of its fleet. "Did the truck look like any of these?" He turned the screen towards her.

"Sort of like the one next to the little one."

"Two axles and six wheels? Roughly seven meters long, with a cabin you can stand in?"

She blushed. "Um, how big's a meter?"

He banged out the mental math. "Three feet and change. That would make the truck about twenty-two feet long."

"Yes. That's what I saw. Two axles with the double wheels in the back."

"Through whose eyes?"

Her cynical tone revealed her frustration. "I didn't ask him his name."

"Could it have been the wraith?"

She shook her head. "No way. I can feel the difference. The wraith makes me sick. The jerk I just linked to is a sleazeball who's trafficking women for the money."

"That doesn't make you sick?"

"Not as bad as the wraith."

"Do you know when this supposed future is happening?"

"June twenty-sixth. Three eighteen in the afternoon, if you want to know the time. I saw the date and time on the truck's radio."

Liam calculated the tight timing, seeing only three days to somehow get Diane into the truck, and then only two days of her working inside the trafficking network before the final triple-tribute homicides. Questions pelted the young hunter's mind faster than answers. "How did you know to look for him?"

She rolled her eyes and inhaled. "I felt the urge to touch my dagger, like it had a message for me. And guess what? It did."

He needed to back off before he infuriated her. He looked to his father. "I'm asking all the questions. I don't mean to monopolize our time."

The elder hunter shrugged. "You're doing fine, lad. I'll stop you if I dislike your demeanor."

Liam continued, probing for her intent. "Okay, let's assume you're correct in interpreting everything you've seen. What's the mission? Are we supposed to rescue these women?"

"No. Aren't you listening? You need to get me in with those Iraqi girls and have me sold at auction."

The concept unnerved him. "I wasn't sure if there was an interim step."

"There isn't. I'll break it down for you. I'll tell you where the truck will be, and when. I don't know anything about ambushing trucks, but I know it's a good spot. You do that and get me into the back of the truck with the other women."

Liam raised his eyebrows. "Then what?"

"Then the traffickers take me to wherever the auction is, you follow, and you find the wraith. *Yulla*. Why are you overthinking this?"

"Because it's my job to keep you alive." As his words replayed in his head, he realized the problem. Keeping her alive was no longer his job. His mission was killing a killer, and the enchanting empath was expendable per his new purpose.

Her eyes became dilated darkness again, but then she closed them.

"Diane?"

Connor tapped the young hunter's arm. "Let her concentrate."

"Yes, Father." Moments later, he felt an invading presence crawling through his mind.

With her lips closed, the empath spoke to his inner ear. "Hello, Liam."

His vision narrowed, and the real world's sounds became muted as he responded within his mind. "Are you seriously doing this?"

"Yep. It's me. I'm in your head."

"Why are you bothering when you're sitting right across from me?"

"Call it a demonstration."

Against his will, his hand rose from the table and approached his face. The dull throb of the healing bone under his cast heightened his awareness to the invasion. "What are you trying to do?"

"You'll see. Or rather, you'll feel."

"I might go along with this out of curiosity."

"You might go along with this because you can't stop me."

As his hand approached his chin, his index finger angled upward. "Bloody hell, woman. Are you trying to make me pick my nose?"

Her metaphysical voice became giggly. "Yep."

"The hell you will." He showered a torrent of resistance at her, concentrating on his dignity, his self-respect, and his desire to remain a pure knight.

Even in his head, he heard her grunting as she strained.

"Get out, witch!"

She left his mind and opened her eyes. "Who are you calling a witch?"

The three onlookers stared at the supernatural duelers with wide eyes. Even Josh took note.

"I mean, where the heck did you park your broom?" Liam glared at her "What the heck was that for?"

"I was showing you what I could do."

Impressed with both her invasion and his defense, he concealed his mixed emotions about her demonstration. "That's fine. I think it's great that you're learning how to use your dagger, but I don't think you can count on having it available if you're being sold as a sex slave."

She smirked as she lifted her hand from her purse and interlaced her fingers on the table. Then, with her mouth motionless, she spoke into his mind. "Maybe I need my dagger for some tricks, smartass. But I can still get into your head without it, and you're coming up with a plan to get me on the inside."

CHAPTER 20

Liam found a private moment with Diane to challenge her desires. During a stroll through the Sultanahmet Meydani public square, he saw his father talking to Nana by a hand-carried candy cart, Josh walking with a tablet in his face–likely reading about the location he was ignoring, and Diane capturing images on her phone.

He marched to her. "Was that for real about wanting to be bait?"

She lowered her phone and scowled. "I thought I made that perfectly clear."

"You did. But we were having, you know, a moment. I thought maybe you got caught up in it."

"No, I don't know. What sort of moment?"

"You were in my bloody head before I pushed you out."

She raised her voice. "Before you pushed me out, huh? I remember getting back in pretty easily, and without my dagger."

He put his finger to his lips. "Quiet. We're talking about things better kept secret."

"Then maybe we shouldn't talk at all." She sauntered away down the inclined and curved path to the Blue Mosque.

Shoeless, and with headscarves around the women, Liam followed his father into the center floor of the mosque. The high ceilings, arching windows, and vertical lines of stone reminded him of mankind's aspirations to send its lofty spirit upward to the divine.

Respecting the place of worship, he remained quiet as he strolled about the holy ground in deep contemplation. Seeking a better solution than Diane's concept of disappearing into a criminal underground, he ran scenarios through his mind.

From his success in Michigan, he considered aerial surveillance, but the idea sputtered for an overabundance of white vans to chase. In Michigan, he'd also used clues to cull a list of properties where the final sacrifice might happen. He assumed the incinerator of Diane's vision could provide a similar clue about the Istanbul wraith's location, but she'd seen so little beyond a concrete floor and a drain to filter a search. With the city's recent rise in construction over the decade, the possibilities were daunting.

Remaining in deep thought, Liam found his shoes, put them on, and followed his father out the mosque's exit. He bumped into Josh and noted the irony of his paying less attention to his surroundings than the autistic young man. "Sorry, buddy."

Josh looked from his tablet and towards the busy water traffic covering the strait separting Europe from Asia. "It's okay."

"What are you reading?"

"It's a book about the Blue Mosque."

Liam could only smile at Josh's love of learning.

"Your dad said you have a new book of prophecy from the hunters you replaced."

"That's true. I haven't seen it yet, although our order supposedly has read it for us and found nothing tactically useful."

"I want to see it."

Liam nodded. "You know, given your track record, I think that's a fair request. I'll ask Father right now."

"Thank you."

The sun bathed the city and its swarm of tourists with warmth, but Liam's heart remained cold as he walked to the elder hunter. "Father, Josh would like a copy of our new book."

"I expected he'd ask. I've already ordered a copy."

"Really?"

"You must think I sleepwalk through our work, lad, but I assure you I pay attention and know that Josh craves the written word."

"Thank you, Father, but what do you mean by having ordered a copy? Can't they just email it?"

"It will be hand-delivered tomorrow in an encrypted format to run on only Josh's tablet and one of your laptops."

"Wow. Cool. Thanks." The promised delivery did little to lift the young hunter's spirits, but he appreciated the teamwork, which had allowed his success in Michigan.

As his team strolled towards their next site, the Hagia Sophia, thoughts continued to bombard him.

In Michigan, he'd predicted Diane's wraith's appearance in Detroit by studying his pattern. But this wraith's compressed lunar cycle left little opportunity for forecasting. In contrast, the Istanbul wraith's geographic limits were tight, and Liam suspected he was already within fifty kilometers of the site of his sacrifice.

He contemplated a fast-reaction tactic to pinpoint the wraith when he would kill his three tributes under the next full moon. With financing, he could lease a helicopter and pilot, and he could arrange for a rapid response the moment his dagger sensed the first of the three homicides. Although judging it an idea worth considering, he tucked it away as undesirable for conceding the first murder and since Diane wanted to become bait before it could happen.

Contemplating her new powers, Liam wondered if Diane could force herself to have new visions. If she could see the wraith's past again or his present activities, she could bring home new clues. She'd learned to do it in Michigan, with ultimate success.

With her dagger, she had a new power to move beyond sensing and into control. When she'd moved the young hunter's hand to make him pick his own nose, she'd demonstrated a new level of abilities. Though she giggled through it, he recognized the gravity.

Why couldn't she simply invade the wraith's mind, make him write down his address, and then shoot himself? He had to ask her, but she seemed hesitant to talk about her experience inside him.

To him, it was simple logic. Invade the wraith ruthlessly until she overcame him or gathered enough clues to find him. But emotions and intuition governed her work more than logic, and overextending herself in Michigan had sent Diane into supernatural slumbers lasting up to eleven days.

There was danger in her trying that again.

Remembering her connection with her Michigan victim's tributes, he tried to outline new connections. She'd seen the world through the terrified women's eyes moments before their death, and she'd helped save one of them. But there were no clues to be gathered from this ability other than helping Liam track the wraith after his next homicide.

The sprawling, ancient former Eastern Orthodox cathedral of Byzantine architecture loomed ahead as he caught up to the empath. "Can I have a moment, Diane?"

She raised her nose. "Only if you come in peace."

"I come in peace."

"Go ahead, then."

She was right. The best available plan was her idea of getting to the wraith from the inside. That's how they'd teamed up to defeat her prior victim, but he needed her help overcoming his objections. "I'm warming up to your idea."

"Great. Now that's got me scared."

"Huh?"

"You've spent so much time thinking about it that you've got me convinced that it's stupid."

"No, I just wanted to think about every other possibility before committing to it."

"Well, have you thought of every other possibility?"

"I have, but I'd like to rule out one other option before we commit to your idea."

She rolled her eyes.

"No, it's not like that. I really think we'll end up ruling it out, together."

"Fine. Spit it out."

He sensed her closing him out. "Only if you'll listen."

"I said I'll listen."

Sensing he was requesting a slap in the face–or worse, he risked his question. "Have you considered gathering more information from him, or even an outright attack against him like you did against me when you tried to make me… you know."

"Pick your nose."

"Yeah."

"That's like me asking you if you've been thinking about ways to burn in hell forever. Does that sound like a logical request?"

"No, but… fine." He accepted his need to support her, and he felt silly for apparently being the last person on the team to reach the conclusion.

She raised her voice. "That doesn't sound like it's fine. It sounds like you don't believe how hard it was to see what I saw, to feel what I felt."

"I'm sorry, and this time I truly am. I have no idea how hard it is because you looked so damned peaceful and beautiful while you were entranced."

She blushed. "Flattery won't work."

"Sorry, for real again. Now I'm embarrassed."

"You can be really awkward, sometimes."

"I don't deny it."

Careful to avoid the cast on his humerus, she stopped walking and grabbed his shoulders. "Don't you think I'd be swimming in his head if I knew how to get back in?"

"Well, actually, I don't know. Not if it hurts as much as you say."

"I would, to save people. To save everyone. I don't know if I'm that strong, but I hope so. I have to believe I can find a way."

Her strength heightened his desire for her, and the guardian angel protecting him from romantic flames was faltering. "I admire your resolve."

"Good. Then stop worrying about me and help me put a stop to this sickening monster."

CHAPTER 21

Edric entered the cell of the next tribute for his Master, the tall and thin Syrian woman he'd won in a two-bidder competition.

She lay on her cot and appeared lethargic, lifting her head as his boots clapped the concrete floor. Lacking sufficient caloric intake, she'd become gaunt, and her body odor filled the room.

Stooping, he placed a two-liter bottle of water in the corner and then balanced atop it the loaf of bread he'd carried under his arm.

"How long's that supposed to last me?"

Infuriated by the insolence of her questioning, he stepped towards her with his backhand raised, but the power of his overseeing spirit stayed his strike. He answered as he tugged her restraints to verify the integrity of the handcuffs around her wrists, the leg irons at her ankles, and the tether to the concrete. "Three days."

"Bread and water to last me three days?"

He reached into his pocket for his Taser and jabbed it into her chest. She convulsed in helplessness, and he watched her until she regained control of her lungs. Since the attack kept her alive and unspoiled, his Master allowed the electronic shock.

"You're a monster!"

Turning, he left her complaint unanswered as he walked out and latched the door behind him. He needed to torment her as much as his domineering spirit allowed, to feed his intensifying craving for playing god.

The impunity he'd enjoyed a century earlier taunted him while in the small warehouse he hid from society's laws and cowered before his Master's rules on his disposition of victims. His hunger to handfuls of women wore down his patience.

He hoped his long life would bring him to a new era in which he could again massacre masses. The repeating themes in human history suggested such a time would return.

Petty punishments of his captives provided minor abatement of the frustration, and he desired better. He needed more.

He lifted his phone to text his flesh peddler.

Expecting his overseeing spirit's veto, he hesitated, but the denial never came. He tapped a request for a meeting, sent it, and glued his eyes to the screen. Moments later, the response arrived with an invitation to talk in three hours.

As he drove his van through tight traffic, the wraith feared his domineering spirit would stop his quest. But the whimsical spirit seemed to permit killing for sport today.

After reaching the bar, parking in its gated lot, and passing through a security frisking, he sat alone in a booth. The space he knew as an auction floor had become a backroom strip club with leering men and exposed female flesh.

He'd hardly noticed the two poles on the stage, to which upside down women clung with their legs.

A lady wearing lingerie approached him. "Can I take your order? A drink and perhaps something from the kitchen?"

Avoiding alcohol to keep his self-control, he picked something benign. "Mineral water."

"Got it. Anything else?"

He dismissed her with a wave.

A wiggling body moved towards him seeking eye contact and money in exchange for a personal dance, but he shooed her away.

Five minutes later, his waitress returned with his water and a complementary bowl of mixed nuts. Nibbling a cashew, he watched another dancer approach him for service, and he scowled. When his waitress saw him again, he waved her over.

She arrived. "Ready to order some food?"

He leaned towards her. "I've got a four o'clock meeting with the owner. He's already five minutes late. Check what's delaying him."

"I'll see what I can find out."

Across the room, a drunk man groped for a dancer's panties, causing her to smack his hand. Two attentive, suited mountains of muscle appeared from a dark corner, and one guard put the offender's hand into a joint lock while the other addressed him with harsh language. The wristlock shifted behind the drunkard's back as the guards escorted him from the room.

The few patrons who'd paid attention to the eviction returned their eyes to their drinks and the strippers, and the sea of sexual arousal and men ogling their fantasies annoyed the wraith.

When the waitress brought him a second bottle of water, he suspected a further delay. "The owner's running late. He sends his apologies and says you can order anything you want on the house. Can I get you a menu?"

Running late. How dare the flesh peddler abuse his power of position. Edric had killed people for less annoying infractions, and he found his dependency on a mortal disgusting. "Did he say when he'd see me?"

"I'm sorry, no."

"Bring me a damned menu, then."

One hundred years of compounding interest had created a nest egg for his essentials, but this year was revealing a need for a larger fortune to control people. This demeaning humiliation of asking for meetings, waiting for a man who considered himself powerful, scrapping for women to kill... it had to end.

He knew money begat more money, and he made note to become more aggressive in seeking investments during the next half century.

But first, he needed a taste of snuffing out life to survive his immediate craving.

The lady in lingerie arrived with the menu. "The boss is ready to see you. If you'd like, you can still order, and I'll have it sent to his table."

"No. I will see him now."

A guard escorted Edric forward into the public bar. He passed a bouncer who controlled access into the back room, and in the dim lighting, the patrons of the establishment's front section appeared as seedy as those in the private auction-strip area.

As his guard angled towards a dark corner, his jacket shifted and exposed the pistol by his hip. When he stopped at the table of a semicircular booth, he raised a large palm to block the eager Edric, and then he faced the boss, who sat with a small entourage.

A dark drink in hand, the short, barrel-chested seller took up a wide expanse of the booth's corner. Beside him sat the eloquent minion of the auction stage, who brushed back shoulder-length black hair as he looked up at Edric. Outside either man sat a broad-shouldered bodyguard, and at the edge of the booth stood a skinny man who curled forward in a pleading and anxious posture.

Combed forward, the boss' coarse gray hair was gelled straight as he tipped his head back with a quick, deep laugh. Though his ruddy face showed evidence of a heart that pumped blood, the coldness of his eyes suggested a callous monster, and he dismissed the nervous man with a gravelly voice. "Your desperation is pathetic. Get out of my face before I have you beaten."

As the guard who'd escorted Edric abandoned him to lead the nervous man away, he exposed the wraith to the boss and his court.

Edric recognized the simple perfection of the seller's game. To demonstrate a hierarchy, the seller had made him wait, he'd forced him spectate the humiliation of his prior visitor, and he'd subjected him to the court at the apex of the king's demonstration of power.

To accentuate the separation between king and pawn, the flesh peddler kept the wraith standing. The dog the seller had just whipped had earned a seat at the booth, but the man in charge deemed Edric unworthy of sitting. "It's always a pleasure. I understand you have a request that is... urgent?"

Edric silently swore to kill the man before he left Istanbul. "I do. I need one girl, just one, and I'm not picky about it."

Seeking submissive laughter, the boss glanced at his companions. "He's not picky. He's not picky. He requests an urgent meeting to buy a girl when I'm not selling, and he says he's not picky."

Using short sentences, the wraith tried to suppress his rage. "Money talks, and I'm speaking."

The boss glared. "I'll be auctioning off a delivery from Iraq in a few days. Surely, you can wait."

No, he couldn't. "I will be interested in that, of course, but I have an urgent need for just one."

"Very well. Money talks. Five thousand liras. I choose the girl."

The wraith was desperate. "Yes, if I can have her soon."

"Come back tomorrow, and I'll have a girl for you."

The next afternoon, Edric parked his van in the private lot, passed through security, and met the long-haired minion in the back room.

His hair brushing his shoulders, the minion led the wraith behind the stage, upon which two strippers entertained sleazy patrons. "She's in our green room." Showing manners to the talent, the minion knocked on the door, looked to the ground, and shouted through the gap. "Make yourselves decent, ladies." He waited several seconds before shouldering open the door.

Bright lights and mirrors illuminated a half dozen women in varied states of dress. The obvious target of Edric's need sat in a corner.

Motionless in a sea of makeup, hair, and clothing preparations, the young girl appeared sixteen years old. She had dark brown skin and cornrow braids.

The wraith's immediate conclusion was that a prior client had found her too young, too disobedient, too undesirable, or some other negative superlative, and he'd just funded the unhappy buyer's reimbursement plus a huge resale profit to the flesh peddler.

She'd suffice.

Aiming his arm to her, the minion shifted into his showtime routine. "She's lovely, is she not? Amazing that we could find her on such short notice."

"I'll take her." He doubted he had a choice, based upon the wills of both his Master and the seller.

"Excellent. After the money transfer, she'll be yours, and I'll have her delivered to your vehicle."

As he drove his van to his warehouse with his solitary victim, he contemplated the final act of scratching his itch–the killing for sport of a terrified victim.

CHAPTER 22

Diane faced the truth she suspected she'd hidden from Liam. She knew how to telepathically attack the wraith, but she feared trying.

Since her trances on the dirt road, she'd had an inkling of how to find and invade the wraith's mind. As she lay in bed, she examined her dilemma.

She wondered if her prophecy of the trafficked Iraqi women had been a call to action against the wraith, urging her into his mind. But she also considered the ghost's call to surrender herself, and entering the wraith's mind didn't feel like a suicide mission.

Or was it? Was she ignoring the risks?

If she attacked via telepathy, she could lose herself in a trance for days or longer, dooming the next three tributes. If she instead tried to infiltrate the slavery network, the outcome was speculative. She could end up anywhere, failing the captive tributes and transforming herself into an imprisoned burden on her friends and family.

The agony of the decision simmering within her rose to a crescendo, and the only solace she could fathom was action.

She caressed her pendant to verify its protective presence. It had helped her against her Michigan victim, but she questioned its value now.

Lifting it, she admired the disk of silver holding a milky iridescent ovular moonstone, which lacey, gothic metal twists surrounded with a sharp point at the bottom. The silvery structure serving as the stone's setting suggested a dagger underneath a full moon.

An initial rush of excitement ran over her, raising the hair on her arms, and then came the jeweled piece's familiar enduring calmness. If nothing else, it begat confidence.

After releasing the amulet, she grabbed her dagger from the nightstand, tightened ten fingers around it, and held it near her heart.

She closed her eyes. "Come on, Diane. Relax and focus."

Seeking the killer, she invoked emotions within herself that sought to connect with his.

But she groped to guess what a psychopath might feel. Arrogance? Entitlement? Contempt? Diane tried to generate the emotions but fell short. Moving to those she could approximate, she probed.

Anger. Envy. Haughtiness.

The combination had worked with her victim in Michigan, and she brought it to the Turkish monster.

Expecting cold and angry resistance, she instead found a twisted welcoming. His words were inaudible, but his meaning was obvious.

"Who are you?"

She remained silent.

"You're a fool for attacking me. I will destroy you."

She kept her inner voice silent to avoid revealing her identity, and she stilled herself like a thief in the night.

The wraith taunted her. "I know you're there."

More stillness. In her mental construct, she held her breath.

"Show yourself."

Courage fueled her retort. "You show yourself first."

"You're in no position to demand."

"I broke into your head. That puts me in charge."

His laugh rose as a haunting mélange of baritone arrogance and high-pitched shrieks of madness.

She became ethereal stone, willing herself motionless while awaiting his next move.

He resonated a deep pain, which he masked under a powerful and defiant ego. "You think you know who I am, but you're mistaken."

Recoiling, she felt waves of wretchedness flow around her, causing nausea to pervade her stomach. She reminded herself that she lacked a physical body in the spiritual exchange and that she could endure it.

"I take it by your silence that you find probing inside me... uncomfortable? I can bear the suffering. Can you?"

From her perspective, calling it uncomfortable was an understatement, but she countered with sustained silence.

"Come now, you're not the first ghost I've faced. Just because you can hide doesn't mean I don't know you're there. You came to challenge me, not to cower. I'll find you, and you'll disappear again for what... years?"

Relieved he mistook her for a ghost, she released a burst of relief. Before she realized her mistake, she sensed his reaction.

He shot out a searing, laser-like scorn. "Ah... there you are. An insolent bitch. I will cut you. I will strangle you. I will burn you."

She tagged his anger as a beacon for future connections. It was an unquenchable angst for all life, the kind so complete and desolate that she wondered how he escaped self-hatred.

"Show yourself!"

Her ethereal heart pounded in her dreamed chest.

"I see your anxiety, your fear. Whoever or whatever you are, you will be exposed."

The rancid evil bathing her motivated her retreat. She tried to disentangle herself and sneak away.

But he had other plans. "Where do you think you're going? You came here to see me. Now see me!"

In a flash, she saw through his eyes, and the reflection of the bound woman startled Diane.

The young lady, no more than a teenager, writhed in a chair. Tape constrained her body, but her mouth was free, and she squealed protests in an unrecognizable language that Diane understood. "What are you doing? Stop! You can't do this."

As Diane's metaphysical eyes focused on the girl's brown skin, she realized she watched a reflection. Behind the captive stood the wraith, revealing himself from the chest down.

Using his forearm at her forehead, he overpowered the girl's neck and elevated her chin. With his free hand, he drew a box cutter to her neck, held it there, and then dropped it. He shook his head as if mocking Diane, lifted a utility knife for her to see, and then jammed it downward.

The victim's eyes opened wide in betrayed, terrified shock, and then life drained from them.

Keeping his face above the reflection, the wraith spoke into the empath's supernatural ears. "I love having witnesses."

Dying with the physical victim, Diane felt an overflow of emotions. Anger, sadness, terror, hatred… they swelled over her, churned her insides, and served as a rip cord, yanking her from further suffering.

Her chest sore, she returned to her body on the bed and opened her eyes. As she dropped the dagger to the comforter, she credited the enchanted knife with extracting her from the horror. She coughed and clutched her heart as she accepted that the wraith had killed another victim.

But it wasn't a tribute. It was another homicide for sport.

She marched across the floor to the bathroom mirror. Turning on the light, she checked her skin for signs of cutting but saw none.

Tears welled in her eyes, and she let them flow in a catharsis. How many more times would she have to endure death through another human's anguish? Was this what the Israeli maiden meant about sacrificing herself?

No, she decided. It would only get worse.

In a moment of lucidity between inner barbs of horror and disgust, she realized the wraith had revealed a clue. The mirror in which she'd seen the homicide hadn't been a mirror, but a window. It overlooked a warehouse of empty metal shelves, and within the space, she saw the top of the white van she recognized from her visions of his past.

She had an identifying feature of his lair.

With that small consolation, she fought against her billowing nausea, knelt before the toilet, and vomited.

CHAPTER 23

Diane dreamt of a young woman burning on a cross, blood pouring from her heart's puncture wound.

Time stopped, accelerated, and slowed again as the surreal nightmarish scene unfolded. The victim seemed distant, and then Diane was the victim. She was a sacrifice–then the savior.

A familiar ghost appeared, an unseen wind flapping a milky gown over her frame as she called out in Hebrew. "Avenge me."

Diane responded in English. "I'm working on it. I volunteered myself as bait, or weren't you paying attention?"

"You were wise to risk surrendering yourself. Only you know if you understand the risk."

"What's that supposed to mean?"

"You are an empath. You know."

She wondered about divine penalties for punching ghosts. Fortunately, her perfect dream-state brain concentrated her attention on the conversation. "You said that if I failed to risk everything, everyone would suffer. You and our sisters wouldn't be redeemed, and Liam would die."

"Correct."

In her dream, Diane frowned. "You also said you wouldn't be able to advise me before the next full moon. Why are you here already?'

"I have come to appraise your commitment."

"Now you're the police maiden?"

"You have offered to risk yourself, but your heart bears not the burden."

The empath reflected upon her days in Istanbul. She had visited sites and had spent vacation time with her family and friends. Yes, she was on a mission, but she had no intention of hiding or sulking while awaiting her moment to act. "You think I don't get it. You think I'm bopping around like everything's fine. Well, don't worry, I've faced a wraith before. I know what it's like to be a captive."

"You are facing much worse this time."

"I know that! Leave me alone!"

The apparition disappeared in an evaporating mist of white.

She awoke and glanced at the clock on the nightstand. It was just after three o'clock in the morning.

Questioning begat doubt, which begat more questioning.

Was the young hunter correct in accusing her of mixing the past with the future? Was her vision of the pending truckload of Iraqi women properly timed? Was she taking more than a calculated risk in offering herself as bait? Was she walking into certain death?

Sitting on the edge of her bed, she looked at her phone. In a moment of weakness, she wanted to call Liam, but she expected him to be sleeping.

Perhaps a text would be permissible, to see if he was awake, running on the same wavelength as her. Lifting the phone, she started tapping a message, but then she reconsidered, erased it, and put the device back on the nightstand.

Was Liam her new confidant? With her friends finding careers and husbands, she'd been looking towards her dependent brother as her companion. But the young hunter had taken root in her mind and in her heart as her first thought for sharing her hopes and fears.

Crawling back under the sheets, she expected a sleepless remainder of her morning.

After hours of tossing and turning, she met the morning sun. She reminded herself that in absence of sleep, quiet laying offered rejuvenation, and she hoped to feel rested during the day as she moved through her morning routine.

Today's agenda included visits to the Basilica Cistern and the Topkapi Palace. She allowed that perhaps the Maiden of Beit She'an had been warranted in verifying her motivation. Her team of family and hunters behaved like normal tourists because they were powerless to do anything but wait for Diane.

She needed to lead them, but she didn't know what a leader was supposed to do.

Liam, however, did.

After the elevator brought her to the lobby, she found the young hunter devouring a continental breakfast. Upon seeing her, he waved and smiled.

She walked to his small table. "Can I join you?"

He chewed a massive mouthful of scrambled eggs and then swallowed. "Of course."

"Where's your dad?"

"I'm not sure, but I think he and Nana were up earlier and are taking a leisurely stroll about the city."

"Ooh, they seem to be getting along." She felt like a dork for saying it, but it was true.

"Yeah. Maybe it's because they're roughly the same age. Who knows?"

"True. I'm going to get some food." She walked to the modest spread which offered fiber in the form of melon, strawberries, and whole grain muffins. With the plate of food in hand, she filled a small cup of coffee and returned to the hungry hunter.

He jammed a complete sausage link into his mouth.

"You eat like a caveman."

With his brain consumed by its reptilian function of ingesting calories, he seemed detached. His eyes looked into the distance as he chewed and swallowed.

"Are you listening to me?"

"Yeah, but last time you said that, you said it was an insult."

"You inhale food."

"Pardon me, Miss Foodie."

"I'm not a foodie!"

He glared at her and smirked.

"Okay, I'm a foodie."

"Don't worry about it. It's kind of cute."

She wondered if that was his attempt at flirting and found it inappropriate on several levels. "I know I'm cute. I've always been cute, but cute's not what I'm going for. I was hoping we could talk about something more serious."

"I'm always serious. That's my problem. I need to lighten up, or at least so sayeth the empath."

She was glad he saw his character flaw, but she needed to capitalize on it. "That's true, but sometimes it's a strength."

"Really?"

"Yeah, focus and determination come in handy in your line of work. Like now. I need your help with something."

He mumbled his comment through a mouthful of oatmeal. "Sure. Go ahead."

"This idea I had of becoming bait, I'm not sure I like it."

He swallowed his grains. "That's understandable. It's scary."

"It's not just the danger. It's that everyone's depending on me. That's a lot of pressure."

"I'll have your back. We're a team."

"Are you absolutely sure it's the right thing?"

The question made him lower his spoon. "I've racked my brain trying to figure this out, and I can't think of anything better. We don't have geographic rules around this wraith. We don't have anything other than your insights."

After she realized her breakfast remained untouched, she nibbled on her muffin and then washed the bite down with coffee. "Okay. I just want to make sure we're taking it seriously enough. I could get killed, or worse. And so could anyone who's trying to help me."

"I know. I've been working out a plan."

His confidence reassured her. "That's great. Were you planning on sharing any of it soon?"

"I wanted to run it by Father first, but I like what I've got."

She offered a smile to melt his shyness. "Could you share some of it with me?"

He sighed. "I'm still not sure if you should bring your dagger or not."

She'd considered it impossible, but the concept excited her. "You think I could get away with it?"

He nodded. "Maybe. It's practically invisible when you're touching it, and you could hide it against your inner thigh."

She swallowed as she realized she might wind up naked in front of leering sleazes. "That's great, if they're only looking."

"Yeah. That's what scares me. If they start touching, and they feel your dagger, you'll be in trouble."

In her dream, the Maiden of Beit She'an had been correct. Diane had been ignoring the weight of the risk she faced. "If they start touching, I'll already be in trouble."

"And if I don't know where you are at the time, you'll be on your own. I don't like it."

Her heart skipped a beat. "Do you think they'd kill me?"

Frowning, the hunter consoled her. "I don't think so, and this is why I'm tending to have you take it with you. Everyone you'll be dealing with will always see your commercial value. You'll be an object worth money, and to scar you would lower your value. To kill you would be throwing away a significant investment."

"You sure know how to woo a girl."

"That's not my job. My job is to keep you safe."

Shaking her head, she suffered a sinking feeling that revealed how right the Maiden of Beit She'an had been. "No, it's not. I'm on the team now. I'm not the object of the mission. I'm… what's the term?"

Unable to face her while answering, he looked at his oatmeal. "Expendable."

"I'm expendable." The ghost's warning hit Diane hard.

He looked her in the eye. "I know I'll find a way to do my duty, but I will never consider you expendable."

CHAPTER 24

That evening, Liam knocked on Diane's hotel room door, and it clicked open.

She appeared relaxed for a slow night, wearing gray sweatpants and a bright green tee shirt. She'd removed her makeup, and her long lashes fluttered as she smiled. "I was just on my way down to read in the lobby."

Her looking so attractive naturally left him helpless to estimate how much time she invested in the flawless daily appearance that made his heart pound. "Before you head down there, I wanted to give you something." He extended a tube of Dermabond.

Reading its label while accepting it, she cringed. "What's this?"

"It's skin glue. You're going to use it to attach your dagger to… well… I haven't exactly figured that out yet, but I think your inner upper thigh would be appropriate."

"You're kidding."

He shook his head.

Her eyes opened wide. "You're not kidding."

"You've got a better idea?"

"I was thinking maybe I could wear a couple of garter belts."

While envisioning a mentally sanitized version her groin area, he tried to avoid looking at it. "That would attract attention."

"So, you basically want me to cement my dagger to my bare leg, near my crotch, and then what? Rip off a foot of skin in a highly sensitive area when I need my knife?"

Reaching for his nape, he fumbled for an explanation. "It wears off over time, a couple weeks for skin, but I'd guess only a day or two for the bronze, depending how much we use."

"We?" She pointed to her private region. "You think you're going to be all up in here slathering sticky goop?"

He wanted to shrink to the size of an ant and run away. "No. Maybe Nana can help you, if you need help."

"And you're only guessing at how long it will hold?"

"Um, yeah. I couldn't find any references online for its adhesiveness to bronze, enchanted or otherwise."

She glared. "Not funny. Have you ever had hair waxed off your upper lip?"

"No! Why would I?"

"Exactly. You haven't. It hurts like a beast. Now take that and multiply it ten times over for ripping off my own flesh."

"You'll probably have access to water to help dissolve the glue."

"Probably? You mean I may not have water at all? What do they do to these poor women?"

His research suggested unpredictable treatment. For the criminals to profit, their trafficked victims needed to appear healthy, but the players in this underground economy sometimes acted before thinking. "I'm sure you will. You'll need restroom access. I can't see them taking you out of the city or asking you to relieve yourself on the sidewalk."

"Good."

"I'm not sure how long it'll take, but the glue will let go of the dagger before it lets go of your skin."

"What does that mean?"

"It means you'll tear the dagger from the glue before you'd tear your skin, whether it's by applying water over time or by brute force all at once."

She put her hands on her hips. "You're sure about that, especially the brute force part?"

He realized he needed to run an experiment. "Yeah, I'm sure. Well, am I a hundred percent, sure? Not exactly. So, I'll test it on myself. I'll need that tube of Dermabond back."

During a roundtrip to the lobby, he borrowed a roll of duct tape from the office and rushed back to his room.

Inhaling deeply, he walked to the bathroom, dropped his jeans, and turned on the shower. He grabbed his razor and shaving cream from the sink and visualized a section of skin on his thigh for removing hair. After running his knuckles under the stream to verify the warmth, he stepped into the tub and ran water down his leg.

The razor against his groin created a weird sensation, and he reminded himself that competitive athletes did it. But he cringed as he exposed straight lines of flesh between his curly leg hairs. Once finished, he shut off the water, stepped from the tub, and dried his leg.

Staying in his underwear, he carried the duct tape and tube of glue to his nightstand. He opened a drawer and removed his weapons case. Closing his eyes, he lifted the lid, grabbed the dagger, and pointed the blade in the direction of the latest tribute.

He opened his eyes, and the weapon adjusted its aim. Keeping it level, he sidestepped to the bed and reclined. Straining his nearer arm, he reached for the glue and the tape. Unsure what would happen, he squeezed a line of Dermabond over his tender, shaven skin and then mashed the dagger against it.

With his teeth and his free hand, he worked lengths of tape crosswise over the weapon to hold it while the glue cured. As he realized he'd forgotten to remove the hairs under the flat adhesive, he trusted that Diane would avoid the same mistake.

He faced a curious decision between closing his eyes or hopping across the floor to find a pair of shorts. Wishing he'd thought ahead to stage his pants, he pushed himself to one leg and kept his daggered limb pointed the way the weapon chose. After modest acrobatics, he reached his drawer of folded clothes.

Again, he closed his eyes, allowing his leg to fall, and then he slid into his shorts. He tapped the cloth to assure it covered the knife, and then he looked in the mirror. The dagger was a lump under his shorts, but since it was concealed from his view, he was free to move.

His awkward first step towards the door unbalanced his gait, and he likened himself to a bow-legged cowboy. He continued his strange movement to the elevator and into the lobby where he saw Diane sitting on an armchair.

She looked up from her paperback. "You're walking funny."

Continuing towards her, he passed an elderly European man who was checking in, and he let Diane draw her own conclusion.

Looking at his pants, she examined his handiwork. "Let me see what you've done."

He stopped short of her reach. "Is it that obvious?"

"Your cast still stands out more, but I wouldn't leave the hotel looking like that."

The dull throb in his upper arm had become a minor bother, but he noticed the deep discomfort and surface itching as he pointed his palm towards his leg. "You mean it's noticeable?"

"Maybe not to a caveman or a hunter that eats like one, but to the rest of the world it is."

"I'm just proving out the concept."

Lowering her book to a round wooden table next to her seat, she stood. "From this perspective it's not as bad, but it's still obvious that there's something there."

He suspected he'd rushed his experiment. "Maybe I should've asked you what you're planning to wear, if you know."

She shot sideways glances to assure their privacy. Beyond earshot, the elderly man and the clerk at the registration desk were the only bystanders. "I saw them in skirts and blouses, which is what you'd expect."

Doubting if the crime had taken place yet, he considered it a future occurrence. "They'll probably be lied to when they're taken, and they'll be dressed nicely. In my research, one way to trick the women is to promise them good jobs in countries with strong economies, and then they head off thinking they're going to be able to send money back home. But then…"

"That's why I have to do this." She stood straight. "This could work. I'll be wearing a skirt, and it should hide everything."

"What do you mean by everything?"

"I was hoping maybe to take my amulet with me."

The pendant hanging around her neck had concealed her identity as her prior wraith's targeted sacrifice, but Liam doubted the Istanbul wraith sought her as the source of his next fifty years of life. "Do you think you really need it?"

She shrugged. "Probably not, but it couldn't hurt, right?"

"If it's hidden well enough, no. Were you thinking to somehow glue it to your dagger?"

She frowned. "I don't know. I just wanted it."

"I'm not sure you'd benefit from it. To this wraith, you're hopefully nothing but a threat he doesn't see coming."

Her mood changed as she sat, reached to the desk, and lifted her book. Her voice was gentle, and she seemed serene. "But you know, it's fine to leave it behind. My dagger should be enough. I love my dagger. My dagger will protect me."

As she lifted her paperback, Liam realized she was using her knife as a bookmark. "You shouldn't have that out in the open."

Her voice was singsong. "Why not?"

The rules of her dagger escaped him and seemed to operate outside what he considered common sense "Oh, never mind. Your dagger's a great line of defense, but we should also consider other defenses."

Her mini-trance ended, and she looked at him. "You can track me with a GPS chip or something, right?"

Having studied the possibility after learning of Diane's desire to become bait, the young hunter had found unfortunate results. Satellite tracking systems were oversized for implanting under the skin, and hiding a wearable system on her body was impossible. "Not really. That's a common myth. GPS trackers are still too big."

She frowned and sat in silence.

Careful to avoid agitating his dagger, he stepped to the chair on the other side of the small round table and sat down. "If you need help, your connection to Josh will be solid like last time. That's a key line of defense."

"Last time you had no idea where I was until the last second."

"You were also kidnapped long before we knew you. This time, we'll be actively following you."

"You could lose me."

He suspected that he'd rather die. "I won't. But if it happens, you'll still have your connection to Josh."

"I guess."

At the risk of projecting arrogance, he attempted to lift her spirits. "Your dagger and your abilities give you powers I hardly understand, but I know the rest of this equation. I know how to track people, and I know how to protect people. That's what I was raised to do. You know I'll do what I have to for you, right?"

She nodded.

"My father will, too."

Lost in her own concerns, she remained distant.

Liam grabbed the armrests and pushed himself up.

"Where are you going?"

"I thought you wanted to be alone."

"Just because I'm not talking doesn't mean I want to be alone."

He sat back down.

"Can't you just sit here and be quiet?"

It sounded improbable. "I'll give it a shot." Careful where he wiggled the glued dagger's blade, he fumbled in his pocket for his phone for something, anything, to read. Lifting the device, he thumbed through random headlines.

"I don't think you'd ever be a good empath. You're too nervous."

He chuckled–nervously. "At least God divvied out our roles in life correctly."

"Quiet. Just chill."

Thumbing through articles on anything he could find kept his mind occupied while sitting with her in silence.

During an hour, a young couple, dressed in Italian sportswear that Liam considered gaudy, checked in at the registration desk and provided the only distraction to his solitude with Diane.

Without warning, she rose to her feet. "Okay, I'm going to bed."

Trying to be a gentleman, he stood. "Um, yeah. Can I escort you to your room?"

"No, thanks. I'm good."

He found her behavior odd. Either that, or he realized he had a long road ahead to get to know her–a road he wanted open to him.

Giving her time to outpace him upstairs, he waited and then took his measured strides towards the elevator. After reaching his room, he closed the door, looked away from his leg, and tore off the duct tape. As hair follicles escaped his skin, he muffled his grunts.

"Bloody hell."

Keeping his shorts over the knife, he slapped, poked, and prodded the metal through the cloth to verify its adhesion. It felt solid.

Intending to test it overnight while sleeping, he hoped he wouldn't cut himself by his tossing in bed. He also made a mental note to beware where he looked during the middle of the night, to avoid spurring the dagger into rapid reorientation across any of his valuable body parts.

CHAPTER 25

At next morning's breakfast, Diane saw the young hunter cramming a heap of eggs balanced on toast into his mouth.

"Can I join you?"

Chewing, he mumbled and nodded.

She placed her phone on the table. "How's the glue situation?"

With glazed eyes, he looked at her and managed a grunt between chews. "Huh?"

She wondered how he could eat with reckless abandon with a day and a half until her undercover insertion into a human trafficking ring. "That thing glued to your leg."

He swallowed. "Oh. I'll rip it off for you when we get upstairs."

"For me?"

"I want you to see it so that you have confidence when the time comes."

"How'd it work for you overnight?"

He sprinkled salt over his ad hoc egg sandwich. "It poked me a couple times, but it stayed put. I think it'll work for you."

"If it comes off."

"It will. We'll check after breakfast."

"Sure. After breakfast."

Her stomach resisting the apple, raisins, and yogurt she'd forced herself to eat, Diane rode the elevator with Liam. She thought she was still hungry, but her nerves were edgy for tomorrow's task. "Does that thing pinch or chafe at all?"

"A little. You get used to it."

As she followed him through the sliding door, down the hallway, and into his room, she figured he was tough enough to get used to anything.

Grabbing the belt around his shorts, he faced her. "This could get a little awkward. We should talk it out first."

"Okay. What do you want me to do?"

"Nothing, really. Just watch. It's the part where I strip to my skivvies that could get uncomfortable."

She rolled her eyes. "Uncomfortable because I'll see you in your underwear?"

"It's not proper."

"Get over it. I've seen Josh in everything and nothing. I used to give him his baths."

"Oh, I see. Well, that's good."

"You need to keep your eyes closed, too. You'll hardly know I'm here."

"Right. You won't have that problem in the field, but I can't risk my knife pointing to Israel without warning. Perhaps I should blindfold myself."

Thinking comic relief might elevate her mood, she toyed with him. "Ooh... kinky! Knives and blindfolds. I feel like a dominatrix. Your safety word is 'submarine'."

Poor at hiding his discomfort, he blushed. "Let's just be quick about it."

"Great. Make sure to rip off as much skin as you can to avoid embarrassing yourself."

"I'm not embarrassed."

"No, you're just turning red."

He raised his voice while marching to his dresser. "Bloody hell. Let's get this over with."

She couldn't resist piling on. "After you blindfold yourself, you'll lick the bottom of my shoe."

He cringed. "What?"

"Ugh. You're no fun. Never mind."

"I'll do it right here." He tied a tee-shirt over his eyes and dropped his pants to the carpet, exposing the bronze blade and his blue cotton underwear.

"Well, finally we're down to business."

"Are you watching?"

She noticed the tip disappearing under the fold of flesh between his leg and his groin. "Yes, I'm watching. Why'd you jam it up so high up your leg?"

"It was the least conspicuous way I could do it."

"You're sure it didn't cut you?"

"Maybe a little. Nothing worth crying about."

She assumed he could withhold tears even if he severed an artery. "Aren't you worried about cutting yourself when you pull it off?"

"That's a good point." He broadened his stance to expose the full dagger. Bending, he lowered both hands to the handle.

"Hold on, buddy. Only one hand."

"Why, for God's sake?"

She raised her voice. "Because you're like ten times stronger than me! If you need two hands, there's no way I could do it."

"Fine, I'll do it one-handed. Do you prefer my broken arm or my weak arm?"

"Just pick one."

He sighed a long, drawn out breath. "Let me think this through. The knife's going to snap out quickly, and it'll rotate in the direction of my wrist. Best I use my right hand to avoid cutting my leg open."

Expecting she'd need two hands, she filed away the wrist-rotation lesson as useless for her future needs. "Whatever. Go ahead."

Widening his stance, he extended his cast forward and grabbed the handle. His arm shook, but nothing happened.

"What's wrong, Hercules?"

"Shut up." His trembling increased, and his skin reddened. The flesh of his upper groin stretched like white rubber as he strained.

"You should stop before you flay yourself."

Grimacing, he ignored her and grunted.

As she saw a portion of the adhesive stretching near the hilt, she ceased her taunting and offered encouragement. "Come on, caveman. You can do it. It's coming off."

An inch-long airgap formed as the blade separated from the elastic glue. "How am I doing?"

"Feel it with your other hand. It's working."

Relaxing, he ran his left index finger along the knife edge, stopped at the hole he'd created, and probed it. "You'll be able to see when you do this. Doing this blind is hard."

"I'm not accepting any excuses."

"Oh, come on! I'm nowhere near one hundred percent with this cast. Stop whining."

Grateful he was blindfolded, she blushed as she conceded she'd been chiding him too hard. "I'll stop whining if you keep going."

He started yanking again, and the air gap grew.

"Keep going. You're almost there."

The gap widened to the width of his hand, and with the lowered resistance, he stopped. He spoke through labored panting. "I've got it now. Just going to take a bit of a break."

With success eminent, she harassed him onward. "You're supposed to be making it look easy."

"Fine." Shaking, he pulled the knife down and away from his body. The last strand of cement resisted but then released the dagger to his overpowering wrist. The young hunter's choice of his right hand proved wise as the blade slashed an arc away from his leg.

"Good job, Liam!"

A knock at the door startled her. "Oh! Who is it?"

"It's Connor. May I come in?"

Enthused by the young hunter's success, she pranced to the door and opened it.

Connor looked at her, gazed beyond her shoulder, and gave an inquisitive look. "Skivvies and a blindfold. I'm afraid to ask."

"Come in before someone sees us." She closed the door behind the elder hunter.

Liam laid the dagger on the dresser and then removed his blindfold. "I tore off the dagger to show her how easy it was."

"Well, now that it's over, may I suggest that you put your pants back on whilst in front of a lady?"

"Yes. Right, Father." The young hunter obeyed.

"May I ask how the experiment went?"

Liam hastened to answer. "Quite well. It came right off, no problem."

"Then why are you beet-red and short of breath?"

The young hunter flipped his wrist. "Just a bit of exertion. She made me do it one-handed."

"That was wise of her. I imagine if you did it with your arm in a cast, then she can manage with two hands."

Diane noticed how the men with bulging muscles trivialized what she considered a feat of strength.

As she prepared for an afternoon reviewing the plan to insert her into the trafficking network, find the wraith, and kill him, she speculated about other challenges they'd underestimated. Would they lose her? Would she end up in a third-world country as a sex slave? Would someone find her knife and kill her on sight?

She thought about complaining and calling the whole thing off, but she remembered the counsel of her ghostly maiden. She needed to risk everything. She needed to be ready to surrender herself to save others.

Unable to defeat the wraith in one-on-one telepathic combat, she needed to attack with her team. And they needed her to lead them.

Fear of failure had to wash away, and she committed herself to trusting her destiny. "Sure, guys. No problem."

Half an hour later, she wore shorts and stood by her bedside with her enchanted dagger, a bottle of Dermabond, and a roll of duct tape staged on her nightstand. A pang of shame shot through her as she realized the trivial task scared her.

An inch in the wrong direction, a few degrees of misorientation, or some other deviation from an unknowable perfection could beget a catastrophe. She needed someone. She needed Liam.

Her phone in her face, she dialed and listened on speakerphone. "Hello, Diane?"

"Hi. Can you come by my room? I need help."

His soft tone implied his understanding. "Sure."

When she heard his soft knock a minute later, she opened the door and lowered her head.

He looked to the carpet, too, as he entered. "I suppose you want help with the adhesive?"

"Yeah."

"Would you like me to do it?"

The burden of the task's execution outweighed the awkwardness of the pending intimate touching. She inhaled and sighed. "It's too important for me to do it. I trust you."

"Alright. Why don't you lay down and pull your shorts up as high as you can? I'll do the rest."

She complied and rested her back against the headboard.

He transferred the items from her nightstand to the comforter beside her. "Um, you'll need to spread your legs."

Rolling her eyes, she blushed while submitting. She felt his weight shift on the mattress as he crawled onto the bed and knelt between her knees. She tried to avoid saying anything about the thoughts his proximity sent racing through her mind.

"You shaved your leg, didn't you?"

With him in her life, she'd made it part of her daily routine. "Of course. I'm not a barbarian."

"Just checking. I made the mistake of keeping my hairs, and it hurt like… well, I imagine like that hot wax thing you mentioned."

"Probably."

"Okay, this is going to feel odd, but I know it works. Here comes the glue."

His squeezing hand produced a steady stream of adhesive running up her thigh.

She giggled. "That tickles."

"Sorry."

"Stop apologizing when it's not your fault."

"I don't like to see you uncomfortable."

"It's fine. Keep going."

"Right." He set the tube aside and then pressed the dagger into the gel. Sliding the blade upward, he stopped it against the tender flesh above her artery. "Done. Now hold it there tightly."

She put her fingers against the knife and stabilized it.

The hunter reached for the duct tape, which he taped against her leg and rolled over the dagger.

She started to elevate her knee.

"No, not yet." He ripped the roll from the strand holding the blade against her inner groin. Moving between her fingers, he applied a second strand closer to her pubic bone. "Now, keep your left hand against it, and I'll help you to your feet." He crawled away, stood, and walked to her side.

As she elevated her free arm across her body, the tape felt taut against her skin. He held her hand and drew her up and forward. With his guidance, she landed on her feet and stood.

He knelt and rolled the tape in complete circumferences around her thigh. "That'll hold. It's not too tight, is it?"

His judgment had been perfect. "No, it's fine."

"Great. Sleep on it and call me if it moves or bothers you. I'll keep my phone on real loud."

"Thanks, Liam." When the moment would come for her dagger, she would remember his gentle strength and let him boost her confidence.

CHAPTER 26

The memory of palpating the empath's supple upper thigh teased Liam and his vow of lifelong celibacy.

Standing at the street corner by a highway onramp, he forced the sweet memory from his thoughts and timed the traffic light one last time. It stayed red for forty-three seconds. "You're sure the truck will pull up here on a yellow light?"

Beside him, Diane sounded annoyed. "How many times are you going to ask?"

"I need to be sure."

"I'm sure."

Bracing for the wrath of an angry empath, he reverified the critical concern. "And you're sure this is the right street corner?"

"I saw the street signs in my vision, and this location feels right." She smacked his shoulder. "Stop asking me. It's right."

He let himself trust her.

The spot she'd envisioned was perfect. The crossroads were quiet with sparse vehicular and pedestrian traffic, and the closest shop was a liquor store with few windows facing the street. Behind him, cement pillars held the highway above the access ramp, which followed a sharp curve underneath the main thoroughfare.

Liam saw the road's curve as an opportunity to conduct his operation beyond the view of trailing vehicles "Then we're ready to rehearse it."

"Does your dad have our other car yet?"

Liam had confirmed with his father an hour ago. "Yeah, he's waiting at the gas station."

"What did he rent?"

"He got a crossover SUV, a Ford Kuga."

"*Yulla.* Let's go."

At the Esso petroleum station, Liam sat in the driver's seat of the Fiat 500X. He rolled down the window. "Are you ready?"

Beside him, his father pointed the Kuga in the opposite direction. "I am. Run ahead, and I'll catch up and pass you."

The young hunter aimed the Fiat into highway traffic and accelerated.

Beside him, Diane craned her neck towards her grandmother in the back seat. "Are you okay, Nana?"

The elder Chaldean Iraqi Christian women responded in Aramaic.

Liam understood a few words, but she spoke too fast for him to achieve a full mental translation. However, he understood her reverent tone.

Nana was uncomfortable placing her granddaughter in danger, but she respected Diane's motivation.

The young hunter navigated through traffic lanes until he reached the right shoulder and decelerated. He stopped the vehicle and waited for his father's Kuga to appear in the rearview mirror. "Here they come. Nana, look up here. Diane, look here and pretend we're lost and playing with our navigation, but tell me exactly when you see Josh and Father drive by."

"Sure. Not yet. Okay! They just drove by."

He lifted his foot off the brake and moved it to the accelerator. The Fiat lurched forward in pursuit of the Kuga, which the elder hunter drove down an off ramp. Liam tried to catch up, but a delivery truck maneuvered in front of him. "Damn."

Diane surprised him with her determination. "Don't worry about it. Even if there's a witness tomorrow, we're going through with this."

While driving down the ramp, the young hunter saw the Kuga moving aside to let the delivery truck pass. "Father's giving us a break today for training, but tomorrow we'll have to move faster. Diane, you'll have to give me five seconds of warning when we do this for real."

"I'll do my best."

As the lead vehicle reentered traffic, Liam nestled the Fiat behind its tailpipe and followed it around a bend, under the highway, and to the intersection. The delivery truck slipped under the yellow light while the elder hunter's Kuga slowed into the red.

Liam stopped the 500X behind the Ford, shifted the transmission into park, and checked his position. The Ford's driver's side mirror was visible, but the curving road hid the vehicle's other reflective surfaces from view. "Go, Diane!"

The empath darted out the passenger door.

Liam wiggled over the console to the passenger seat and grabbed bolt cutters from the floor. He followed Diane out her door, and with the tool tucked under his arm, he trotted towards the SUV.

Wearing a skirt to hide her dagger, Diane labored forward as he passed her. "It's hard to move."

"Pace yourself. Better to arrive late than to trip and fall."

"I'm not that clumsy." She tripped and stumbled the final steps to the Ford. "Okay, maybe I am that clumsy."

Reaching the hatchback, Liam stopped, lifted the sharp steel to the door, and began a ten-second mental countdown. "Don't worry about speed. I'll need a few seconds with the lock anyway. Take your time walking so you don't break your ankle."

"How long's this normally take?"

"I'm allotting ten seconds, but I plan to cut through in half that time. Five seconds is a long time over this short distance. Just walk calmly." As his countdown timed out, he lowered the bolt cutters to his hip. "Okay, you're in."

"What do I do now?"

"Practice what you'll say to the girl you'll be replacing."

"I'd tell her to get out and join you."

"Say it in Aramaic."

She rattled off words he partially comprehended.

"What was that? I heard you say 'hurry' and 'walk'." He lifted a new lock from his pocket to simulate hanging it on the truck. From his other pocket, he pulled a magnetic GPS tracker and pressed it against a flat surface under the bumper."

"That's what I said, more or less."

"Good enough for now, but practice with Nana tonight. Let's go." He marched back to the Fiat's passenger door, slid the cutters to the floor, and crawled over the console into the driver's seat. The light turned green before Diane could sit, and the impatient driver in the Renault sedan behind him honked his horn.

When Diane reached her seat, she complained. "I'm moving too slow for this."

"I have no idea how fast the Iraqi girl will move or if she'll even come with me. She may just run away from the truck and never look back. As long as the traffickers count five women when they get where they're going, that's fine." Liam drove through the intersection and hailed his father through the cabin's microphone.

The elder hunter's voice issued through the cabin. "Hello."

"Can you pull into the liquor store?"

"Yes, of course. One moment."

Liam angled the 500X into the parking lot, stopped it next to his father's vehicle, and hung up as he rolled down the window. "How was it from your perspective?"

"I was concerned when you became separated from me. That delivery truck swooped in fast, and you'll need to account for that sort of driving. That would play out poorly tomorrow if it happens."

"It won't."

"Don't be too eager, either. You need to stay inconspicuous."

"I'll handle it."

"We'll rehearse it again to get the timing down."

Liam trusted himself to get it right, but he knew better than to challenge the elder hunter's conservatism. "Yes, Father. We'll rehearse it again."

"How was the breaking in?"

"Fine. It'll all depend on how fast I can cut the lock and on how receptive the Iraqi girl is to Diane's orders."

"Of course. One more time, then, from the gas station. Also make sure to track me on your GPS. Give me a five-minute head start to allow separation."

That night, after a second and successful rehearsal, Liam paced across the length of his hotel room, replaying his mental vision of tomorrow's ideal scenario for the hundredth time. Then he probed for his thousandth possibility of failure.

The Iraqi girl Diane planned to replace would stay in the van. The lock would resist the bolt cutters. The truck would run the red light. The traffickers would hear the doors open. A hostile witness would interfere. Diane would trip over her undersized feet.

He considered a preventative measure for every failure and a mitigation to each unsuccessful prevention. His mind buzzing with tactics and alternatives, he made himself anxious.

He paced faster.

A timid knock on the door offered a welcomed distraction. He darted across the carpet and twisted the knob. "Diane."

"Can I come in?"

"Yeah."

She sat on the edge of his bed. Unsure if he should sit, he walked to the desk and twirled its chair towards her.

As he sank into the seat, she shared her worries. "I know it was my idea, but I'm scared. It really wasn't my idea, though. It was a vision, or a calling."

"You mean anything specific, or the entire idea of tomorrow's infiltration?"

"The whole thing. Just because it's a vision doesn't mean it's a guaranteed success. In fact, a ghost keeps saying I need to be ready to surrender myself. Does that make sense?"

Her fear concerned him because everything depended upon her perceptions. "I guess so. I can tell you that what we're doing is inherently dangerous, and I can tell you that I'm going to do everything humanly possible to protect you, but only you know what's going on beyond the humanly knowable."

She frowned. "Does that mean I'm not human?"

He found her hard to talk to, for an empath. "It means that you're more than the average human."

"I'll accept that."

"What's this about surrendering yourself?" He hoped it was metaphorical.

Her gaze drifted towards the ceiling. "The ghost said I needed to be ready to surrender myself. I can't say exactly what that means, but it could mean everything."

That cut to his core. "Everything? Like your life?"

"Let's not talk about it." She lowered her eyes to his. "But just in case anything happens to me, I want you to promise me that you'll take care of Josh."

He sprang from his chair. "No!"

She scowled. "What's wrong with you?"

"What's wrong with you? Stop this bloody defeatist talk."

"I'm just being real."

"I don't want to lose you." Her silence made his heart pound as his words lingered in the air. He wondered how many sacred lines he'd just crossed with his comment, and he had to break the silence himself. "You know what I mean."

"I do. That's the problem. You don't have me to lose. I'm not yours. You saved my life, but I'm not a prize." She flicked her wrist towards the dresser. "I'm not some trophy you get to put on your mantle."

"You're right. I'm sorry."

"Just promise me."

He knew he'd find a way to care for her brother if the unthinkable happened to the empath. "I promise. If anything happens to you, I'll take care of Josh like my own brother."

She stood and walked to the door. "Thank you."

"Of course."

As she disappeared into the hallway, he committed the image of her beauty to memory, accepting that tonight might be her last in safety.

CHAPTER 27

The next afternoon, Diane sat in the passenger seat of the unmoving Fiat 500X. She looked beyond her grandmother and out the back window at approaching traffic.

From the driver's seat, the young hunter grabbed her attention.

"Look at my hands. Watch for the truck from the corner of your eyes."

She aimed her nose at the console where Liam held his phone. "What are you looking at?"

He thumbed the screen. "Nothing really. Random headlines. I'm just distracting myself since I'm nervous."

The pit of anxiety in her stomach dwarfed the Grand Canyon. "Yeah. No kidding. What time is it?"

"Three ten. We're early, but I wanted to be situated."

Wanting to talk about anything other than her pending task, she rambled. "Are Josh and Connor ready?"

"Ready and waiting. Hopefully, we won't need them."

"Josh looked real funny, didn't he?" She remembered him wearing a blue bandana over his head, a shirtless jean jacket, and mirrored sunglasses, like a military veteran motorcycle enthusiast. Liam had suggested dressing her brother in drag to maximize the distraction, but the consensus had been the subtler solution.

"A hoot. Make sure you're watching the road."

She yelped. "I am! Just because I'm talking doesn't mean I'm not paying attention."

From the back seat, Nana volunteered her support in Aramaic. "You know you'll get it right. You're special."

Her nerves numbing the foreign-language section of her brain, Diane responded in English. "Thanks, Nana. That doesn't make this any easier, though." In her mind, she appended the words "or less dangerous."

The hunter brought her back to her task. "Do you see it yet?"

"No."

"Do you feel it yet?"

Despite her fear, she did. "Yeah."

"Is it getting closer? Can you tell?"

Her connection with the truck's driver had been weak since seeing the proposed future through his eyes. But it lurked in her mind like the recollection of a pending dentist appointment, an annoying reminder of an encroaching, necessary evil. "Not really. This is intense for me, but it's business as usual for him. So, there's no major emotional signals coming from him, and I'm too wound up to notice them anyway."

"Yeah, like a saturated reception antenna. I get it."

She ignored the technical jargon and kept her peripheral vision on the approaching traffic.

Exposing his impatience, Liam stole a glance through the Fiat's rear windows.

"Don't you trust me?"

"Sorry." He looked back to his phone.

"You don't even know what the truck looks like."

"I said I was sorry."

Her breathing became shallow. "I see it."

"How close?"

She saw a truck's grill in the distance, but she waited upon confirmation from her empathic ability to identify it. "How should I know? Just start driving."

"Bloody hell." He moved his leg and accelerated the Fiat down the shoulder.

The cement barrier crept towards her passenger door as the off-ramp approached. "What are you doing?"

"Aggressive driving is normal around here from what I've seen. Better to drive like an ass than to let another car come between us."

The side mirror scraped the barrier as Liam whipped the Fiat behind the white truck. An Opel sedan's horn blared, and Diane twisted her neck to see a scowling, reddened face and an unpleasant upward-moving hand gesture.

"Don't worry about him. Our mission's ahead of us." The young hunter drew the Fiat into drafting distance of the truck.

Despite her fear, Diane sensed the Iraqi victims. "That's it! That's the truck. I'm sure."

"I never doubted you."

While she ran her fingers up her skirt to caress the blade for certainty, she left unchallenged his dozens of historical second-guessing comments. Although the glued dagger provided some insights while attached to her leg, she found its strongest power in her hands. She was right. They trailed the proper vehicle.

Liam brought the 500X to an abrupt stop behind the truck.

Nana protested from the back seat. "Easy!"

"You don't have to drive like a maniac!"

Ignoring her comment, he raised his voice. "Get out, Diane!"

"Don't be an ass!"

Whether she intended to depart or not, he was halfway over the console. "Bloody hell, woman, get your ass on the street."

Expecting him to carry her if she resisted, she popped open the door and hit her labored stride. With the dagger glued to her groin, she used a limping trot to reach the broad façade of double doors behind the truck.

Carrying bolt cutters, Liam joined her. He aimed the steel blades at the single deadbolt, which matched the image in her prophetic vision, and he snapped it open. Quickly, he slipped the severed lock into his jacket pocket and pulled a door open with minimal squeaking. "You're in. Go."

With her knife pinching her, she reached for him. "Help me up."

His rapid footwork surprised her as he moved to her backside and lifted her from the waist. Like a feather, he elevated her to the truck's bed.

She didn't stop to glance back and see if he grimaced with pain in his broken arm or to scowl at him for grabbing her ribs without permission. Time ticked away.

His command was stern. "Hurry."

She stood in the dim space, illuminated by one bulb. The five women matching her prophetic vision sat with their legs tucked underneath their skirts. Spying the one she intended to replace, she locked eyes with her and spoke in Aramaic. "I'm here to rescue all of you, but only you now. I must take your place."

The woman ruined the plan with one sentence. "I can't leave my sister."

Overwhelmed, Diane turned to the sunlight and the hunter's silhouette. "She says she can't leave her sister."

"Bloody hell. Hold on." The young hunter pressed the Bluetooth receiver against his ear. "Father, I need more time. I need a distraction." He moved to the edge of the truck, waved, and tried to give the captives a friendly smile. "Tell them there's a team of professionals saving them all, but we need to exchange you for one of them to get you inside."

Diane turned back to her body double and explained Liam's thoughts in her best Aramaic.

The Iraqi woman still refused to abandon her sister, the younger one beside her whom Diane pegged as sixteen years old.

"She won't leave!"

"Tell her what I did for you. Tell her how I have no choice but to save them all. Sell it like you mean it!"

"But they're not your mission. They're just a means to an end."

Even with the sun backlighting him, his face showed his resolve. "Can you see me leaving them behind if I have any chance of stopping it?"

Accepting his commitment, Diane turned and knelt before the scared Iraqi woman, clasped her hands, and refused to harbor another rejection. "His name is Liam. He and his father risked their lives to save me from a similar problem. He took bullets to his chest and arm. His father nearly bled to death. They will follow me and save you all."

"Including my sister?"

"Especially your sister."

"What must I do?"

The truck's horn honked, filling the cabin with instant anxiety.

Liam's voice echoed off the cabin's walls. "That's Josh and Father pulling off some antics in the crosswalk, but the bloody light's already green! Hurry up."

Diane stood and extended her hand. "Stand and leave. I will take your place. Go with Liam and do whatever he says. Hurry, please!"

The woman accepted her hand and rose with featherlike grace. Diane escorted her to the back of the truck, cupped her hands under her armpits, and helped lower her to the hunter.

Liam spoke while pulling the new lock from his pocket. "Tell her to get in the back with Nana."

"Get in the back seat with my grandmother."

The woman nodded and walked away.

Diane crouched to the floor and sought an opportunity to kiss her hero goodbye, but he had other plans.

"Take care of yourself, and please communicate as often as you can through Josh." He swung the door shut and closed it.

As she heard the replacement lock slide into the latch, she stood, turned, and faced her new teammates. Her Aramaic proved strong when needed, although she wondered if the dagger's enchantment helped her along. "Hello, my name is Diane. Tell me what you've been through together, what village you're from, and anything else you can to make our captors believe I'm the lady who just escaped."

CHAPTER 28

Liam bumped his knee against the shifter and banged his shoulder against the driver's door. The truck carrying Diane had already raced through the light, and he fumbled with his body parts, enduring the repeated horn of the Opel stranded behind him on the curved ramp.

Confident he'd dabbed enough glue in the replacement lock, he watched it hold halfway between open and closed as it held the doors shut behind the departing vehicle. He trusted the traffickers would assume they'd unknowingly left it unlocked, and that the defective device needed replacing.

He also hoped Diane could pass as a replica of the young lady in his back seat, whether through the trafficker's ignorance, her dagger's divine influence, or the empath's acting.

Liam set the car into motion. "Nana, ask her what her name is."

The Chaldean grandmother engaged the newcomer in a conversation that lasted longer than gain rapid intensity.

As he passed under the light, Liam shot a sideways glance at Josh and Connor, who'd reached the crosswalk's far side.

The autistic young man mimicked a perfect rendition of an American pro-motorcycle, pro-military, open-road bike rider while his father had dressed in the most unfashionable garb a grandparent could wear, with high leg cuffs exposing his unmatching socks.

Liam turned into the corner liquor lot and kept the 500X crawling towards the back. Behind the store, he found the Kuga, parked beside it, and addressed his father through their vehicles' windows.

"She says her name is Nadine."

The young hunter twisted to face the women in the back seat. Forcing a smile, he tried to put the young lady at ease in his broken Aramaic. "Hi, Nadine. I'm Liam."

"Hello."

Nana translated the new arrivals' concerns. "She says her sister is still in the van. We need to get her. She also says she knows all the girls in the truck. They're from the same village."

Although unconcerned about their origins, the hunter suspected that Nana needed to expound. "What village?"

"Bazwaiai, right outside of Mosul."

Liam sensed a convergence of forces ramping up the Chaldean grandmother's motivation. "You're from Mosul, right, Nana?"

"Yes! We have to get them all back."

"Of course, Nana. That's what I'm doing. I've got to move to the Kuga now, since they've seen the Fiat." He opened the door and got one foot onto the pavement.

"No, I'm coming with you. Connor, he gave me my own gun."

"Again! I think my father's in love with you."

Nana smirked and shrugged. "Maybe."

"Well, it's up to Father where you ride and what you carry."

The elder hunter rounded the liquor store's corner and appeared in front of Liam with Josh at his side. "Nice work, lad."

"You, too, Father. How'd you manage with the distraction?"

"Oh, it was rather simple really. I just feigned turning my ankle while walking in front of the truck. Then Josh did an admirable job pretending to help me to my feet."

With his bandana covering his head down to his sunglasses, Josh looked like a new person, but he seemed uncomfortable without a tablet near his face. "You mean you were faking?"

"Yes, Josh, I was."

"That's lying."

"You're right, Josh. It is. I shall make amends later with those whom I've offended."

Josh aimed his sunglasses at the elder hunter. "How?"

"If I see them again, I'll either apologize to them, or I'll kill them. Perhaps apologize, then kill them. Shall we be on our way now? You'll ride with Liam."

Unfazed by the elder hunter's directness, the autistic man followed Liam to the Kuga while Connor entered the Fiat on its driver's side.

Without a word, the young hunter shifted the manual transmission Ford crossover SUV into gear and zipped away. "I know you want your tablet, but can you manage the GPS tracker for me, Josh?"

"I can do everything on my tablet."

"Good point." Liam whipped his cast and broken arm behind the console and fished for his young companion's device. "I'm not finding it. Can you get it?"

"Sure." The autistic man rummaged through the back seat and then faced forward. "I found it." The tablet appeared in front of his face. "It's hard to read."

"You can take off your sunglasses now. You can also take off the bandana. In fact, you should, so that they don't recognize you."

Josh removed both items. "I can see better now."

"Great. Can you call up the GPS tracker? I'm going from memory at the moment."

"I see the GPS."

"Can you call up a course to follow it?"

"I already am."

"Not that I don't trust you, but can you turn up the volume? I'd like to hear the program call out the turns."

"Sure. You don't have to trust me."

One thing Liam liked about Josh was his passive compliance despite subtleties that might offend others. "Thanks, Josh."

"Why are all the drones in the back seat?"

"That's a great question, my friend. It's to help get your sister back. Just in case we need to track more than one vehicle, I've got GPS trackers mounted on each of the big drones. I can magnetically mount them under trucks and vans if I have to."

Liam's companion kept his face in his tablet. "Did you practice that?"

"Well, yes, but just once. It's easy enough to nudge one of these babies up to a leaf spring, and the laws of physics take care of the rest."

"If you say so."

The experiment the young hunter had run on the Kuga happened so flawlessly, he'd forgotten to repeat it and learn from his mistakes. But he needed the trick to work, possibly several times. The time for second guessing had passed. "Yes, I do say so, buddy."

"We're supposed to turn right up here."

Liam followed the GPS tracking software's recommendation through congestion. Though he slogged the Kuga through nasty traffic, the same lethargic vehicular flow restricted Diane's progress away from him.

"Do I get body armor?"

"Was it that obvious that I'm wearing mine?"

"Yes."

Liam had hoped to be less conspicuous, but he admitted the light jacket he wore over his armor in June's heat was a beacon for onlookers. He'd considered leaving the armor off, but he'd been one loud noise away from gunplay when inserting Diane into the truck. "Yeah. There's a suit back there. You want to try it on?"

"You'll need to help me."

At least the kid knew his limits. "Sure, do your best now and I'll help you when I can. This traffic will be stop and go for a while. There should be a vest for you on the floorboards behind your seat. We'll deal with helmets and other stuff later."

"We're only two miles from Diane."

Growing accustomed to his partner's rapid segues, Liam agreed the offhand comment made sense. "Right. That's comforting. I uh... don't suppose you've heard from her yet, telepathically?"

"No."

"Do you think you should reach out to her, just to make sure she's okay?"

"I can't reach out to her."

Liam frowned. But if you were highly emotional, she'd seek you, wouldn't she?"

"Yes."

The hunter flagged a data point in his brain to stimulate emotions in Josh if he ever needed to summon Diane.

"She's okay."

Liam shrugged. "Not my area of expertise. I'll trust you."

"She'd contact me if she needed me."

"Cool." He abandoned the subject as the next turn brought the Kuga to slower traffic, and Liam suspected the onset of rush hour. "I have to admit these human traffickers are patient."

"Don't let that stop you from pulling the trigger."

Liam guffawed. "Bloody hell! Now, that's an attitude I like." From the corner of his eye, he saw Josh pulling his vest into his lap.

"Where do I start?"

In his mind, the young hunter reverse-engineered the procedure. "Uh... if you can get your head and arms through it the right way, that would help."

The empath's brother fumbled with the armor. "How's this?"

Shooting a glance, Liam surmised the effort. "Well, it's backwards. So, just try it again the other way around."

Tufting his matted hair, Josh lifted the vest and tossed it to his feet. "I don't want to. This is stupid."

Diane's wisdom guiding him, Liam let her brother's frustration wear itself out. To change the subject, he hailed his father on this phone.

"Yes, lad. How are you?"

"We're fine up here. I don't see you on GPS. Can you call it up on all your phones, please?"

"Right. Sorry. I was wary of my battery constraints. I shall address it now."

Liam stole a glance at his passenger's tablet and saw his father's phone's location appear half a mile behind him in traffic. "How's the new young lady holding up?"

"I'd say amazingly, given the circumstances. She's calm and coherent."

"Did you let her know she has no obligation to help us?"

"Of course, but she wants to stay until we get her sister back. I defy you to win an argument against two incensed Iraqi women. She's formed a quick bond with Nana, and I'm not committing political or literal suicide with a counterargument."

"Oh, bloody hell, Father. You didn't give her a gun already, too, did you?"

"Nonsense, lad. She'd have to prove herself first, as Nana did. But something about her temperament tells me she'd welcome it."

Liam drove in silence for miles, coaching his calmed companion into his vest and trailing Diane's truck. When the GPS showed the targeted vehicle turning into a restaurant's parking lot, he asked for his passenger's help. "Can you send that destination to Father?"

"Okay." Josh tapped his screen. "I sent it."

The young hunter elevated his chin toward the cabin microphone. "Do you see it yet? They're in a parking lot."

"I've got it. Careful with your drive by. I'll assess the nearby lots for parking."

Diane's truck passed through a motorized chain-link fence and into a lot that oozed a desire for privacy. "Josh, can you take a video from down low in your window? I'm going to drive by the back and through this neighboring lot."

"Yeah. That's easy."

Liam stopped at the last intersection before the establishment of interest. "Easy, huh? You got it rolling yet?"

"Yes."

He wanted Josh to video everything, but he respected the limits of his understanding. "You're doing great, Josh. Okay. Get a shot of all the trucks you can. Once that's done, let me know."

The light changed, Liam rolled the Kuga forward, and the lot came into view. From the corner of his eye, he counted the two men from Diane's vehicle greeting a lone guard at the door."

"Go ahead, Josh. Get the trucks."

"I got the trucks."

Aiming his nose towards traffic, Liam minimized the suspicion to witnesses, but he knew if anyone saw Josh with his phone, the mission would blow up. "Wait! Never mind."

"Never mind?"

"Too many people are looking around now." Liam suspected the traffickers would become paranoid as they moved the girls from the truck to the building.

"There they are!"

Behind the private parking area, Liam turned into a convenience store's lot. Adjoining its retail neighbor, the small store shared a tall chain fence with a wall of ivy. The young hunter slowed the vehicle in hopes of giving Josh a view. "Anything?"

"No, it's too thick."

"Did you see Diane?"

"No."

"But they're unloading the girls from her truck into the building, right?"

"Yes." Josh's autism frustrated Liam during rapid exchanges.

"Okay, then this is the place. I'm going to circle back to the other side of the road at what looks like a bridal shop. It'll have lower security protection than a convenience store."

The elder hunter's voice filled the cabin. "Can you see the lot from the bridal shop?"

"Yes, but not all. They have ivy covering a lot of the view. Josh was able to video the trucks through the gaps, but it'll be tough."

"You don't see a better option?"

"I don't. We could back out of traditional surveillance and leave this to the empath and GPS trackers." The suggestion sounded weak as he uttered it.

From his phone connection to the Fiat, he heard Nana's protest. "Bridal shop? What's wrong with you? I owned one for forty years. You send me in. I take care of everything"

CHAPTER 29

With both cars parked behind the bridal shop. Liam followed his five-person team into the store's foyer. Though gaps in the ivy across the street allowed modest spying, the vantage point was insufficient.

Unless he could see better, Diane would be carted away on a random outbound truck, and he'd need her telepathy to identify the vehicle carrying her.

But Nana was leading the charge, frowning as she caressed frilly, laced dresses of off-white colors hanging upon racks.

With a spunky posture, a short woman in her mid-sixties greeted Nana in Turkish. "May I help you?"

The Chaldean grandmother shifted gears, responding in Arabic. "Do you speak Arabic or English?"

The patron cocked her head. "I prefer English. Many of my clients come from America or the UK."

Liam translated the comment to mean the owner knew her inventory's value to Western buyers, and he observed the Chaldean matriarch's counter.

Nana used the high-volume-purchase argument. "I have my granddaughter, her fiancé, her fiancé's father, and my grandson, who's the best man. We need a wedding dress, a groom's tuxedo, six groomsman tuxedoes, and six bridesmaid dresses."

"That's wonderful. Do you have a theme for the wedding party?"

Nonplused, the Chaldean grandmother struck hard. "That dress over there in your display, the Giovani. You say it's this year's, but it's four-years old."

Everyone but Nana and her jousting partner meandered towards safe corners. The patron kept her poise under pressure. "Giovani's style has been constant for years. Perhaps you're mistaken."

"I doubt it, but what about that McDougal? You price it at four thousand liras. That's five times the wholesale price."

"We offer free alterations. That helps quite a bit, if you're on a tight budget." The woman's glare was a barb precluding any pity about pricing.

As Nana scowled while formulating her counterattack, the owner switched subjects. "Are you here to buy products or to do something about those god-forsaken human traffickers across the street?"

Unable to contain himself within the charade, Liam marched to her. "What makes you ask that?"

The patron pointed to his chest. "You're wearing body armor under your jacket."

Liam had hoped she'd figure it out and accepted the opening. "Well, silly me. Looks like I've blown our cover. Now that we can talk seriously, we have someone on the inside pretending to be a victim, and we'd like to set up surveillance from here. Since the police won't help you, we will."

The woman squinted. "Who pays you? Parents of the victims? Village elders at the source cities? I'd be surprised since half of them profit from this."

Before Liam could ruin the conversation with an awkward version of the truth, Connor spared him. "We work for a European human rights agency that targets small groups like the one across the street. We hope to stop this horrific practice with enough small successes, one at a time, if we must."

The patron seemed to accept the elder hunter's argument. "I've been wanting to retire for years, but these evil men set up shop about three years ago and cut my profits in half. What can I do to help?"

The building's tactical possibilities inspired Liam. "Can you get me roof access?"

"Yes, of course."

"Great. Father, can you help me bring the drones up there?"

"Indeed. I think I see where you're going with this, but what else is on your mind?"

"Another distraction. I see an entry point into the parking lot at the corner of the chain-link fence. It's out of site of the loading dock, but I need a backup plan in case someone walks too far on their smoke break."

"I've already been the distraction. So, I can't help you. Neither can Josh."

"Oh, I'm not convinced of that."

On the bridal shop's roof, Liam doublechecked the coordinates of the parked vans. He sent the three drones with the GPS trackers mounted atop their cargo bays over the lip of the dress shop's roof, down to the sidewalk, and to a resting position beside the chain-link fence. He spoke into his wireless headset. "I'm ready to go. I don't see anyone watching."

Below him and nearer to the intersection, Josh wore bright red lipstick, a fuchsia dress, and a gay rights sign around his neck written in English and Turkish.

Connor owned the final decision. "Josh, do you see anyone looking towards Liam's drones."

"No."

"Send the drones, lad."

Liam tapped an icon on each of the three controllers lying on the tarred roof. The day's heat wafted upward, causing him to sweat. He watched the trio of aircraft rise above the nearest fence and then float to ground level, behind the vehicles. Within the forbidden parking lot, the drones did his bidding.

The first settled under a van, and he used its camera to bring it under the left rear leaf spring, farthest from the lone sentry. With gentle alignment, he aligned the craft with the curved and layered pieces of metal and then slow, upward movement brought the GPS tracker to its magnetic mount.

He backed the drone away and took a parting glance at the GPS device. Success. He tapped a command to order the drone to its landing site behind the bridal shop.

After moving to the second hovercraft's controller, he played the same game and yielded the same results.

But with the third tracker, he couldn't get it to stick. He wondered if excess dirt on the truck's undercarriage precluded the connection. Instead of forcing the bad situation, he ordered the final drone back.

"I got two of three loaded. That's all I'm doing. Bring in Josh." He shot a glance across the roof to Connor, who lay five meters away looking through the scope of his Heckler and Koch 416 rifle with a suppressor. "Can you see anything, Father?"

"Nothing yet. This could go on all night and into the next. The next full moon isn't for two days, and there's no guarantee the wraith's even here. We're trusting our empath."

Liam pondered the permutations. "Five trucks are expected to depart, and we'll have to assume the women from Nadine's village will be split across at least two of them."

"I doubt that divine providence would consider making it any easier on us. We could be stretched thin."

The young hunter continued his assessment. "Until we can get more intelligence from Diane, we're forced to watch and guess. The original truck with Nadine's colleagues still has a GPS tracker. Diane's truck will obviously have Diane, and she'll have to suffice whether it has GPS or not. I've got one GPS tracker each onto two other trucks, but I missed one."

Connor's confidence was reassuring. "Let Diane handle her own end, lad. Unless she's facing the wraith, I pity whomever leaves this lot with her. And if we need to follow the truck without GPS tracking, I can do it the old-fashioned way."

"You'll trail it? Visually?"

"Of course. With Nana and Nadine. That seems a good separation of duties."

"Should we bring them up here? A few extra pairs of eyes couldn't hurt."

"No, it could hurt, unfortunately. An extra reflection from an untrained surveyor's phone, weapon, or clothing would ruin the mission. Sorry, lad. It's just father and son up here tonight."

"Do you have eyes on the target?"

"At the moment? Yes."

Liam rolled and stared at the stars. "Tell me a bedtime story."

"Hah! To put us both to sleep?"

"No, Father. To celebrate that we're both here after defeating a wraith in Michigan, and to get our minds around the concept of defeating the next one."

Ten minutes later, Josh appeared on the roof. His dress was gone, but a tenacious wiping effort remained ahead of him to remove the lingering lipstick.

"I thought you didn't want anyone else up here."

Connor answered over this shoulder. "I didn't. Josh, get down please."

"Never mind, Josh. Just head back down and I'll follow you." Liam crawled to the roof access door and descended rickety wooden steps to a back room. "What's going on?"

"Diane contacted me."

"Telepathically?"

"Yes."

"What'd she say?"

"She said she's okay, but the place is seedy and disgusting."

"Did she show you any images of her truck's drivers?"

"Yeah, just to be sure we were in the right place."

"And are we?"

"Yes."

"Did she add anything else, like how they're going to separate the women?"

"It looks like an auction."

Complete randomness and unpredictability. "Well, we'll deal with that when the time comes."

CHAPTER 30

Edric paced the floor in front of the auction stage.

Something bothered him.

Unsure why he'd shown up, he questioned if his Master had urged him to buy one or more girls. After killing for sport three days ago, he expected to survive without scratching the itch again until the full moon tributes of his three Syrian captives.

But he was here, intending to purchase Iraqi toys from the latest inventory.

Given his limited jail cells, he found the concept illogical. Three of the four pens held Syrians, and he saw the acquisition of new women distracting. Then, sensing the buzz and energy of the other bidders, he rationalized that killing, cutting, and incinerating his purchases required no storage. He could buy all he needed, and he trusted he'd find a way to dispose of them.

But the hunger was missing. Every appetite, even killing, followed a natural rhythm of feeding, digesting, resting, and hungering again. Nothing within him suggested a growing hunger for committing casual homicide.

He stopped pacing and listened to the questions circling his head.

Why was he here? Was he ignoring a burning desire to snuff out a life? Was the craving already billowing inside him, ready to eat at him when it would later make itself obvious? Why was his lording spirit spurring him into action at the auction?

His solitary comfort was the beefy sum he'd placed in his buying account. He had plenty of money to buy at least one woman, and he'd let his domineering spirit guide him through his bidding.

An island without need for companionship, he noticed a twisted sense of camaraderie among the buyers. Though he was the newest, the others accepted him into their ranks, a phenomenon he attributed to the need of the powerful to brag to someone who understood.

Standing next to the German who wore a tailored suit, sunglasses, and a ponytail, he sensed that need.

"How have you enjoyed the Egyptian woman you bought in our side deal?"

Edric recalled having killed her in tribute two months ago. "She was perfect."

"Then, no buyer's remorse?"

"None."

"Excellent. Then we had ourselves a favorable business exchange. I hear this new Iraqi crop is quite lovely."

Since supernatural prodding had driven him to the day's auction, the wraith had neglected reviewing videos of the inventory. "Yes."

"You seem at edge today, a bit nervous. Your account is funded, is it not?"

Edric nodded. Despite the common bonds between bidders, each sought an advantage against the other. He kept his answer curt. "I will never make that mistake again."

The German scoffed. "My loss. But I unfortunately believe you."

The wraith scanned the room for other buyers and recognized the familiar groups. As usual, they seemed engaged in impatient and anxious chatter. He glued himself beside the German who appeared to respect silence.

Wearing an eastern European imitation of an Italian-cut, a single client entered the room and greeted the seller and his minion.

His nerves prompting him, he broke the silence with his German companion. "Why do you think he does that, showing up at the last minute every time?"

"Perhaps he thinks he earns a psychological edge against us. I can think of no other logical reason."

"Does he not know that the cut of his suit at the waist gives it away as a forgery? Does he live in a dream world?"

The German scoffed. "We all live a dream, or a nightmare, of some form. I prefer to keep it on the dream side."

A hush overcame the crowd as the raven-haired minion climbed to the stage and made his announcement. "Everyone's here. So, let's get on with the excitement." His mane brushed his back as he moved to the side of the stage. "Today's five beauties hail from Mosul, Iraq with ages ranging from sixteen to twenty-five. You've all seen their videos. Now get ready to meet them, starting with number one."

Bright spotlights lit the stage as a girl appeared from behind a curtain. Wearing high shorts and a tight tee shirt, she squinted and stood defiantly against the lighting.

Edric assumed she was the youngest of the group, and since she was first, he feared the prices would be high today for the small number of women. Though short of stunning, she was attractive with an average height, alluring curves, and well-proportioned facial features.

But something about her struck him.

Every other victim he'd seen had cowered on the stage. This one portrayed a confidence in her eyes and posture that unsettled him. He wondered if anyone else noticed the anomaly.

Gesturing with a circular wiggle of his finger, the minion spoke in a passable Syrian dialect of Arabic. "Turn all the way around. That's it. Keep going. Now face us again and stop."

As she obeyed, she retained her confidence and poise.

The minion swept his arm towards the woman. "The bidding begins at fifteen hundred liras."

The audience remained silent.

"Come now, who will bid fifteen hundred liras for this young woman with such exquisite appeal?"

The last client to arrive raised his finger. Edric considered the late arrival in the fake Italian suit his greatest threat for the early bargains.

"Excellent. Now who will bid seventeen hundred? Seventeen hundred liras?"

The wraith lifted his finger.

"I have seventeen hundred for this Iraqi doll. Who will bid nineteen? Nineteen hundred liras?"

The buyer in the imitation Italian suit made his second bid.

"I have nineteen hundred. Who will bid two thousand liras for this healthy girl?"

To add drama, Edric waited.

"Will no one offer the pittance of two thousand liras for this gem? Nineteen hundred going once. Nineteen hundred going twice."

The wraith pounced. "Two thousand."

"Two thousand! I have two thousand. Do I have twenty-one hundred? Twenty-one hundred?"

Edric knew his competitor's limits and expected the late arrival to shy away from bids above two-thousand liras.

"Two thousand going once. Two thousand going twice."

The challenge came from across the room. "Twenty-one hundred."

Edric snapped his jaw towards the bidder, a man he recognized as one of the wealthier buyers who preferred the choicest selections of the later rounds.

"I have twenty-one hundred. Do I have twenty-two?"

The wraith raised his finger.

"I have twenty-two hundred. Do I have twenty-three?"

The wealthy buyer raised his voice. "Let's stop playing games. Three thousand."

"I have three thousand. I shall remind our seller to return soon to Iraq for his sourcing. It seems the ladies from there are considered most desirable by our discerning clientele. Do I have a superior bid to three thousand liras?"

Forecasting his craving to kill, the wraith risked more than twice his usual purchase price. "Thirty-five hundred."

Before the minion could invite a counter, the wealthy buyer volunteered it. "Five thousand."

Unable to stomach the price, the wraith shook his head and relinquished the girl to the victor and hoped for a more habitual process with the next captive.

A guard escorted the young lady offstage to a waiting area, and then the next woman passed through a curtain onto the stage.

Like the first, she wore cheap, revealing clothing. She was short, made of lean muscle, and above average as measured by the metrics of beauty the other buyers considered. Walking away with any woman would be costly today.

She displayed a disturbing confidence like the first, and Edric entered a quick bidding war with his usual competitor in the fake Italian suit. But this time, the wealthy buyer remained quiet.

Relieved to be alone bidding above two-thousand liras, he bought her.

Then he bought the next two, completing a trio for purposes that remained murky. Perhaps his Master was thanking him for good work and letting him kill three for sport.

But then the last one appeared. When she faced the crowd, her long straight black hair bounced.

He noticed her pleasing face, with expressive thoughtful bright eyes, and sharp and long nose. He like her defined lips, long neck, and her soft, smooth skin. Her legs were ideal.

Like the others, she portrayed unwarranted confidence, but her demeanor bordered on an insulting presumption of authority.

The minion aimed his palm towards her. "This is your last chance to purchase a piece of Iraq. She is stunning, is she not?"

Before ordered, the woman turned to let the crowd examine her profile, her backside, and then her front again.

"Let the bidding start at twenty-five hundred liras."

Edric wanted to add her to his collection. She was perfect. "Twenty-five."

The wealthy bidder countered. "Again, let's not play games. Four thousand."

The wraith would give up the others he'd purchased today for her. "Five thousand."

"Six."

Edric shot a glance at his competitor, who seemed unaware of the visual challenge. Would he not even look at him? "Very well, then. Seven thousand."

While the minion recounted the status, the wraith returned his gaze towards the woman he wanted. But he noticed a hazy sort of mirage near her inner thigh, and he questioned if it were an invitation or a warning.

The wealthy buyer dashed his hopes of finding out. "Let's end this silliness. Ten thousand liras."

A pit formed in Edric's stomach. Despite his precautions, his account lacked such funds after winning the three previous bids. He shook his head, and the auction ended.

As his frustration rose, he sensed his rising desire to kill, and the three Iraqi purchases would have to suffice.

CHAPTER 31

In the green room, Diane sighed in relief.

As she'd instructed them, each of her four colleagues had appeared courageous on the stage, despite the danger and the humiliation. They'd created an air of value, driving up their worth and making them desirable to the one they needed to track to his lair. Somehow, perhaps guided by the dagger or by her own empathic intuition, she'd known that the hungriest bidder in the audience was the wraith.

And he had been there. She remembered his appearance.

Morphing in her memory's vision into a disgusting demon, the man's face became a twisted aberration of sagging and torn skins. Fangs protruded from the slimy mouth, and the long, crooked nose hinted of a devil. The beast, its inner essence exposed in nakedness, had a body of scarred and blighted leather, and at its extreme ends, horns, a pointed tail, and cloven hooves.

In her final moments battling the wraith in Michigan, she'd seen a similar image, and she realized that wickedness in its varied manifestations remained ugly at its core.

Her powers with her dagger were growing, and she'd impressed herself with her control of the wealthy buyer. From the green room, she'd tapped his mind to win Nadine's teenage sibling, and then she'd hammered him with the craving to purchase her in the final auction to keep them together.

Feeling responsible to Nadine for protecting the teenager, Diane was grateful to the dagger for allowing her purchase by the same man. Although her exposure on stage had prevented her from grasping her weapon, it had helped the empath manipulate the wealthy man into buying her.

However, her gratitude toward the blade stopped there.

When she'd recognized the wraith in the audience leering at her, the dagger had remained silent. It lacked fire, lightning, or even a gentle nudge suggesting it would have supported her throwing it at his heart. And since the bronze blade was a living being, she'd seen no choice but to honor its will.

Honoring it was different than agreement, and she wrestled with a lingering frustration. Why hadn't the dagger allowed her the kill shot from the stage?

Perhaps he'd have seen it coming in time to dodge or parry the tip, or perhaps the dagger had considered the attack suicidal for Diane, who'd stood in front of half a dozen armed guards. Whatever the enchanted weapon's motivation, it had stayed her hand. It had let her be sold, continuing with the Irish hunters' plan.

Then she remembered they needed to trail the wraith to his lair since he may already have possession of his next three tributes. The dagger never panicked. The dagger always had wisdom.

Clearing her mind of burdensome speculation, she examined her quiet surroundings. Since a lone guard oversaw the sold captives, she assumed the green room lacked an exterior door. Barred windows at the far end suggested the door in was the only way out.

As she moved to the chair that held her clothes–replicas of Nadine's clothes–she addressed her colleagues in Aramaic. "He bought me. So, three of you are going with the one we've been hunting, and the other two of us are going with the rich guy."

Heads nodded agreement.

The guard said something in Turkish and pointed at the skirt and blouse on Diane's chair.

From the auction experience, she knew he'd watch her change, and asking for privacy was pointless. But she wanted him distracted from seeing the translucent knife glued to her thigh, and while looking at herself in the mirror, she debated invading the guard's mind or using a mundane tactic.

Drained by her attack on the rich man, she chose the natural path and called out in Aramaic. "I need you to distract him while I change. Pretend to argue."

Three of the Iraqi women prattled off curses at each other, and their vocal volume jumped from nothing to jet engine levels.

From the corner of her eye, Diane glanced at the guard.

He cringed and looked at the yelling women, but he was wise enough to avoid interfering with the angered women.

The empath noted his size–he was smaller than the other guards, but he moved with graceful poise. And he lacked a weapon, meaning he could monitor the changing and half-naked women without allowing an armed revolt.

Diane stripped to her underwear, making deliberate movements to avoid flexing the dagger while keeping it from the guard's direct or reflected view. She stepped into her skirt and lifted it, concealing her secret, and then she called an end to the charade. "That's enough, ladies."

Their continued arguing was so convincing, Diane wondered if she'd opened a true wound.

Replaying the words she'd overheard them spit at each other, she noticed animosity about who had encouraged their departure from home in search of work, who had ignored which warning signs, and who had led them to this horrible place. The empath raised her voice. "Enough!"

Silence.

At the far end of the room, the Turkish guard gave a quiet sigh.

Remembering the Maiden of Beit She'an's warning to risk everything for others, Diane steeled her resolve in the unbreakable code of Aramaic. "It doesn't matter how you got here. I vow on my life that you'll all get out."

Her tingling thigh caught her attention, signaling the dagger's desired interaction. With her peripheral vision on the solitary guard, she slid her fingers under her skirt until she caressed bronze.

In a flash, she knew the weapon's will. It wanted her to invade the spirit of her guard.

Wary and hopeful that the dagger's plan included control of the unarmed man, she probed him. Expecting resistance, she sent a burst of awareness into the man's mind, like slamming her imaginary shoulder into an ethereal door.

But as she staggered through the open entrance, he welcomed her. "Hello."

She stabilized her awareness within him. "Excuse me?"

"My name is Ozan. What's your name?"

"Wait. Seriously? Aren't you upset that I'm in your head?"

"No. Should I be? I can't blame you, and you seem friendly."

Stunned, she had no answer. Everyone else, even the young hunter, had resisted her. "I guess not. Aren't you surprised that I'm capable of this?"

"A little. But I could tell that something strange was happening tonight. The bidders were behaving bizarrely, and I thought there might be someone behind it."

His nonchalance made her feel less special. "And you just assumed some sort of mind-control game was going on? You've seen this before?"

"I've suspected. I've seen many victims from ancient cultures pass through here. I've sensed probing in my mind before, but as you can see, I have no weapons and am useless as an ally for attempting escape."

Diane's empathic alarm spiked. "Victims? Then you understand we're victims and you're part of a horrible crime?"

"Yes. It's terrible. But since I can't stop it, I add humanity to this grotesque tragedy. I'm often the last caring face a young lady will see. If I can give a little compassion, then it's worth something."

The dagger's intent with inhabiting this man's mind became murkier as she sought answers. "Empathy? Like you know what it is to be in our place?"

His deep sadness rose to his surface and was overwhelming.

"You're being forced to do this job, but it's not you who's in danger. They've threatened someone you love. Multiple people."

"Yes."

"I sense them. Younger sisters?"

"Yes, and a niece. They will be trafficked if I fail to comply in my duties."

"The local police forces can't be trusted?"

"No. The boss here has bribed the local precinct's chief. I am powerless."

She sensed something else he was hiding. "You're gay."

"Yes. You saw that quickly."

"If they find out, you're afraid they'll fire you and sell your family into slavery."

"Yes, and they'll probably kill me and my partner. My partner lives in secrecy and fear with me, pretending to be a roommate."

"I'm sorry. This is terrible."

"Everything in this building is terrible, but I make the best of it. I try offer some comfort to those in need."

Diane understood the dagger's intent. "Ozan, I think you should call in sick the next few days. There's a good chance I'm going to blow this place up before the end of the month."

"I appreciate the warning."

The burning question arose. "Do you know the address, name, or phone number of the man who bought three of my colleagues?"

"I'm sorry. They tell me so little."

"I understand. Can you give me a few minutes of privacy after I leave your mind? I need to contact someone else." She was planning to give Josh a download of everything she'd seen in the auction.

"I can delay, but I can't promise how long."

"Do your best, and keep this exchange a secret." She released him from the link and glanced at him.

A mere ten paces away, he squinted and looked at her to verify his experience had been real.

She put her finger to her lips and nodded. Yes, it had been real, and it had taken much less time in the material world than they'd sensed together in their disembodied conversation.

A knock on the door completed Diane's sensual grounding in reality. The latch clicked open, the auctioneer with shoulder-length black hair entered, and he spoke in passable Arabic of the Syrian dialect. "You did very well on stage, ladies. Now it's time to move on. This way, please." He swung the door back, exposing armed escorts behind him.

Per his agreement, the unarmed guard marched across the room and engaged the auctioneer. After a dismissive nod, the long-haired man departed, but the door remained ajar.

The guard stood next to Diane and spoke in broken Arabic. "One minute. Maybe two."

Tapping her dagger, the empath made quick work of contacting her brother, who accepted the information.

As the auctioneer returned, his attempt to hide his contemptible role in subjugating women behind politeness angered Diane, but since she knew the truth, she kept him on her mental kill list. Unlike the guard the dagger had chosen to spare, the auctioneer would find no pity.

But his presence meant one thing—it was time for her to leave.

Moving with confidence, she stood, gestured at Nadine's sister to join her, and walked towards her armed escorts.

CHAPTER 32

Envy swelled within Edric as he watched the wealthy bidder drive away with the tall and beautiful Iraqi he'd wanted.

Although the wraith had three women to the winner's two, the other bidder had spent more money and had earned the privilege of leaving first.

But leaving second required little patience, and as he followed his three new possessions and their escort towards the parking lot, he sensed he'd done his Master's bidding. He sensed his dagger's spirit approving his purchases, guiding him, and protecting him.

Protecting him... as he approached the exterior door.

His escorting guard twisted the knob and opened the way to the warm summer air. Dusk was settling, bringing the concealing darkness the wraith preferred.

Though he found the outside atmosphere alluring, he received a defensive trigger he knew came from his domineering spirit. He slowed his gate and scanned the parking lot. Then he raised his gaze to the convenience store. Continuing his search for danger, he stuck his head through the doorframe, looked to the left, and saw two amorphous auras of azure and blue pulsating atop the bridal shop across the street.

Fifty years.

After half a century of safety, the gunmen who had hunted him in Israel had reappeared.

He'd considered them dead, killed by soldiers during the raid in Beit She'an, but then he remembered they were mortals who needed to replenish their ranks.

Dead or alive, they would always find ways to make themselves reborn to come for him.

A short buttress around the shop's roof concealed their human silhouettes, but to his eyes, their pulsating energy fields were as obvious as a full moon in a dark sky. Before granting his supernatural enemies an easy shot at his head, he stepped back and formulated an alternative exit plan.

Sharing the news of the enchanted hunters was impossible. The seller and his staff would doubt the paranormal story, and if they bothered to give him the benefit of doubt, they'd probably hand him over for a possible reward.

He groped for a believable reason to change his departure, and the idea came. "Can I arrange to grab a sandwich on the way out and have you meet me in the front with my van?"

The guard scowled at him. "All exits are from the rear."

"Yes, I'm not an idiot. I know the women need to leave from the back, but I wish to get dinner and leave from the front."

"I said it's not allowed."

"For a two-hundred-lira tip perhaps?"

The guard's tone softened. "This is highly unusual."

"But you understand why I can't stop and order food elsewhere any time soon, not with my cargo."

"I understand that, but I didn't say I'd help."

"But I'm sure you could make it happen for three hundred liras."

"You want me to personally load the ladies into your van, drive around front, and wait for you?"

"I wouldn't want you to wait with the women on the public street. That's too dangerous. I would have you wait in the parking lot until my sandwich is ready. Then I'd call you and have you meet me out front."

The guard smirked. "That's all you want for say… four hundred liras?"

Edric pushed back on the price hike to hide his desperation. "I'm not that hungry. The final offer was three hundred."

"Let me see what I can do." The guard marched by the wraith and the three blindfolded Iraqi women, back into the main building.

Their wrists bound behind their backs, the women began talking in that accursed unbreakable code-like language known only to Iraqi Christians, Aramaic.

He snapped in his best Iraqi Arabic. "Silence!"

Minutes later, the guard reappeared with a menu and an assistant.

Edric's spirits rose. "I assume this means we have a deal?"

"It's your lucky day. The food is complementary, provided you have the tip in cash."

The wraith had learned the value of cash in his pocket. "I do."

"My colleague and I will load your cargo. I've done it before, and I know how you like it. Just head to the front bar and order what you want, and then call me when you're ready."

Edric got the man's phone number, left him his vehicle's keys, and walked to the bar. Hungry, he ordered a sheep's head sandwich. While awaiting his dinner, he considered the surprise threat.

The hunters' presence felt obvious now, like a lowering of barometric pressure before a violent storm. Since he hadn't sensed their presence on his drive to the restaurant, he hoped they'd arrived after him and were unsure which vehicle was his.

He needed to hope they remained unsure, since he lacked a second vehicle for carrying his women, and he couldn't leave them on the premises for a later pickup without generating suspicion from the seller. He'd consider himself fortunate enough if he could escape out the front with a sandwich and his life.

A waitress brought his dinner in a plastic carton, and then he called the guard to deliver his van. He watched the street through a window as his van appeared, took a U-turn, and stopped.

He stuck his head out the door and looked for dangerous bluish auras. Relieved to see no spies, he placed his dinner on the passenger seat and then followed the guard to the rear for an inspection of his cargo.

The sentry cracked opened a door. "They are secured to your liking?"

Shackles held three bound Iraqi women to the floor of the cargo bay. "Yes." The wraith closed the door and locked it shut.

"Good. Then I believe this settles our arrangement."

Edric took the hint, dug the cash from his pocket, and paid the man his tip.

"That was easy money. If you want to do this again, I'm your man."

"Of course." As the man departed, the wraith walked around the other side of his van looking for the GPS tracker the hunters may have flung against it. He then stepped onto the front tire to give himself a view of the roof, which he also found void of obvious spyware. Delaying a deeper search in hidden areas for probing gadgets, he sank into the driver's seat and turned a tight U-turn to avoid exposure to the hunters atop the bridal shop.

Once pointed away from danger, he met rush hour traffic. The lethargy of movement was fine with him, since he assumed some form of tracking device gave his position to the enemies he'd left behind, and he aimed his vehicle away from his warehouse.

As the first traffic light brought him to an extended stop, he popped open the hood, scurried in front of the vehicle, and examined the engine compartment. Nothing stood out as a tracking device.

He slammed the hood and returned to the driver's seat in time to flow with traffic to the next light, where he darted from his seat and inspected the underside of the nearest tire. Nothing.

Repeating the stop-and-inspect process at successive lights, he saw a block-shaped plastic device under the left tire's leaf spring. Terror gripped him as the fear of being hunted became a fact, but opportunity beckoned as he detached the tracker and took it into the van.

Pondering how to turn the tracker into a tactical advantage, he continued driving until he saw his next move. Ahead, a bus with an advertised destination far from his home was loading passengers.

He stopped next to it, turned on his hazard lights, and stepped from his van. Despite the honking protests of the angry motorists he trapped behind him, he walked to the public vehicle and mounted the GPS tracker to a flat surface in a wheel well.

Ignoring the curses from enraged commuters, he returned to his van and drove behind the bus carrying the device he hoped would lure away the hunters.

At his first chance, he doubled back towards his warehouse, relaxed, and bit into his sandwich.

CHAPTER 33

As his father fought the Kuga through commuter congestion in pursuit of the wraith, Liam watched the GPS tracker on his phone.

Connor glanced at his son's hand. "Is the signal still strong?"

Liam was enthusiastic about his prospects. "Yes. We'll follow him all the way to his lair. This is looking favorable."

While Connor followed the signal to the wraith and his three Iraqi captives, a phoneline kept them connected to Nana, Nadine, and Josh in the Fiat 500X. He raised his voice to the cabin speaker. "Nana, I still have a strong signal, following the van to the east. How are you doing?"

The Chaldean grandmother was excited. "I'm still following Diane to the north."

The empath had clarified to Josh that she could see through her wealthy captor's eyes and was waiting for a hidden stretch of road to make him stop and do her bidding. She wanted to avoid witnesses.

Liam wondered, however, with everything going to plan, how had the wraith escaped the auction building unnoticed?

Diane had seen him in the audience, but he and his father had missed his exit. It was possible he'd paid a driver to deliver his purchases while he'd walked out the front door, but it was unlike a wraith to trust others.

With Connor able to push the smaller Kuga through traffic faster than the van, the hunters had reached three quarters of a mile from their target, but it remained out of view. "Traffic is a challenge."

"You're driving well. I like how you ignore traffic laws when needed."

"It helps to be old and foreign, sometimes. For example, watch this." The elder hunter whipped the wheel to the left into oncoming flow and passed a slow meat truck.

With angry oncoming motorists honking, Liam feared for his life but appreciated the effort.

After another pair of high-risk maneuvers, his father placed them within half a mile of their target.

Liam expected more difficulty. "I don't like this. We're catching him too easily. I'm sending a drone."

"For what purpose?"

"To make sure we're chasing what we think we're chasing."

"A drone would be a dead giveaway and negate our advantage of surprise."

Conceding, Liam countered. "That's true only if I send it close enough for him to see. I'll send it high but keep it distant."

"Does a drone have the speed and endurance to come back to you?"

Traffic had slowed to a crawl. "It will in this congestion."

"Go ahead."

The young hunter glanced in the back seat at the drones and found the one with the most charge. He identified it on his phone's application, set it to fly fifty meters above ground, and programmed it to return to his phone's coordinates after its mission. He pulled the hovercraft to his lap as the car lurched forward. "Next stop light."

"That won't be long. There are plenty of them."

As the car slowed, Liam rolled down his window, balanced the drone on the sill, and used his free hand to order the aircraft's flight. Its rotors spun to speed, and he released it.

"You're sure that's legal?"

"It's no worse than your driving."

"I thought I was impressing you with my tactics."

"You are, but the point still stands." Liam ordered the airborne camera to point towards the latest incoming GPS coordinates, and grunted as he disliked what he saw.

"What's wrong?"

"I don't see the bloody van."

"Are you sure? This is a unique perspective."

Liam understood the inaccuracies of GPS, but within several meters of the latest feedback from his tracker, he saw a bus, passenger cars, and a furniture delivery truck. "Something's wrong. I don't see any bloody vans, nothing that even closely resembles what we should see."

"Perhaps he just turned."

"GPS struggles with turns, but that would have a minimized effect. The accelerometers in the tracker would compensate for it."

"So, we're wasting our time? We've been foiled."

An idea made the young hunter feel stupid. "Father? Did we expose ourselves to him?"

"We were perfectly hidden."

"I mean to his supernatural view of us. He can supposedly see us as something different, like we can see him. Perhaps that allowed him to see us behind the roof's wall."

"It's possible, yes."

"Then why weren't we wearing our amulets that protect for that? Bloody hell, Father. Were we stupid?"

The elder hunter shook his head. "We indeed forgot nothing. I thought of using them, but you need to learn that the amulets are only good for twenty-four hours per use. Once we put them on, that's all we get until they're blessed again by our order."

The young hunter realized the wraith had seen him and his father on the rooftop. "I don't feel as stupid as I could, but don't you think that's something we could have discussed ahead of time? We could have had a kill shot."

"I doubt it. Whether he saw us or not, didn't you notice the loading procedure with the first group of women?"

"Yeah, Diane and Nadine's sister."

"Didn't you see how the trafficker's used the ladies as human shields against a shot from this roof? The truck protects them from the convenience store roof, and they use the women to protect themselves from the bridal shop roof. There was no kill shot to be had, even if the wraith had gone out the back."

Liam wanted to scream, but his father's composure helped him stay calm. "We've been outsmarted by an immortal killer. To me, that's the makings of a bad day."

"If the wraith knew of our GPS tracker, he may have warned the others at the auction."

"I don't think there's any such thing as honor among these thieves, Father."

"But he wanted to purchase Diane and was outbid. It's possible he knows where her buyer operates and is seeking her there."

A pit formed in the young hunter's stomach. "We need to get Diane into action. She can't wait any longer."

From the cabin's speakers, the grandmother's voice crackled. "I hear you talking. This is bad news. Josh knows to tell her next time she contacts him."

"That's good thinking, Nana. I'll turn us around and come join you. There's no more sense in us chasing the wrong vehicle."

"Hold on, Father. I'm going to see if I can verify which vehicle has our transmitter."

"How?"

"Since I no longer care who's looking, I'm going to overfly the coordinates and look straight down to be sure I didn't botch this up."

"Go ahead."

In the crawling traffic, Liam needed two minutes to place the drone above the latest coordinates. The downward view included one vehicle in common with the prior video. "That's why we've been gaining on it. He stuck my transmitter on a bus."

"Can you set the drone to follow the bus a bit longer to be sure?"

"Yes, I'll do that. It's got some time left before it needs to come back. But you may as well turn back and head towards Diane."

The Chaldean grandmother's voice filled the cabin. "She just contacted Josh. She's going to take over her truck. What do I do?"

Impressing Liam, Connor remained calm. "Liam will send you the address where to meet. When she's done, pick up Diane and Nadine's sister and we'll regroup."

CHAPTER 34

Diane sat cross-legged in the delivery truck's dark cargo hold. Filled with hanging garment bags of dry-cleaned clothing, the space was hot and stuffy. She wiped sweat from her brow and welcomed the moment to liberate herself. "Are you ready to get out of here?"

Conserving her energy, Nadine's sister peeped. "Yes."

"Here we go." She tapped her dagger and brought her awareness into the wealthy man who'd bought her. Her view materialized within his body in the passenger seat of the truck's cabin. As she feigned awe and fear of the man, she found his resistance nonexistent and wondered if he recognized her presence.

The more likely truth, she realized, was that his fragile true inner self cowered in a corner, trembling before her power. Arrogant men were superficial, and unless they benefited from unnatural support, they were easy to invade. She grunted to assure herself of control.

The driver responded. "Everything okay, boss?"

Diane understood the Turkish words through her puppet's ears and answered with the wealthy man's voice in the same language. "Pull into the next side street."

The driver gave a hurried response. "Boss?"

"The next side street."

"Why? Are we being followed?"

Curious how the driver would react, Diane fished for data. "It's probably nothing. But let's see what happens."

"Should I call for help?"

That's what she was looking for. Help required a call, implying it wasn't automatic, which meant she could make her move. "Let's see what happens first."

"You're the boss." The driver angled the truck into a side street, which was a dead end. He stopped and parked. "I hope you're just paranoid. There's no room to turn around."

Diane reached inside the wealthy man's blazer for his silenced pistol, withdrew it, and glanced at the side mirror. "I may have been. We'll know in a minute."

The driver withdrew his pistol and looked at his side mirror. "What are we looking for?"

The empath aimed the weapon at the driver's chest and pulled the trigger twice. As the body fell limp, she returned the pistol to the blazer and forced the wealthy man to step from the truck. She walked him to the rear doors, compelled him to roll the tumbler to the four digits she fished from his memory, and made him pull open the latch.

Then, from within his mind, she pounced on him.

She buried her fury into him and ordered his pistol to his own temple. As she curled his finger, she heard a scream from a voice she recognized as her brother's.

"No!"

Keeping the silencer aimed at her victim, she turned and saw Josh running from the open door of the parked Fiat 500X. Confused, she held her breath and forced her inhabited puppet-man to do the same.

"Don't kill him!" Josh covered the distance in impressive timing and appeared in front of her.

She addressed her brother through the wealthy trafficker's voice. "What are you doing?"

"Liam has a plan. We need him alive."

"Take the gun." She handed him the butt.

He grabbed the weapon and stood like a statue.

"Can you tie him up?"

Nadine appeared in the alley. "No, but I can. I found handcuffs in a backpack in the back of the car."

Diane slid the wealthy man's wrists behind him and felt the Iraqi woman tighten the bonds. "Help him into the back of the truck." She accepted Josh and Nadine's balancing and lifting as she forced the man to stagger upwards into the cargo hold.

He tripped, fell, and smacked his face against the flat floor.

Diane abandoned him before impact and heard the flurry of Turkish curses issuing from him with her human ears. Her adrenaline pumping, she pushed through the forest of clothes, urging her teenage companion to join her. "Come on." When she reached daylight and the wealthy man, she pressed her heel against his back.

Nadine and her sister raced to an embrace.

Diane felt terrible cutting the reunion short as she interrupted it in Aramaic. "Get some clothes and tie this guy up better. Tie his feet together and tie his feet to his handcuffs."

Nadine nodded. "What about the man up front?"

"I'll take care of him, at least temporarily." Diane strode to the passenger seat, gulped, and grabbed the bloody corpse. Pulling its arm, she dragged the driver's body to the floorboard and left it there. After closing the passenger door, she returned to the cargo hold.

Nadine and her sister were looping a long evening gown around the wealthy man's ankles.

"I thought you'd be done with that already."

Nadine nodded at the man's head. "I had to shut him up first." A knot behind the man's neck held a white dress shirt in his mouth.

"Good work. So, what's Liam's new plan?"

Nadine shrugged. "They talked in English. I don't think Nana understood it well enough to translate."

She looked to her brother. "Josh?"

"I don't know."

"Did Liam say why to leave him alive?"

"He said it was to get information."

Knowing the young hunter's mind, Diane suspected more. "Did he say anything about a trap, too, Josh?"

"Maybe."

"Maybe he said it, or he said he'd maybe set a trap?"

"He said maybe he'd set a trap."

"Thank you, Josh."

With her sister, Nadine jumped from the cargo hold's lip. "He's not going anywhere."

Josh seemed impatient. "We need to go. Liam gave us an address to meet him."

Diane did the quick math on who was driving. "If he wants this rich trafficker, I assume that means he knows I need to drive his truck."

"Yes. Nana drives the Fiat. You drive the truck. That's what Liam wanted."

Wearied from the telepathic overtime, Diane wanted the crutch of modern technology. "I need a phone."

"You can use mine." Josh extended it.

"You're sure?"

"We're all using Nana's in the car."

"Thanks, Josh. Can you get me a charger, too?"

He pulled the cord from his pocket. "See if there's a USB port in the truck."

"I'm sure there will be. You're a lifesaver." She hugged him and then trotted to the driver's seat.

Within the vehicle, she tasted the coppery smell of blood as she tried to ignore the corpse on the floor. She found the truck clumsy but manageable as she backed it into the main road in front of Nana, who had created a small gap in the traffic flow with the 500X.

Charging her brother's phone, she turned on its speaker and dialed her grandmother.

"Yes, Diane. Can you hear me?"

"Yeah, can you hear me?"

"Yes, but I just hung up on Connor."

Diane drove forward, following the navigation program her brother had preset in his phone. "You wait, Nana. I'll call him and we'll arrange a three-way conference call. So, hang up now."

As the line went dead, Diane found the elder hunter's number on her brother's phone and dialed.

"Yes, Josh?"

"No, this is Diane."

"Lovely to hear your voice, young lady."

Death was becoming familiar. "I killed the driver but spared the guy who bought me."

"Good. Liam and I wanted that. There may be value in him yet."

"I've got our meeting address. I'm taking the truck there now with my buyer bound inside it. Nana's following me. GPS says I've got about twenty-five minutes."

"Excellent. We'll see you soon."

"Can you dial Nana on conference call? Things are moving fast, and we all need to get back on the same page. People are going to start dying fast in the next day or two, and I want to make sure it's the bad guys."

CHAPTER 35

Edric unloaded the third Iraqi woman into the tiny jail cell. With one shackle cemented into the ground, the three new captives shared the tether to their pen, making them three-times as strong in tugging against his craftsmanship. He had to remember that the next time he opened the door.

He locked the door to their cell and trotted upstairs to his solitude, his sanctuary, and his dagger.

Standing with his blade in hand, he looked through the panoramic window overlooking the warehouse. In his thoughts, he commanded the master of the dagger to give him information, but he knew better than to utter such a challenge to the dagger's spirit, his Master.

Instead of defying his domineering lord, he posed his demands as questions. "Have I not done your bidding as you commanded, Master? Have I not earned an explanation as to why you made me purchase these extra Iraqi women?"

The spirit responded in its rapid, wordless flash, and in an instant he knew.

One of them would be his sacrifice under July's full moon, to become the source of his next fifty years of life. But the spirit kept hidden the identity of the precise Iraqi woman of the trio.

That meant one was crucial to him and the other two were kills for sport. "Excellent, Master. In two night's time, I shall give you your Syrian tributes, and I shall have adequate jail space for all the Iraqi women."

He wanted to ask which woman held the source of his life, but he opted for patience. The domineering spirit was fickle, and to provoke him would be foolish.

But he could instead provoke the women.

He returned to the warehouse floor and went to his tool bench. There, he found a special toy he'd reserved for his most insolent prisoners.

Unsure if his lording spirit would allow its use against a possible sacrifice, he clutched the Taser and marched to the Iraqi women's cell. He rushed to the latch and pulled open the door, revealing all three of them seated together on the solitary cot. Their eyes grew enlarged at the sight of his nonlethal weapon.

He used his best Arabic. "It's time for answers."

They cowered as he approached. Hoping to see a red aura arise around his chosen sacrifice, he became enraged.

Grabbing the nearest by the forearm, he lifted her from the bed and made her stand. "Which one of you is from Nineveh?"

She shrugged. "We all are."

"Wrong answer." He released her and jammed the leads into her torso.

She shuddered and collapsed.

He grabbed the next and lifted her. "Perhaps one of you has special blood? Royal blood? Huh? Magic blood?"

The second woman shook her head. "We are all from the same village. None of us is special. We're all just commoners."

"Wrong answer." He abused her as the first and then looked to the last. "Perhaps you have some insight."

Defiantly, she stood and met his gaze. "I have nothing to add."

"Nothing? You know of nothing that separates one of you from the others?"

"I do not."

"Then I see no reason to punish you any differently." He zapped her, and she fell to the concrete in convulsions. As he walked from their cell, he called out over his shoulder. "I know you can all hear me. I can do this many more times until I get the answer I want. Can you?"

Alone in his chambers that night, he lamented the complexity. In the past, his Master had kept it simple, but then again, the murders had been easier to hide.

The Assyrian genocide had made his first life-giving kill trivial, but his second sacrifice had already become dangerous, even while he'd hidden it within the raids on the Israeli settlements. Perhaps now his lording spirit was forcing his caution by making him hold his target under his roof until her death.

It was a lot to manage. Three Syrian tributes, each two days from death. Three Iraqi captives, one a sacrifice and two for sport, or would his Master demand a different mix before the next killings?

He needed to be flexible. He needed to be ready.

Above all, he needed to avoid those who pursued him. The hunters had revealed themselves, and a month was a long time to hide.

But the city was large, and his warehouse was quiet and stocked. He had enough rice, bread, and basics to last the remainder of his killing cycle, and he saw no reason to leave his home until he possessed his next fifty years of life.

Except he needed to offer the tributes as far from his home as he could take them, to keep the hunters off his back.

Then there was the messy issue of needing to scratch the itch.

With six women under his roof, he questioned if his Master tested him. Was his lording spirit strengthening him to resist the urge to kill, or was it a form of temptation for torment? With the capricious whims of the dagger's spirit, the wraith never knew.

He needed to drive the van out and back one more time to offer the tributes. Other than that, he would transform the warehouse into a fortress.

He darted back up the stairs to his lounge and energized the monitors to the security cameras. The building's owner had done an admirable set up of the video feeds, and Edric admitted he'd been lazy in watching them. That ended tonight.

A quick check showed all cameras working under his control through their full sweeps.

Next, he checked his arsenal. Dragging his chests and cases from his bedroom to the lounge's panoramic window, he counted three shotguns, two assault rifles, two pistols, and enough ammunition to kill two hunters ten times over. He visually verified the low wall below his panorama was made of concrete block thick enough to stop bullets.

With the high ground and the ideal overview of any battle, he set out to block the entry points.

Other than the vehicle door and loading docks, the warehouse had seven human-accessible entrances. The wraith dedicated hours to verifying each door was latched and deadbolted shut and to blocking each one with stacks of leftover supplies and construction debris.

He wrapped coils of concertina wire behind the loading dock doors, stacking three layers of helixes. The razor wire would slow any trespasser enough to become fodder for Edric's assault rifle from above.

The last defense—the one against a ramming vehicle—would be tedious to install and remove, but he needed it.

The broken and scavenged forklift leaning against a wall retained its wheels, and he found its motor working and its gears functional in its slowest mode. With the machine's battery dying, he drove it towards the garage exit and stopped it short of the door. He left it in neutral, steady in its place.

He illuminated the floodlights outside the warehouse and checked the exterior cameras on his phone's security application for intruders. Seeing none, he risked opening the garage.

He jumped into the driver's seat of the van and turned it sharply on the concrete, pointing it towards the forklift. With a gentle nudge, he pushed the broken equipment forward and into the night. Lacking his hand at the steering wheel, the decrepit machine veered off his desired course, but it stayed close enough to serve its purpose.

The wraith got out of the van, set the forklift's transmission into park, and withdrew its key. He backed the van into the warehouse and examined the gap.

An oncoming vehicle would be unable to ram his garage door without first having to address the heavy machine blocking its way. But if needed, Edric could drive his van in a tight, slow arc around his protection against ramming.

He trotted back up the stairs and spread his full suit of body armor across the floor. He wanted it ready to wear with a moment's notice, since his barricades were good but imperfect.

Reconsidering, he put on the vest as a precaution before laying down for the evening. With his Kalashnikov AK-47 rifle and infrared vision googles by his side, he risked a night of sleep.

CHAPTER 36

Liam examined the top of the parking garage and noticed that his group was alone. The Kuga, the 500X, and their former occupants stood outside the trafficker's truck. "You're sure we're safe here?"

His father sounded confident. "I wouldn't call it safe, per se, but it's ours to use without interference by the police, yes."

"Thanks to the order?"

Connor nodded.

Ancient rules prevented Liam and his father from seeking help from outsiders, but the young hunter understood the curt nod's meaning. The order would prevent law enforcement's meddling and could get them access to a parking garage that was closed for maintenance. "What do we do with the body?"

"Nothing yet, and perhaps nothing at all. Let's see how this plays out before we address that."

"Diane needs to get him on the phone."

The elder hunter displayed a calmness Liam found impressive. "Let's see what Diane knows, first."

"I'm standing right here, guys. What do you want to know?"

Liam started with the basics. "Okay. Does the buyer know where the wraith lives?"

"No. They only meet at the bar when there's an auction."

"Does he have any direct way to contact him?"

"That's not how it works."

"Well, you've been in the buyer's head. Is there anything in there to help us find the wraith's lair?"

She reflected. "There's nothing direct. They only see each other at the auction. There's no networking beyond that."

Liam shifted towards his plan. "Will the auction house broker a trade or a resale between bidders?"

"I guess so. When I'm in his head, I don't learn everything all at once, but I got the sense it's possible."

"You ready to give it a go?"

"You tell me what to have him say."

In the back of the truck, Liam saw the wiggling, hog-tied human trafficker. He pulled his gag to his neck and heard instant swearing. Although the words were foreign, the wealthy buyer's angry threats were obvious. The young hunter climbed onto his back, fished his phone from his blazer, and grabbed it. "Would you recognize which number connects us to the auctioneer?"

Diane shrugged. "I should get into his head and find out."

"Right. Make yourself comfortable."

She sat on the edge of the cargo hold, leaned into a pile of clean clothes, and tapped the dagger under her skirt. "Should I try to remove this from my thigh?"

"Not yet. Let's see what happens with this phone call. Do you know what to say?"

"More or less. It was pretty simple as you explained it."

"Sure." Liam lowered his laptop case to the cargo bed and pulled out his computer. He energized his cell tower tracking program and connected the wealthy buyer's phone to his USB port. "I'm ready. Get inside his head."

She became quiet.

"Are you in his head yet?"

The wealthy buyer answered for her. "Yes. It's me in here."

He put the phone in front of his face. "Which number is the auction house?"

"Scroll down recent calls."

He thumbed through them.

"Stop. There."

Liam called to the elder hunter. "Father, will you hold the phone please? I want to be in front of Diane in case she needs coaching."

Connor took the phone and held it near the possessed man's cheek. "Sure."

"Wait for my signal. I want to make sure I can communicate with Diane." Liam moved to the seated empath. "Can you hear me in there?"

She answered through the buyer. "I can. You worry too much. I've got this."

"I may need to talk to you out of earshot of the phone."

"It'll work. Can we make the call? Let's go. This is tiring."

"Right. Go ahead and dial, Father."

The auctioneer answered in English, which Liam assumed was the language of his local peddling trade. "Hello, sir. What can I do for you?"

Diane spoke through the wealthy buyer. "This is client twenty-one. I'm interested in a secondary resale."

"From today's event?"

"Yes."

"Do you wish to buy or sell?"

"Sell, primarily, but I wish to buy as well."

"Then I assume you'd like a secondary market with client thirty-three?"

"Yes, can you put me in contact with him?"

The auctioneer hesitated. "That's unusual but not without precedent. For a ten-percent fee, I can broker direct contact between buyers. Are you willing to accept that fee?"

Liam nodded and gestured for Diane to press forward.

She gave her prepared retort through the buyer's body. "Yes, but I'm sure you understand that I'd like to give my own sales pitch."

"Of course, but may I ask about your opening offer?"

"I'll offer my second purchase of the day, the one I purchased for ten thousand liras in the fifth auction, in exchange for all three of his purchases of the day plus an additional eight thousand liras, and your fees to be paid by him."

"That's demanding. He may reject it outright."

"Client thirty-three wanted my woman but lacked the funds at the time. I think he'll be willing to pay now."

"I'll speak to the boss and see what I can do."

"Should I wait to hear from you, then?"

"Yes."

The line went dead, the wealthy buyer started cursing in Turkish, and Diane opened her eyes.

As a test, Liam checked his laptop and noticed that the brief talk with the auctioneer had pinpointed the call within a four-kilometer radius of the restaurant and its backroom auction block. "If we can get the wraith on the line for even thirty seconds, it'll help."

Diane frowned. "I can do better than that."

"Do what you can, if you get the chance."

"He'll let us talk to him."

"You're sure?"

"I'm an empath, remember?"

Liam tried to remain positive. "That's my concern. In Michigan, you were able to see through the wraith's eyes. Here, you're having trouble."

"You don't understand."

"Of course, I don't. I wish I did. Why's it so hard now?"

Her voice rose an octave. "Did you think it was easy in Michigan?"

"No, that's not what I meant. Why's it impossible now?"

"I tried it, and he was too strong. He toyed with me."

He remembered her saying the wraith had made her watch him kill for sport through his eyes. "But you still learned from the invasion of his head, whether in real time or in his past."

"I didn't say I was giving up. Let's try your plan with the phone call before we do anything else."

The phone in the elder hunter's hand chimed.

Liam looked at Diane. "Get in his head."

A moment later, she spoke through the wealthy buyer. "I'm in."

Connor lowered the phone to the hog-tied buyer's cheek. "I'm answering."

The auctioneer's voice was crisp. "I have client thirty-three on the line."

The wraith's voice was ice. "I'm here."

The young hunter felt his heart pumping as he ran his cell tower tracking program.

Diane responded with the possessed buyer's voice. "Client twenty-one here. I recognize client thirty-three's voice. Go ahead."

The auctioneer kept control of the phone conversation. "We have interest from both parties, but we don't have an agreement on price. The opening offer is item number five in exchange for items two, three, and four, plus eight thousand liras, plus the ten-percent fee payment. The counter is to client thirty-three."

Liam verified his laptop recorded the conversation, in addition to locating the cell towers nearest the wraith.

"I'm keeping the three I have. I'll purchase item number five for eleven thousand liras plus the commission fee, giving client twenty-one an instant ten percent profit."

Surprised with the counter, Liam orchestrated a lie, which he whispered to Diane. "You're running a business. You need more assets, not less."

Speaking through the hog-tied man, she followed his lead. "I'm running a business. I need more assets, not less."

The wraith countered. "You can buy several assets for the price I've offered."

Liam whispered again to Diane's ear. "You need Iraqi assets. Your clients value them at a premium."

"I need Iraqi assets. My clients value them at a premium."

The auctioneer interjected. "Given this recent valuation of Iraqi assets, we can arrange for another shipment within a couple months."

The young hunter looked to his laptop, liked the progress in filtering cell towers, and whispered. "That's too long to wait. Unless client thirty-three is willing to give up his Iraqi assets purchased today, this isn't going to work out."

Diane conveyed the answer through her puppet. "That's too long to wait. Unless client thirty-three is willing to give up his Iraqi assets purchased today, this isn't going to work out."

"I cannot give up the ones I have."

Liam sensed the wraith's resistance turning into suspicion, but his cell tower tracker had done enough, pinpointing the wraith's phone to within several blocks. "Thank you, but we're done here."

"Thank you, but we're done here."

The auctioneer retained his public persona. "Contact me again, either of you, if you have future needs. It's always a pleasure doing business."

Connor hung up the phone. "What did you get?"

"As close as the program can get me. A few city blocks. It's still a lot to cover, but it's the closest we've been."

"Good."

"What about him?" Liam pointed at the cursing buyer.

"Help me carry him up front to the passenger seat."

With his father's help, the young hunter slung the trafficker over his shoulder and carried him forward. The elder hunter opened the door, and Liam dropped the man into the seat. "Now what?"

"Now his driver shoots him in a one-for-one deadly exchange."

"Gruesome."

"Would you like me to handle it?"

"No, best that I get my hands dirty." Without hesitating to overthink it, Liam probed the corpse on the floorboards for a pistol, withdrew it, and aimed its silenced barrel at the wealthy man's chest. He pulled the trigger, stopping a tirade of curses. With his father's help, he untied the restraining garments from the man's feet and wrists and removed the handcuffs. "Do we leave them here?"

"You would prefer to burn them?"

"It would be cleanest."

"It would also suggest a third party, which could lead them back to us. Without burning, the police can simply say that they killed each other."

"For that to be true, the driver would need to have moved from his seat to the passenger floorboards postmortem."

Connor shrugged. "Don't overestimate the police's effort in this. We're giving them the gift of two dead criminals in a plausible mutual-shooting scenario. I think they'll appreciate it."

Wondering if the secret order would make his father's prediction come true, Liam trusted the elder hunter. "Right. Let's regroup with the team and start figuring out how to find the wraith in his lair. We're two days from a full moon."

CHAPTER 37

Diane rode in the passenger seat while the young hunter drove the 500X. "I'm hungry."

Convincing Liam to eat proved easy. "I imagine it's a good time for dinner. We've got two days of hunting ahead of us."

"Are you sure it's only two days? And are you sure he's not going to kill before then?"

"No, I'm not. I was hoping that you as the esteemed empath could tell me. All I know is he's allowed to start killing his three tributes at eight-forty-nine in the evening two days from now, and I've still got a few thousand addresses to comb through to find him."

She grew short with him. He was the hunter. He was supposed to know how to find the bad guy. "What do you want from me? Are you saying we just did this phone trick for nothing?"

"No, I narrowed down a lot of geography, and you have access to three women on the inside now. Start talking to them."

Laying back in her seat, she felt like an idiot for forgetting her three new colleagues under the wraith's control. Everything was happening fast, and her energy was low. "Can I take a break? I'm tired."

"I'll call Father and pull us together to get some food. We could use a break."

In the restaurant, the growing team nibbled on crispy disks of hot bread and a plate of raw vegetables. Diane rolled pickled cabbage into a wrap, bit into it, and swallowed. She felt the discomfort of multiple eyes that silently ordered her to do something impressive. She poked the ribs of the young hunter, who sat next to her.

"What?"

"I'm going to contact one of the women."

"Right now? You're sure?"

"Look around the table. Nobody's asking me yet, but they all want me to do it."

"Understood. Do you know which one to contact?"

"Dunya. She was the second oldest after Nadine."

"I'll make sure nobody disturbs you. Happy telepathing."

Diane gripped the dagger glued to her thigh and concentrated on the young Iraqi woman. With the enchanted weapon's help and the captive's affinity for Diane, the link was strong.

"Diane?"

"Dunya? Can you hear me?"

"Yes. It's like you're in my head."

"I am. Are you safe? Can you talk?"

"Yes. I'm alone with the others in a jail cell."

"I made it out with Nadine's sister. You three are the only ones left to be freed."

"No, there are others here. We talk in Arabic between the walls. There are three Syrian women from Aleppo being held captive. They're in danger, too, I'm sure."

That complicated the rescue effort. "I understand. We'll find a way to get you all out. Did you notice anything about the building?"

"He parked his van inside the building and blindfolded us one by one as he moved us into our cell. It's some sort of big warehouse, judging by the echoes."

The report aligned with Diane's visions. "Can you let me see through your eyes?"

"I guess so. I don't know how."

"Just don't resist me. Here we go." Diane saw the small room and shackles at Dunya's feet. Her two companions were leaning against the wall at the edge of the single cot. The space appeared to have been a floor supervisor's office prior to the addition of a toilet, a deadbolted door, and a central chain mounted in concrete. After seeing what she could, she eased her sensory connection to the Iraqi woman. "I can't see anything useful in your cell."

"Unfortunately, this is all we can see."

"He hasn't hurt any of you, has he?"

"He's used an electronic shocking tool."

The Taser rekindled Diane's nightmares from Michigan, but it suggested something promising. "The electronic shocks are the cruelest thing he can do without disfiguring you. That may mean you're safe at least until the full moon."

"All of us?"

The addition of three Syrian women muddled the math. "I don't know. Maybe. I'll ask Liam. Have the Syrian women been beaten?"

"One was, but they haven't seen her since the first day. The other three say they've had nothing worse than the electronic shock."

"This is good information. I'll see what I can learn."

"Please. Hurry. We'll fight him any way we can, but we're scared."

Diane reappeared inside herself and scanned the faces around the table. As she accepted how time moved faster within her links than in reality, she realized she could jump in and out of them with a measure of secrecy.

"You were hardly gone."

She glanced at the young hunter. "But I learned a lot."

His eagerness betrayed his ignorance of his enemy's location. "Something about where he is?"

"No, nothing that good. He's holding three women from Aleppo in jail cells, in addition to our three new friends. There were four from Syria, but they've lost track of one."

The young hunter scowled. "The Syrian women were there before our Iraqi colleagues?"

"Yes."

"Then why the bloody hell did he need our Iraqi ladies?"

"You're the hunter."

"I know. I'm just thinking out loud. I'm sure he killed the first Syrian woman for sport. The other three, I'm not sure. Three Syrian women support three tributes, but three Iraqi women also support three tributes. Maybe he hasn't made up his mind yet, or maybe his Master hasn't made up his mind yet."

A chill overcame Diane. "But if he makes up his mind right now, that's three women he can kill for sport, right? We're racing a clock, and we don't even know when it runs out."

"I'm afraid you're right."

On Diane's other side, her brother stirred. "No."

"Josh? Did you have something to say?"

He kept his face in his tablet. "Yes."

"Josh, can you share what you're thinking?"

"Yes."

"Josh, what are you thinking?"

He looked away.

"What did you want to tell me, Josh?"

"It's about the hunters' books."

The conversation around the table died, and Diane continued extracting information from her brother. "Josh, what's in the hunters' books?"

"The first chapters of both hunters' books are the same."

Diane looked to Liam and then to Connor beside him, before continuing. "We know that Josh. They're the same, word for word, and they relate to Nana's book's first chapter."

"But it's obvious!"

"What's obvious, Josh?"

"Oh, why are you all so stupid?"

Diane exhaled and reminded herself to be patient. "It's not nice to call people stupid, Josh."

"But it's so obvious."

Liam talked out the autistic man's solution. "The first chapters in all three books, Nana's, Father's, and the other hunters', have three hundred and forty-three characters written in the shape of a cross. Three hundred and forty-three is seven to the third power, which was purposefully mystical. You also discovered that applying the encryption scheme from Father's book to Nana's book created a new chapter about the power of Diane's dagger."

Josh opened up. "Not just the dagger, the good spirits inside it. It said that evil spirts can't see what the good spirits hide."

Diane raised her hand to stop Liam, who seemed ready to pounce. "Are the good spirits hiding something from the evil spirits, Josh?"

"Yes."

"What are they hiding, Josh?"

"The wraith didn't know we switched you for Nadine."

The profound insight weighed upon the table, but Diane noticed a lack understanding in the hunters' faces. As the waiter brought plates of cubed and shredded meats, she waited for him to leave before recommencing her inquiry. "He bid for me at auction like he wanted me, but I drove the price up too high with the other bidder. Are you saying he specifically wanted Nadine?"

"Yes. Sort of, but he didn't even know it."

"Do you know why?"

"It's obvious, but the wraith can't see it. He can only see part of it."

"He can't see it, because the good spirits are hiding it?"

"Yes."

"What are they hiding, Josh?"

"Don't be stupid. There's only one answer that makes sense."

Diane sensed her brother was correct, despite his cryptic claim. "I'll believe you, Josh. I know you're right. You can tell me."

"Nadine's supposed to be his sacrifice for the July full moon."

"Wow, that's big, Josh. But I believe you. I feel it."

"You don't know what it means."

With his cast riding over her back, the young hunter huddled beside her. "I think that means the wraith doesn't know if he possesses his sacrifice, right Josh? He suspects it's one of the three Iraqi women, but he's also not sure if it's Diane, or Nadine. We turned him around sideways at the auction."

"Oh, you're still so stupid!"

Liam backed off from Diane's side. "I guess I was off a bit on that theory."

"Josh, can you be nicer to everyone?"

"I'm trying, but nobody else is trying."

She understood his meaning. He grasped concepts that eluded those distracted by the mundane concerns he ignored. "I'm trying, Josh. You can tell me."

"If he thought you or Nadine was really his next sacrifice, he would've bought you when you called him on the phone. But he wanted to keep the women he already has."

Again, Liam crowded her. "So, I was half right? He thinks he has his sacrifice. It's one of the three, but he's not sure which one?"

"Yes."

"But that doesn't explain why he tried to bid for me, Josh. Do you know why he wanted me?"

"I can't explain why people are stupid!"

The elder hunter's voice was calming. "Perhaps I can. I believe we have an excellent theory here, thanks to our young detective, Josh. The wraith was indeed thrown off when we substituted Diane for Nadine. That explains his erratic behavior. But now that he's in the comfort of his lair, he can't fathom the concept of failure. Diane got away and, therefore, couldn't have been necessary to him, which means his other three Iraqi captives are sufficient for his needs. He was still working through this thought process when we called him for the trade, and he drew his conclusion on the phone."

"That's sort of illogical, isn't it, Father?"

"Not if you're an egomaniac. Consider his supreme arrogance, and you'll see that the logic is flawless."

CHAPTER 38

Watching the setting sun through an open window, Liam leaned against the pillar of the unfinished building's fifth floor. As a matter of good luck, the rising edifice provided a central point within the possible locations of the wraith's lair, and his father's call to the order had produced an elevator code giving access to the uninhabited structure. "This could take a while."

His father seemed an infinite source of calm energy. "How long is that?"

"I've narrowed it down to fifty-two properties. I figure a fifteen-minute fly time for each gives four per hour, and that's more than half a day of drone work. But we'll need breaks."

"And fortunately we can take breaks, thanks to this young man's insights." Connor slapped the back of Josh, who frowned and nearly dropped his tablet.

Liam wanted to believe the empath's brother's conclusion, but his doubting nature nagged him. "That's true if the wraith thinks one of the Iraqi women is his sacrifice."

Nana led the two young Iraqi women in the chorus of protest.

Diane balked. "*Yulla!* Stop doubting me."

Liam pointed at the rescued sisters. "Wait, I made my comment in English. When did you two learn English?"

Nadine shrugged. "We know a little."

"Okay, fine. I get it that he thinks one of the ladies from Mosul is his sacrifice. But what's to keep him from killing the Syrian women? We know the last wraith had flexibility with tributes."

Connor's tone was its usual soothing tonic. "We don't know, but this young wraith's on a shorter leash than the prior killer in Michigan. He's probably a psychopath, which gives him a stronger resistance to Diane than we expect, but he's also viewing his Master in the same lens through which he sees himself."

"A madman?"

"Precisely. He's afraid to challenge his Master. If his Master told him to acquire three Syrian women, he'd consider them precious until he's finished his Master's bidding with them."

"Then we have two days to find his lair and storm it. I'll need to manage the flybys, but I could use help setting the coordinates into the drones and keeping a constant charging of backup batteries."

The empath stood defiantly. "And how do you plan to manage the flybys?"

Liam caressed his nape. "I was going to take still lifes and short videos for ease of storage and then show them to you in the morning. Then the ones that looked like your visions would go on the short list for a closer look."

"That sounds awfully inefficient."

"I wanted you to get some rest, that's all."

"Let's find the lair. Then I'll rest, if there's still time."

"It's already late, and it's going to be a long night. Unless we get lucky, it's going to go all night."

Nana raised her voice. "Josh can help with the drones. I will get blankets and pillows so we can rest. If Diane needs to sleep, she can take a nap, then she can wake up and look at pictures. We get enough blankets and pillows for everyone. Connor, we have the place to ourselves all night, yes?"

"Indeed, we do, and through the rest of the month."

The Chaldean grandmother continued. "The girls, they can make hot tea. I'll buy snacks, too, for sugar to keep us alert."

Liam knew sugar would help for half an hour and then turn him into a quivering ball of exhaustion on the floor, but he knew better than to argue with Nana. He'd pretend to eat whatever snack she'd bring. "That would be wonderful, Nana. Thank you."

Proving the defiance running in the Nineveh blood, Diane stood with her hands at her hips. "Well, are you ready to get to work?"

With late night hunts, his father had trained him to stay awake long hours. "I sure am. Let me pop open a few laptops."

"Hold on, lad." His father marched across the sparse floor to a foldout table and then dragged it towards the window. "You can set up here for a better view and a better work environment. You'll fatigue too quickly if you work on the floor."

"Thank you, Father." He placed his hardware on the table, found a map on one computer, and clicked on the first property within the search radius that resembled a factory or warehouse. He'd tagged his targeted properties numerically, and he moved his cursor to the front wall of number one. Then he copied the coordinates and pasted them into a field that controlled one of his drones. "Josh, will you take that hovercraft to the window, please?"

The young man complied and carried the drone to the glass, which was cracked open enough to slide the aircraft outside vertically. Backlighting Josh, the sun's highest red arc was setting below the horizon.

"Now turn it on and hold it with both hands at its sides. I want to test the rotors." Liam sent the aircraft through a propulsion burst.

Josh held the aircraft, which rose in his hands. "It's working."

"Great. Now slide it through the window and hold it for a second. I'm going to set that point as the return-to-home location."

"Okay."

Liam set the home coordinates as Josh held the aircraft outside the building's façade. "Okay, done. I'm going to release it now. Just wait for it to fly out of your hands." The young hunter ordered the aircraft to the first building on his list. "Here we go."

Josh released the first hovercraft.

Liam watched it veer into the encroaching darkness, which he assumed would aid his attempt to keep his flying spies stealthy. "Let's do this first one together as an exercise, so that we all know what's going on."

As the drone flew, the team gathered around the table, some of them bringing chairs and paint buckets to sit on.

On his laptop screen, the airborne camera showed an urban center with the silhouettes of skyscrapers. Interior lights lit a sparse matrix of windows for cleaning crews and late workers. Minutes later, the video showed an expanse of wider and flatter buildings as real estate became cheaper and allowed a spread of factories and warehouses. Security lights illuminated parking lots and entry points, and Liam saw several candidate buildings.

Connor stepped away from the table and moved to the window. "I'm going to see if I can open this up a bit to make retrieval easier."

"Sure, Father. Just make sure it's not a hazard for falling."

"Nonsense. The window only opens above waist height."

"I don't want Josh taking a spill. I'd still feel better if we tied something around his waist."

"I believe I saw safety harnesses around the corner. I'll see what I can find."

On the laptop, the camera view settled as the drone hovered and awaited Liam's command. He tapped an icon, ordering the lens to swivel towards the first building. "Diane, can you see anything yet?"

Her sarcastic tone told him he'd be muddling through their communications until they found a working cadence. "Yeah, I can see a building with windows."

Before the young hunter could defend himself, the Chaldean grandmother interjected. "You talk to him like you're married."

In unison, the empath and the hunter objected. "Nana!"

The grandmother shrugged. "Sorry. It's just what it sounds like."

Liam returned his focus to the mission. "I mean, Diane, can you rule it out from here? I don't want to announce to the wraith that I'm spying on him by bumping my drones into his factory windows."

"Just get it a little closer so I can look inside."

"Sure." He nudged the controller icon, and the drone walked towards a second-story plate of glass. Liam saw rows of automotive parts stacked to the roof. "That's not it, is it?"

"No way."

The young hunter thought out loud. "I can probably do this faster if I move on to the next target, and possibly the next."

Diane's sarcasm sounded flirtatious, so he hoped. "Yeah, you think?"

"Look, I've broken you into the back of a truck, I've watched over a slave auction house through a rifle scope, I've tracked a killer across town only to learn that he outsmarted me, and then I killed a human trafficker."

"Your point?"

"It's been a taxing day, and it's just getting started."

"Would you like to compare diaries? I've still got a sharp piece of metal glued to my crotch."

He sighed. "Sorry. I get it. It just doesn't help when you're short with me."

Nana took the opportunity to extract herself, Nadine, and her sister from the quarrel. She led the women to the elevator to find the promised sleeping and drinking supplies. "*Yulla. Imshi.* We go."

Liam examined the numbering and geometrical pattern of his targets. "I numbered them clockwise in a shrinking circle. So, they aren't grouped together in any real meaningful way. We'll have to manage this by eyeball."

When she withheld her sarcasm, she was a welcomed presence by his side. "Looks like two, seven, and nine are all pretty close."

"Yeah. The drone should have enough battery to hit them all, depending how fast we can rule each one out."

"Go for it."

He copied the coordinates for the second building and pasted them into the drone's GPS navigator. "Here we go to target building number two." The aircraft covered the short distance.

"It's four stories tall and too narrow."

"You can tell already?"

"I'm an empath. I'm supposed to trust my instincts."

"These buildings can rise higher than you'd expect. It's to allow stacking and inventorying of every conceivable kind of product."

"That's not the building, Liam. I just know."

The irony struck him that she knew about this building so quickly but had used sarcasm to make him move the drone closer to the window of the first. He was wise enough to leave the discrepancy unchallenged, but he couldn't restrain an extended sigh.

"What?"

"Nothing. I'm just settling into a long night." After checking the drone's remaining battery capacity and flight time, he committed to the third building. "Off we go to building seven."

Connor appeared with a safety harness which he tied around Josh, who held still like a willing puppet. The elder hunter then wrapped the free end around a neighboring window latch and clipped it tight, holding Josh safe from a fall.

With Liam's guidance, the drone flew by building seven and then building nine. When the empath rejected the structures as the wraith's lair, the young hunter ordered the aircraft back to their makeshift command center. He prepared the second drone with the coordinates for target building three. "Josh, please get the second drone ready for launch."

The empath's brother complied through the pre-flight test and then held the hovercraft outside the window.

"Here we go." Liam ordered the second drone into the night. "Father, are the spare batteries charging?"

The elder hunter stepped away to an array of secondary chargers and extra batteries plugged into a far wall. "All the lights are glowing red."

"That's good." Liam glanced at the map showing the first drone's location. "Get ready, Josh. The first drone's about twenty seconds away. Father, please make sure he doesn't fall out the window."

"Yes, lad. Of course." The elder hunter marched to the empath's brother and stood beside him as the first drone returned to the window and hovered. "Go ahead, Josh. I've got you. The harness has you. And somehow, I think Liam could fly across the room to grab you before you could fall."

"Funny, Father. I'm trying to keep everyone alive. That's all."

Josh reached for the drone and pulled it into the room.

"See, lad. He's fine. No need to worry."

"Wait until we're bleary-eyed twelve hours from now. It could be a very long night, and nobody's dying on my watch."

CHAPTER 39

Lying on her side, Diane awoke with a coppery taste on a pile of blankets. Examining her surroundings, she saw everyone else sleeping except her grandmother and the young hunter. "What's going on?"

"You were so tired. You passed out. Me and Liam have been using the drones all by ourselves."

Despite trying to conceal his fatigue, the young hunter sounded exhausted. "Yeah. Josh needed a break, and Nana's not bad at all with the drones."

The empath looked out the windows at blackness and then checked her phone for the time. It was almost four in the morning. "So, the two of you haven't slept a wink yet?"

Her grandmother waved her hand. "I'm fine." But she sounded more tired than Liam.

"Can't we get Josh to handle the computer stuff so that you guys can rest?"

Liam shrugged. "I imagine, but I'm fine. We've covered half the targets."

"No, you're not fine. You're about to fall over from exhaustion. Both of you. How long has Josh been asleep?"

The young hunter looked at her. "A couple hours. But before we move on, you should look at the properties we've recorded. You've got a backlog of almost twenty."

Diane rolled to her feet.

"Hold on. Let Nana retrieve the incoming drone. Then we'll all take a break." The hunter walked to the window and braced the grandmother's arm as she reached for the arriving and hovering aircraft. He took the drone from Nana and carried it to a charger.

Two steps behind him, the grandmother moved to a break area where she'd set up tea and snacks. "I'll make us some tea."

Liam stooped, set the drone's expended battery in its charger, and then walked to the table holding his laptops.

Diane joined him. "Let me see what you recorded."

He yawned while playing through the videos. "You can control it here." He pointed to the icons for the video player.

Sipping tea her grandmother had made, the empath cycled through the images, but none of them seemed like the wraith's lair. "Nope. We need to keep looking."

"Right. Perhaps you had a point that I could use a short nap. If you're up with him, I imagine Josh can manage the drone flights."

"I'm sure we can manage. I'll wake him."

Ten minutes later, after he'd freshened himself, Josh sat at the computer. "The next drone is going out to target number thirty-one."

Keeping her voice down to avoid disturbing those who rested, Diane carried the drone to her brother. "This one?"

"Yes."

"What do I do with it?"

"Just hold it while I make sure it works."

Without warning, the rotors whirred to life, and the drone jumped from her hands and steadied above the floor.

"I said hold it."

"I was. Never mind." She grabbed it from midair. "Now what?"

"Take it to the window and make sure you don't fall out or Liam will get mad."

"Cute, funny man." She carried the aircraft to the window.

"Now let it go. We figured this out hours ago."

As it flew from her hand out the open window, she watched it disappear into the darkness. Despite her nap, she felt fatigue's lingering claws creeping up her frame.

"Diane."

She heeded her brother's call and joined him at the table. The computer showed the drone's camera spying on yet another failed attempt to identify the wraith's lair. "Nope."

Josh navigated the drone to a nearby building, then another, and finally a fourth before bringing it back. "You have to send out the next drone while this one comes back."

After trotting to the mass of plugs that charged the two remaining aircraft and the array of spare batteries, she pointed. "This one?"

"No, the other one."

Kneeling, she unplugged the hovercraft and carried it to her brother.

"This time, hold it while I test it." Again without warning, he energized the rotors.

This time, she held it down.

"Now take it to the window."

Watching her step to avoid tripping, she brought the aircraft to its launch point and waited for it to fly away.

"Stay there. The first one's coming back."

Seconds later, the first drone arrived and hovered within reach outside the window. Diane braced herself against the sill and grabbed the aircraft, which felt light as she pulled it into the room. "What do I do with this?"

"Swap out its battery for a fresh one and charge its battery."

"Um, what?"

He sounded irritated. "Never mind. I'll do it." Trotting, he moved to her, took the hovercraft, and crossed the distance to the charging stations. He swapped out the batteries, set up the drained one in a spare charger, and then returned to his seat. "Come here."

Diane walked to her brother and then looked at the screen. "That's not the right building."

"Okay, I'll try the next one."

A minute later, Diane stared at a long line of second story windows. "Move in closer." She held her breath as the barren inventory floor appeared. "Can you get closer?"

"No, but I can try another angle from a different wall."

"Please!"

She knew the answer before the camera steadied, but seeing the van parked on the concrete floor confirmed it. "That's it!"

Josh surprised her with his coolness. "We do what Liam said. First thing, I bring it back immediately." He tapped an icon to withdraw the hovercraft. "Now we wake him."

"Okay." She stood like a statue.

I'll do it." Excited, Josh yelled. "Liam! Liam! We found it! It was number thirty-seven."

Everyone who had been resting rolled awake.

Within a minute, Liam retook control of the laptop and the hovercraft. "We've got about an hour until sunrise. I want a full infrared sweep of that place for human heat signatures. We'll find out where he's keeping his prisoners and where he sleeps. I'll handle that. Josh, can you handle a drone and take a video looking straight down while flying it around the building?"

"Yes."

"Good. I'm also going to send the third drone in reserve. I may need it for some closeups. Let's get them launched."

The elder hunter was awake, and, despite any lingering fatigue, sounded alert. "I'll work on getting blueprints. I should have them soon after businesses open, if not sooner."

Diane assumed he meant he'd call his order, but she was more interested in the visual data from the drones, which Josh was launching from the window.

With the aircraft in flight, her brother sat beside Liam and took control of a drone from his tablet.

Ten minutes of transit brought the first drone to the building, and the young hunter switched its camera to infrared mode. "Nothing yet. Let me fly around the back. Josh, you've got your drone capturing video from overhead, right?"

"Yes."

"Is it picking up the locations of the security cameras?"

"I think so. So far, I see them."

The young hunter's computer screen showed bright forms inside the building. "There. That looks like three bodies and then three more in a tighter space."

Diane's heart pumped. "That's how Dunya described the jail cells. That's them."

"Let me find him now." Liam elevated the drone to the second floor, and a solitary bright form appeared. "That's him. He's got the second floor to himself."

Connor spoke with his usual calmness. "That's logical. He would select a location that gives him an elevated position. Try a look through all the windows to get a better sense of the layout."

Liam switched to the visual camera and drove the drone by each window with slow caution. "The warehouse is rather boring, but you can see how he's already barricaded the doors."

Connor pointed. "And look there. He's got concertina wire behind the door to each loading dock. He's certainly expecting us."

"I don't see any traps, though. No explosives. That's a nice change from our last wraith."

"We'll want to review these video recordings in finer detail to be sure of that, but I hope you're right."

"I think we've captured all we need, Father. Unless you can think of anything else we need, I'll bring them back, before he wakes up and sees our hovercraft."

"Sure. Bring them back. That's good reconnaissance. Now, for the important part–the planning of our raid."

Diane hoped the hunters would allow time to rest. "We've got a day and half until the full moon."

Connor affirmed her hopes. "And we'll make proper use of the time. Let's clean up everything from here and load up the vehicles. I suggest we all take naps at the hotel, plan in the afternoon, prepare in the evening, and then conduct our raid tonight at dark."

The tired team nodded silent approvals.

"So be it, then. Let's get some rest and target lunch time for our planning session."

CHAPTER 40

That evening, Edric replayed his security camera feed again. With his Master's prodding, he knew the hunters had spied on him in the last hour of the morning's darkness.

He'd counted three drones working in the service of his enemies, but the knowledge added little to his defensive strategy. His preparations were complete. They had him penned in like a wild animal, and if they challenged him within his lair, a wild animal's wrath they would suffer.

He triple-checked his preparations–his weapons and his body armor, verifying his readiness for battle. To complicate any rescue effort, he had set up additional concertina wire in front of the jail cells. His enemies faced a monumental task against him.

With shotgun shells and exploding glass, they began their assault.

"Bastards!" The wraith stooped, trotted to his panoramic window, and saw rappelling lines dangling through the broken glass of two second-story windows, suggesting that the assailants had come from the roof. He scanned the floor and saw two human forms running behind his empty metal shelves.

To slow their advance, he grabbed his AK-47 assault rifle and shot away a pane of glass, which required a final kick of his boot to clear. Hiding below the sill, he aimed rounds in the general direction of his assailants. As they returned fire, he crawled to his spare body armor components and donned his helmet, limb guards, and gloves.

He crawled to his weapons and clipped a holster with a pistol at each hip around his waist. Then he stuffed spare magazines and shells into his vest, and he grabbed a shotgun. With a rifle in one hand and the shotgun in the other, he worked back to his superior vantage point above his enemy.

Below him, they aimed shotguns at the concertina wire he'd spread in front of the jail cells. He found their solution to his razor wire clever as they shot out its mountings and made it unravel, but it cost them precious ammunition. Expecting his cartons of bullets and shells to outlast whatever the assailants had brought, he smattered AK-47 bullets at their feet, enticing them to shoot back.

As they took the bait and forced him below his window sill, he realized they lacked the azure glow he expected. But he knew they were the supernatural pair who hunted him, since his Master had made it clear during a nonverbal flash.

Though they outnumbered him two-to-one, he liked his position. They were trapped behind empty shelves and faced a long, exposed path under his elevated position to reach his prisoners. He lifted his rifle barrel and squeezed off a few more rounds to remind them of their disadvantage.

He whispered to himself. "Is this the best you cretins can do?"

One of them tossed a grenade towards a loading dock door. Edric ducked before the detonation, which blew away its razor wire barrier and created an exit into the night. As he examined the damage, he considered it desperate. The assailants still faced a long distance under his bullets to release the prisoners, and then they'd have to double back further to get out. It seemed folly.

Most importantly, he was safe in his position. There was no threat of them storming his elevated defenses. Even if they did escape with some or all of his captives, they showed no intent of attacking him.

Though carrying grenades, his assailants lacked the strength and accuracy to throw the heavy weapons into his personal space. They also lacked any riot weapons like teargas cannisters, given the light load they could carry based upon their swift entrance.

But his domineering spirit prodded him to take the precaution of holding his dagger within reach. Though a night away from the full moon, Edric obeyed. He crawled to its case, lowered his rifle, and took up the bronze knife in his hand.

"It is illogical tactically, but if you insist, Master, I shall hold it."

As an experiment, he slid the blade into a vest pocket, freeing his hand.

"Is that good enough, Master, just to have it on my person?"

The unspoken answer was affirmative. Edric exhaled, picked up his AK-47 assault rifle, and sent rounds at the hunters, who had remained in their safe positions. To improve his aim, he repositioned at the leftmost window in his panorama, shot it out, and gave himself a superior field of fire. Although their return fire was easier, his shots were now direct, removing the shelves as their cover.

As long as he showed the courage to take shots at them, they were thwarted. His mind raced to rationalize how his enemy had gifted him such an advantage. Having understood the basics of warfare his entire long life, he judged their attack foolhardy.

Then, as he sent rounds towards the assailants, he saw a female form appear in the gap blown through the loading dock door.

Edric felt a rush, and he saw a red aura rise from her, filling the warehouse. The sanguine light blossomed in his vision, and the woman and her life force became his complete world.

His Master was painting her as the next sacrifice.

The red illumination receded, returning Edric's normal view of the visual spectrum. In the dim light of his warehouse floor, the bulletproof riot shield, with a viewport and a lightweight design that would stop any caliber he possessed, revealed itself. With her small body, the shield protected every angle against her.

Thoughts raced through his mind, and he panicked.

This was the one woman his lording spirit had selected for him as the source of his next fifty years of life. Why did his enemy have her? How could she be used against him?

He feared that killing her now, more than a month before her time, would destroy him.

As he hid below the window, he heard clamoring from the direction of his intended sacrifice, and he guessed from the clinking and the sliding that she'd grabbed additional riot shields from the evening's darkness and had slid them towards the nearest hunter.

One of the hunters, with the weathered voice of an aged man, cried out to him. "Do you speak English?"

Terrified, the wraith remained silent.

"I know you do, and I know you recognize this woman. We have her, and I don't imagine you can risk shooting her, can you?"

Edric wanted the hunters dead. "I'll kill you all."

"I think not. You won't risk hurting her. If you'd care to look, she's already next to me, and I've put a protective amulet around her neck. Whatever means you had of identifying her is gone."

"I said I'll kill you all!"

"That's unlikely. But if you kill any of the women, you'll have no way of telling them apart."

"Damn you! I will simplify this and kill you all." His ire rose, clouding his thoughts.

The hunter remained silent.

Edric risked a look over the sill, and he saw three riot shields racing down the aisles towards his jail cells. The hunter had been correct, and the wraith was afraid to kill his sacrifice. Instead, he aimed at the lone shield in the passageway, which protected a hunter. He unleashed a burst from his assault rifle, but the rounds bounced off the plastic. Without return fire from his enemy, he studied the shield for weakness but found none. Even the handles were protected.

Below him, a small explosive detonated, opening the way to the first prison.

"Damn them!" The wraith shifted to his shotgun, extended it outside his window, and aimed at a shield. He pulled the trigger.

The defense held, but the buckshot knocked the hunter to his backside while the other hunter risked exposure and aimed a pistol at Edric's head.

His instincts forced him to pull back into his room, and the bullets sailed by his window. Fearing a second detonation, Edric waited, but the next loud sound was a deep thud. Sticking his head into the warehouse, he saw nobody. The three intruders were hidden from his view, below him, inside the nearest jail cell.

The deep thud echoed again.

Realizing a hunter had brought a sledgehammer to break down the drywall between the jails, Edric credited his assailants with the foresight to have brought bolt cutters as well. He was helpless to stop them unless he went to the warehouse floor–exposed, outgunned, and in the weaker position.

He hoped they failed to consider his resolve to risk that trip. Strapping his assault rifle over his shoulder, he grabbed his shotgun and stood. Whether he ended up hurting or even killing his sacrifice, he trusted his Master to sort out the fallout.

Action would be rewarded, and he turned to descend the stairs and face his enemy.

CHAPTER 41

While his father took over the hammering duties to break down the wall of the final prison cell, Liam led the first three captives, the Syrian women, towards safety. He backed out of the first jail cell and aimed his Heckler and Koch 416 rifle at the window above him. Seeing nothing, he sprinted half the aisle's distance, turned, and aimed again.

The first Syrian woman gazed at him with hopeful eyes.

He gestured for her to raise her riot shield and to walk backwards towards him.

She obeyed, as did the other two.

Stealing a glimpse from the corner of his eye, the young hunter saw what he'd hoped to see.

In the darkness of the blown-open loading dock door which marked the prisoners' exit, Diane stood with her dagger cocked by her ear. With its enchanted azure glow, the weapon was poised to end the battle.

"Come on, show yourself one more time, you bastard."

Through the radio earpiece, his father responded. "Say that again."

"He's not showing himself. I don't have a shot. Diane can't see him yet, either."

"Take advantage of this to get the women out."

"Of course. *Yulla! Imshi!*"

Sidestepping behind their riot shields, the women followed Liam towards Diane, who marked the exit.

The young hunter kept his rifle barrel aimed high but saw nothing. But as each Syrian woman handed him her shield and disappeared through the dock's door into the safety of darkness, a little pressure came off his chest. He slung two of the riot shields over his shoulder and carried the third in front of him as protection, remarking at their bulletproof lightness. As he reached the midway point of his return to the cells, he broke away from the back wall and headed down the empty aisle.

Diane's scream announced her dagger throw.

Expecting to see the azure arcing towards the wraith's second-story nest, Liam was surprised when the knife cut a light blue swath towards the bottom of the stairs. Though he watched in a timeframe that seemed like slow motion, he knew the divine force behind the empath's toss was deadly as the blade's tip careened towards the wraith's exposed neck.

A fraction of a second before the kill, the wraith's dagger glowed sanguine, appeared in his hand, and whipped a red arc of defiance. It caught the empath's dagger inches from his flesh and sent the flying knife against the wall.

The plan's climactic assassination had failed.

Dumbfounded, Liam looked through the shelving at the wraith, who stared in a similar trance at his own dagger, wondering how he'd cheated death.

Though she wore body armor, Diane was unarmed and exposed to the wraith's weapons.

To distract the savage, who appeared like the horrific demonic beast he'd expected, Liam yelled while sprinting towards the jail cells. He dropped the two extra shields by the wall and kept the third in front of him.

The ruse worked, drawing the enemy's shotgun attack, but the impact of the shells sent the young hunter sideways to the floor. "Father, I'm down. The wraith's on the ground floor. Diane's exposed. He parried her dagger."

"Dear God, lad. Can Diane get to her dagger?"

"Only if he keeps coming for me. He's coming now."

"Keep your head down. I'm shooting my way out." The fourth jail cell's door erupted in splinters as the elder hunter's shotgun burst it open.

"Negative, Father. The concertina wire's still in the way. You can't get out."

"I know that, but I distracted him, didn't I?"

Stealing a glance over his shield, Liam saw Diane sprinting to the wall where her dagger lay on the ground. The wraith moved towards him, and he wanted to keep it that way. He worked the barrel of his rifle aside his shield and aimed it at the animal. He squeezed off several rounds and yelled. "Come and get me, you bastard!"

The wraith tucked himself behind the corner of the stairway, dodging the volley. He then noticed Diane sprinting towards her dagger, lifted his shotgun, and aimed.

With perfect timing, the empath dove to the floor below the buckshot.

His shotgun empty, the wraith lifted his assault rifle from his shoulder and pointed it at Diane.

Forgetting his own safety, Liam dropped his shield, clutched his rifle in both hands, and charged the savage. He released a primal scream to distract him, and he sent bullets into the animal's back.

The wraith's armor took the pounding, and he kept his weapon on Diane. He pulled the trigger, releasing automatic rounds at the empath.

As Liam sprinted towards the animal, he watched in awe as Diane whipped her dagger in a defensive demonstration of azure arcs. The clank of bullets hitting bronze announced each deflected shot.

Thinking he had the better of this enemy with Diane consuming his attention, Liam raised his barrel towards the wraith's head. Though covered with an armored helmet, the savage's skull was still vulnerable to the concussive forces.

Before the young hunter pulled the trigger, the wraith turned and glared with demonic eyes. With impossible speed, he lifted his red dagger and hurled it at Liam.

Guided by supernatural evil, the tip slid between the seams of the young hunter's armor and lodged itself into the artery under his arm. Liam fell to the ground in pain as the mortal wound took its toll. As he glanced across the warehouse floor, he was at least relieved to see a successful rescue.

His father was leading the other women out with the riot shields in two groups of two, including Nadine whom they'd snuck in as a decoy. The final group of two were making their move and would reach safety.

The wraith appeared over Liam, kicked away his rifle, and tossed the pistols from his jacket. He reached for his knife. "I'd cut your arm off and watch you bleed to death, but I first need to deal with this harlot." He yanked out the blade, accelerating the bleeding and leaving the young hunter in a spreading pool of his own blood.

After stifling a yelp as the knife left his wound, Liam whispered into his communications set. "Father, lead them to safety. Get Diane out of here."

"There all out now, lad. It's just you, me, and Diane against him. I'm not leaving you."

Diane interjected her command over their shared communication circuit. "I'll deal with him myself. Save Liam."

The wraith countered them all. "If you want to save the boy's life, throw down your weapons."

Liam felt his life waning. "Don't do it, Father."

"I... can't seem to help myself. I'm lowering my weapons. I'll be there with the first aid kit." Unarmed, the elder hunter sprinted across the concrete and arrived at Liam's side.

The pressure in his arm was comforting. "I told you to leave me, Father. You're unarmed and exposed."

As the elder hunter pressed gauze into the wound, he glanced over his shoulder. "Diane seems to be holding her own."

Liam lifted his head and saw the empath's light blue blade swinging against the reddish glow of her enemy's knife.

She wielded the charmed dagger like a superhuman, parrying a punch and slicing her assailant's forearm. Then she clashed bronze against bronze, and the weapons exchanged a multi-colored bolt of supercharged lightning.

The wraith moved with concise, expert motions, awing Liam with his natural abilities and his supernatural speed. Though he'd seen Diane outclass a skilled fighter in Michigan, he watched an even battle now.

A woman possessed, Diane dodged and parried, stopping three slashes and four thrusts that would have killed a lesser foe. But with his Master fueling his rage, the wraith cut her forearm, and she cried in pain.

"Holding her own, maybe, but not for much longer. Can't we help her, Father?"

"I wanted to, but she wouldn't let me."

"She was in your head?"

"Yes. Rest now. Let me patch you up."

With his father's assuring tone, Liam released himself to his care and lost consciousness.

CHAPTER 42

Diane prayed her gambit would work.

As her confidence plateaued, she doubted shed could do anything else. She thrust the point towards the wraith's exposed neck, and he blocked with his crossguard. Mystical sparks flew as bronze scraped bronze. With a crazed shriek, she pulled her weapon back and then whipped the blade upward with incredible speed, but her enemy matched her with a rapid parry.

Recalling the words of the Maiden of Beit She'an, she understood that this was the conflict about which the ghost had warned her. This was her risking everything.

Losing ground in her knife fight, she took solace as she saw from corner of her eye the elder hunter dragging his son towards the door. She was relieved to see Liam escaping, but the glimpse cost her.

The wraith sliced open the backs of her fingers, and only the dagger's divine essence kept it in her hand.

Diane stepped backwards as the wraith pressed forward. With her profile to the blown-open door, she judged the time perfect for her final move. She called out telepathically. "Now, Nana!"

Within her grandmother's mind, Nana protested. "I can't."

"You have to."

"No. I'm afraid."

"You can do it. We can do it together. You aim, and I'll help you pull the trigger."

Bullets pounded the wraith's helmet, and he collapsed.

The empath seized her moment and pounced on him. She rolled him to his back, straddled him, and raised her dagger.

As she recited her incantation, her voice echoed off the walls like a haunting symphony, blending the voices of two dozen dead victims.

"I avenge. I free. I redeem."

Two handed, she plunged the coppery knife through her enemy's armor and into his heart.

White light cracked though the wraith's skin and clothing, and ghosts wearing milky white dresses emerged from his dying form. Two dozen apparitions escaped their killer, rose to the warehouse's ceiling, and ascended beyond sight.

As the final victim flew away, the savage's body turned to bones, falling into its proper state of decay for a one-hundred-and thirty-three-year old man.

Diane enjoyed the rush of power and sensed herself growing stronger. With her newfound energy, she sprang to her feet and sprinted across the floor. "Liam!"

Connor stopped her with his raised palm. "He's in danger. He's lost a lot of blood."

"He'll be fine." It was a statement of hope–not empathic insight.

"I'm calling for emergency help."

Glowing, Diane's dagger summoned her attention. She lowered it towards the young hunter's wound.

"What are you doing?"

"I don't know. The dagger's doing it."

"I don't see how that can help him."

"I don't know either, but lift the bandages out of the way."

"I can't do that. He'll bleed out."

"That's what the dagger wants."

"Oh, dear. For a moment, I suppose. But whatever you're doing, please hurry." The elder hunter unraveled his handiwork.

Diane let the blade guide itself into Liam's wound. Though it was cool metal in her hand, its edge seared the young hunter's flesh. "What's it doing? I don't understand."

"I think it's cauterizing his wound."

She lifted her dagger from its patient.

"Mercy me, his bleeding has stopped. That was brilliant. How?"

"It wasn't me. I have no idea. I just… well, you saw it."

"I still don't believe it, but you're full of surprises. What does my son call you, again?"

"The Lady of the Dagger."

"The Lady of the Dagger, indeed."

Aiming her Heckler and Koch 416 rifle towards the ground, the empath's grandmother appeared beside Liam. "Is he okay?"

"Thanks to your granddaughter."

"I saw. That dagger, it's something special."

"Absolutely." Relieved that his son's life appeared spared, the elder hunter gave a confounded look. "It has the power to stop bullets and to heal a wound, but why do you suppose it was unable to defeat this wraith in hand-to-hand combat?"

Nana stood and slung her rifle over her shoulder. "Maybe that stays a mystery, but you'll hear no complaint from me. It gives me a chance to shoot him, and I hadn't shot in three weeks. My trigger finger was getting... how do you say it?"

Diane scoffed. "Itchy, Nana?"

"Yes, itchy." Reliving her recent glory, the grandmother lowered her rifle to her cheek and aimed it at the pile of bones that had threatened her team. "But I'm glad you make me do this, Diane. I wasn't sure I could, but I feel great now."

"If I'm the Lady of the Dagger, you're Machinegun Nana. I'm not the only one coming out of this with a cool nickname."

That evening, the team gathered in Liam's hospital room. Diane leaned against the counter by the window and watched the full moon rising over a city she'd made safe for the victims of a supernatural savage. "How are you feeling."

One arm in a cast from month-old bullet wounds, and his other arm bandaged and immobilized, the young hunter used his broken limb to balance peas on a fork. "I'm starved."

Connor smiled. "That's a good sign."

Diane waved a dismissive wrist. "He's always hungry. But, yeah, it's good to watch him shovel food into his mouth. Come on, we're crowding him. Let him eat in peace."

Liam mumbled. "No, it's okay. I don't mind the company."

The elder hunter waved the women away. "Josh, you can stay, but I think the rest of the gang needs a little girl talk."

Diane followed Nana, five Iraqis, and three Syrians to an empty waiting room and joined a circle around the matriarch.

The Chaldean grandmother spoke in slow Arabic. "You're all free, but you're not home. Does anyone want to go home? Does anyone want to go to Western Europe or even the United States?"

A mix of shrugs, nods, and head shakes revealed the complexity of Nana's question.

As an empath, Diane thought she could help. "I could talk to each of you individually to help decide. I could even do a tarot reading, if anyone wants one."

The reception was positive, and Diane knew how she'd spend her evening. But before invoking prophecies, she needed to return to the hunters without her female colleagues. She walked to Liam's room and closed the door. "There are eight women in there who may be afraid to go home. Can your secret order help get them somewhere safe with opportunities to start over?"

"I'm optimistic, young lady, but don't make any promises until I research each specific case. I'll do my best, of course."

Diane returned to the waiting women and started her tarot card readings. As she progressed through each individual situation, her interpretations aligned with her expectations.

Facing persecution at home, the Syrian women needed to find someplace new. The Iraqi women had murkier futures, each with a path to happiness and prosperity at home in Mosul or in distant lands. After a private debate, the five Iraqis decided to return to their friends and families.

The empath walked to Liam's room and found the young hunter sleeping.

Seated in a large chair, her brother slept with his face in his palm. Beside him, Connor was sleeping but stirred when she entered the room. "Is there a decision?"

"The Iraqi ladies would like to go home, and the Syrian ladies would like a fresh start. Can you help with that?"

"I'm sure the order can help the young ladies get home, and creating new starts for three people is a lot easier than for eight. Let's say that I'm quite optimistic."

CHAPTER 43

In the morning's early hours, Diane dreamt of a woman on a cross, blood pouring from her wound.

She called out in her nightmare. "Why are you here again?"

The blood ceased to flow, the cross evaporated, and the unwounded misty maiden appeared. "Help the others."

"I don't understand."

Like a lifting fog, the whiteness drifted from the Israeli sacrifice, revealing a human being. Raven black hair framed a face with dark eyes. "You helped me. You redeemed all of us whom he killed. But you must do more."

"Why? I freed you all. I've killed two wraiths already."

"You destroyed two monsters, but there are more like them, and there are deceased victims like me in need of redemption."

"Am I really going to be called to kill a third?"

The Israeli woman smiled. "This will be the last time we speak before I pass. So, please forgive me, but I must remind you that you already know the answer."

"Because I'm an empath, and I know?"

"Yes. Thank you, Diane. Good bye."

The empath awoke in her hotel room.

Setting aside the prophecy of the freed maiden, she reached to the nightstand for her dagger, and she knew it was time to close a loose end.

She sent her spirit across the city, seeking a man she remembered from a darker day. Taking over his body, she felt her awareness materialize in the auctioneer of shoulder-length black hair.

Standing on the stage, she saw the familiar faces of the traffickers who bought and sold women. The short and barrel-chested boss-seller was present, too. The opportunity was perfect.

She made her possessed puppet walk off the stage and into the green room. He knocked on the door and waited for the security guard she considered worthy of saving to open it. The auctioneer followed him into the room.

The guard gazed into his eyes. "Is that you, Diane?"

"Yes."

"Are you ready?"

"Yes. Hand them over."

One at a time, the guard extended four grenades.

Diane accepted them and slid them into the auctioneer's pockets. "Get the girls into the bathroom for safety."

"I will. We'll be fine. I can't thank you enough."

Returning to the stage, the auctioneer faced the seedy crowd. Without speaking, Diane grabbed the first grenade, pulled its pin, and lobbed it to the far left. She then sent one to the far right. To the middle left, she sent a third. Finally, she walked the fourth to the middle right, pulled its pin, and held it over his head.

Her awareness returned to her body, and then she called to the friendly guard. "May I see through your eyes?"

"Yes."

"Are you okay?"

"The green room's door blew off, but we're fine in here. The girls are fine." The guard walked towards the devastated smoky back room, found a dead guard, and picked up his rifle.

"Can you get the girls out of there to safety?"

"I think so. It will be good to use a weapon against these bastards. Hold on." Aiming the rifle at a surviving guard who writhed on the floor, he ended the man's suffering. Then a sentry from the front door raced into the room, and the friendly guard gunned him down.

"You got this, Ozan?"

"Yes, I do. I'll grab the keys from one of these animals and use their truck to get the women to safety. I thank you again. My family thanks you."

That evening at dinner, Diane joined Liam with his father, Josh, and Nana. In celebration of the young hunter's release from the hospital, she'd let him choose the restaurant.

A wise man, he'd deferred to what Diane wanted and selected Mediterranean fare. While she picked at pickled cabbage and warm bread, she watched the young hunter devour meat and rice wrapped in grape leaves.

Diane risked the question. "Do we need to get ready to take on a third wraith?"

Connor kept his response calming. "The order hasn't revealed a next assignment, if that's what you mean."

"I've got a feeling we're going to be called on again."

Liam powered through his food and swallowed. "Bloody hell. If you've got a feeling, then it may as well be written in stone."

"Not true. My feelings are just feelings. No future's certain."

He jabbed his fork into another stuffed grape leaf and aimed it at her. "Really? Name one example where one of your feelings proved untrue."

She frowned at him. "Don't be a smartass."

"My son unfortunately can't help himself. I sure hope he didn't get the habit from me."

The young hunter spoke through hurried chews. "I'm not being a smartass. It's a fair question."

Diane dropped her cabbage and bread to her plate. "Fine. I'll answer. When I threw my dagger at the wraith, I thought it would hit."

Liam glared at her. "Are you sure?"

She looked away. "Ugh. Okay. No, I'm not sure. I also kind of knew I was supposed to place myself in danger against him."

"I knew it! That's why I asked. You're a walking prophecy."

Unable to stop herself, her grandmother made it worse. "That's true. This has been going on in our family for generations."

"Nana! You're not helping."

"What? You want me to lie?"

"Just don't help him."

Chewing a piece of crispy bread dipped in olive oil, Josh lowered his tablet and offered a rare moment of eye contact with his sister. "Why not help him? I like him."

Liam chuckled. "Thank you, Josh. I like you, too."

Diane scrunched her face towards her brother. "What made you say that, Josh?"

"I like Liam."

"We all like Liam, but that was random."

Josh looked towards the ceiling. "I was thinking he'd be a nice brother-in-law."

Flushed with embarrassment, Diane looked across the table at Liam, who also turned red and had trouble holding eye contact with her. "Um, don't be silly, Josh. He's taken a vow of chastity."

"Oh, why is everyone so stupid?"

Connor tried to calm the frustrated autistic man. "She's right, Josh. As wraith hunters, we all must take the vow of chastity."

"I've read your books. There's nothing against getting married and starting families."

Diane intensified her scowl and raised her volume. "Josh! You can't tell Connor and Liam their business."

The elder hunter waived his palm. "No, I don't mind at all. That's true, there's nothing written against it. It's all been a matter of tradition. None of us has married in generations due to the nature of our work, but it's well known that the first hunters were indeed married."

Liam frowned and nearly coughed out a mouthful of falafel. "It's not well known to me."

"Well known to those in the order whose job it is to know."

The young hunter swallowed. "Were you going to wait until you died of old age to tell me?"

"You're well ahead of yourself, lad. There are time-honored rules, there are exceptions, and then there are even rarer exceptions. What we're talking about here doesn't even register in the rarer exceptions end of the spectrum."

Undeterred, Josh continued his argument. "Your vows were for chastity, not celibacy. There's a difference."

The elder hunter tried to keep the table calm. "I agree. Chastity is a virtue that a married couple can share. Do you believe that Liam and Diane are destined for marriage, Josh?"

"It doesn't matter what I think. Ask Diane."

As all eyes turned to her, she wanted to disappear. She knew the answer, but she'd melt into a pile of gooey embarrassment if she shared it. "Can I answer that later, like maybe when I'm alone–with Liam?"

THE END

About the Author

After graduating from the Naval Academy in 1991, John Monteith served on a nuclear ballistic missile submarine and as a top-rated instructor of combat tactics at the U.S. Naval Submarine School. He now works as an engineer when not writing.

Wraith Hunter Chronicles:

PROPHECY OF ASHES (2018)
PROPHECY OF BLOOD (2018)
PROPHECY OF CHAOS (2018)
PROPHECY OF DUST (2018)

Rogue Submarine Series:

ROGUE AVENGER (2005)
ROGUE BETRAYER (2007)
ROGUE CRUSADER (2010)
ROGUE DEFENDER (2013)
ROGUE ENFORCER (2014)
ROGUE FORTRESS (2015)
ROGUE GOLIATH (2015)
ROGUE HUNTER (2016)
ROGUE INVADER (2017)
ROGUE JUSTICE (2017)
ROGUE KINGDOM (2018)

PROPHECY OF BLOOD

www.ingramcontent.com/pod-product-compliance
Lightning Source LLC
Chambersburg PA
CBHW030306200626
46816CB00002BA/787